BLEEDING KANSAS

THE SAGA OF THE DEAD SILENCER

BOOK ONE

BY

L. ROY AIKEN

ONE

MAYDAY

1

This is it, the day we've been looking forward to for so long, and it's not starting well. Claire wakes up feverish and phlegmy, too sick to drive me to the airport. There's not much to say but sorry, hope you feel better, before she crawls back into bed.

The next thing I know I'm loading my luggage into the trunk of the cab because it turns out the cab driver should have called in sick himself. "Hey, sorry, man, you know how it goes!" he says. "Ya don't work, ya don't get paid!"

"Tell me about it," I say, settling into my seat.

"Airport, huh?" The cabbie sneezes wetly, brings his hand up after the fact. "Where ya headed?"

"Kansas City."

"Kansas City! Kansas City, here I—!" God help me, he's trying to sing that old song but a burst of coughing cuts him short. I pull a handkerchief from my pocket and cover my nose and mouth.

He composes himself, sniffs loudly. "So what's out there?"

"Job interview."

"Yeah? All the way out there? I hope they're paying for it!"

"Oh yeah."

"Must be nice! Wish I could get a gig like that!"

"Me, too."

"Ha! I hear ya! So whatcha been doin' all this time?"

"Unemployed."

"Oh. Nowhere?"

I have to wait for him to finish his latest coughing fit before I can answer. "Pretty much."

"You don't seem all that enthusiastic about this."

"Lot on my mind."

"Oh." A short, barking cough, followed by a long, gurgling wheeze. "Yeah. It's tough out there."

"Yeah."

"So how long you been outta work?"

"Long enough." Four years, but who's counting?

"Me, I *got* to work, know what I'm sayin'? I'd go crazy stayin' at h—!" The driver explodes into another round of coughing, his entire body bucking and convulsing behind the wheel. It's all he can do to keep his eyes open to see the road.

After a terrifying stretch of seconds in which I wonder if he's going to run the red light we screech to a halt, the taxi's rear swerving with the force— "Here, you want a piece of none-of-your business to chew on?" I say. "If I don't make this flight my house goes into foreclosure and my family is homeless as of next month! If you can't make it to the airport, I need someone who can!"

"Whoa, man, it's okay, it's okay! I got this!"

"Can you do it without interrogating me like some nosy old biddy? Can you keep fucking *quiet?*"

"Hey, what's with the language? I'm just making conversation!"

"Just get me to the airport! I'm running late as it is!"

"Jeez, mister, I said okay!"

The light changes and we roll. I'm embarrassed for letting the f-bomb slip. Professional class people don't do that in front of their lessers. My problem as an old-fashioned working stiff is that, as much as most people annoy me, I don't think of them as my lessers.

I take some satisfaction that the cabbie is keeping quiet, which, in turn, has eased his coughing. Still, I keep the handkerchief pressed to my face until he pulls up to the white zone at the airport. He pops the trunk and I step out into the blessedly germ-free air to grab my luggage.

I don't know what the tip scale is for cab drivers. I can barely afford to pay him, let alone tip. I give him 15 percent. It's more than this Chatty Cathy by way of Typhoid Mary deserves. Maybe

I'll get more than I deserve.

"We good?" I ask the driver before I walk away.

"Look, good luck," he says. "I know you must be nervous."

"Yeah. Try and get well."

I'd like to think that's the end of it but I'm running a gauntlet of sneezing, coughing people all the way to the fat lady at the ticket counter. She got a red Hitler mustache of raw skin under her nose from wiping at it with her third wad of tissue.

I wish I had some tongs or latex gloves with which to take my boarding pass. For God's sake, I can't afford to get sick, not for the best chance for gainful employment I've had in years! It's probably a matter of time, though. Turning away from the counter every other person I see is suffering from some degree of the "Mayday Malaise."

That's how the logo reads behind cable news queen Stefani Dunham on TVs all over the airport. "Now this is a *different* kind of cold bug," she says. "Aside from the fact that one out of three people come down with it, you can actually sort of function through it! Of course, some are saying it's because Americans with jobs are afraid to miss work for any reason, given the economic situation." Our head cheerleader-cum-broadcast journalist makes a face to let us know what she thinks of *some* people.

"Whatever the case, doctors say it's an aerosol virus, which means *it's all up in your air!*" The shot cuts to a gray-haired eminence mumbling authoritatively in a plush office. Back to Stefani: "And we're not immune here!" She coughs theatrically into a handkerchief. "All this and a runny nose! A big shout-out to my make-up people here in the News Center for keeping me presentable! Hey, we carry on, what can you do?"

With my Irish luck, that's the strain I won't be getting. Claire struggled to make it to the bathroom and that poor dumb cabbie I rode in with was barely functional. I call my contact at the company in Kansas City. Giselle finally picks up. "Mr. Grace! To what do we owe the honor? Aren't you still in Colorado Springs? You're at the airport, right?"

"Yeah, I'm right here at the gate. I just wanted to make sure the interview was still on."

"Why wouldn't it be?"

"That cold that's going around. Everybody's sick!"

Giselle laughs. "Oh, that! We've had a few people call in, but that's not enough to stop us. *You're* not sick, are you?"

"Oh, no, no! I'm fine! I was…concerned."

"Well, give me a call when you make it to KC. Hopefully you can get here before Rob leaves for the golf course. You play golf?"

"It's been a while," I lie. "If nothing else, I'd make him look good." I despise golf and the kind of people who play it. But this is the world I'm trying to bluff my way into. From out of the slave market and into the world of the Professionally Overpaid.

"Sounds to me like you'll all get along. Again, give me a call when you land."

"Will do. Thanks, Giselle."

"Don't get sick!"

Right. If my wife didn't give it to me, if the cab driver didn't give it to me, if the lady at the counter didn't give it to me, if half the people at the airport didn't give it to me—now I'm ducking into a narrow aluminum tube, settling in to breathe recycled air people have been coughing and sneezing into since last week.

We're getting fresh germs all the time, too. Barely half the seats on the plane are filled but half of those people are sick. The flight attendants sit at their seats along the fore and aft bulkheads and scowl at us over their surgical masks.

If I can just stay well for 24 more hours. Twenty-four hours. Lord, that's all I ask.

It's a mercifully short flight. Eventually, I find myself in another TB ward of an airport, squinting through clouds of aerosolized phlegm to get to my luggage. I call Giselle. "Welcome to KC!" she says. "You know how to find us, right?" she says.

"Oh yeah. See you soon!"

At the rental car kiosk I check my pockets for the directions I'd printed from the Internet. "Uh, hey," I ask the guy behind the counter. "Can I get some directions printed up here? I left mine at home."

"What do you need those for?"

"To find my way to my job interview."

He's looking at me vaguely horrified, like I just pissed myself.

"Your vehicle has GPS."

"Oh."

"Man, *really?*"

Walking out to my vehicle, I have to work the keychain remote several times just to be sure this magnificent black luxury SUV is really mine. The new car smell is intoxicating. Nothing is slammed; the rear hatch closes with the touch of a button. I walk around to climb into the cab. Can't slam this door, either. It's like burping a Tupperware lid.

I turn the key and the air conditioning blows on full. The radio plays symphonic music in full-immersive surround sound and none of this seems a strain on anything. I turn down the music and give myself a minute to familiarize myself with the GPS. Not that I need a whole minute. It works on voice command.

The traffic is light on the way into downtown, allowing me to work on my breathing and concentration. I screwed up in my first call to Giselle. The rental car clerk's attitude towards me was also telling. Going all the way back to the cab driver, if he spoke with such annoying familiarity to me it's because I didn't give him the proper nonverbal cues telling him not to.

I can't afford to be friendly. I can't show surprise every time I come across some delightful, if appallingly expensive toy the Courtesan Class takes for granted like hot and cold running water. If it's apparent to anyone at the company that I'm Not of Their Tribe—say, someone who's been driving the same car for ten years, doesn't own a smartphone, etc.—they'll throw me right back into the stagnant, dying pond I come from. One does not get a seat at the Kool Kids table out of kindness, or even ability. It's because you're already a Kool Kid and that seat has belonged to you since before you were born.

With that in mind I step out of the elevator and stroll across the sumptuous lobby like I own it. I've never met Giselle but I know her on sight: a meticulously groomed McMansionland beauty working the Hot Librarian look in her horn-rimmed glasses and a navy blue power suit worth two or more of my mortgage payments.

She blesses me with a cinematically white, straight-toothed smile: "Thank God, something's going right today!"

"That's what I'm here for," I say, dry as a bossman's martini.

"First, I need to apologize. I thought Rob was going to be here today, but—guess what!"

I raise an eyebrow: *this had better be good.*

"In the four hours since we spoke this morning we've had

people going home right and left. Rob sometimes doesn't get here until ten so I imagined he'd at least be here to welcome you to the city. He ended up calling in."

"Given how I left my wife this morning, I can tell you, if you're sick, you're really sick. And I know what I saw in both airports on my way here."

"Yes, sir, and I *do* apologize! I honestly didn't see this coming! We've got so many people here working through their sniffles just *fine*. Anyway, it seems there may be some…consequence to this."

"Yes?"

"Assuming Rob's among the group of the Really Sick we'll have to postpone the interview."

"How long are you willing to put me up here?"

"How long are you willing to stay?"

"I came to talk to Rob. If it's not too much of a problem, I'll wait."

"Even with your wife sick back home?"

"My teenage children can take care of her."

Giselle puts an envelope on the counter. "There's a voucher in there for a really good steakhouse in the Power and Light District. Should be enough in there for breakfast and lunch tomorrow at any number of places close to your hotel. Call me in the morning before checkout. Either I'll have another envelope or a plane ticket."

I smile tightly as I slip the envelope into my inside jacket pocket.

"I hope you don't mind eating out so much!"

"Not at all. Thanks, Giselle."

"Okay. We'll talk to you tomorrow, then."

"You bet." I turn and walk out of the lobby. I manage to make it inside the blessedly empty elevator car before letting out a sigh of relief to blow the doors in.

2

I really don't want to call. After weeks, months, years of the same old drag, day after day, I'm finally back among the living. I'm not losing my mind sitting at my laptop in my tiny basement office, my wife twiddling away at her computer just outside the door. Things are happening!

Still, a man's gotta do what a man's gotta do. So, after the most pretentious breakfast I've suffered in my entire life—a runny spinach omelet from some foo-foo yuppie bistro I wouldn't go anywhere near if the meal wasn't free with this voucher—I finally reach my son Jack by phone. It turns out Claire's been bedridden since I left yesterday. She appears to be resting, though.

There's talk of closing the schools until this blows over. He's staying home today, regardless: "We did nothing yesterday, Dad. Nothing. It was a total waste."

"Same here," I say. "What can I tell you? Just look in on your Mom from time to time. Try not to get sick."

"Dad, come on! If we were going to get sick don't you think we would have by now? I took a regular snot-shower from all the people sneezing and coughing yesterday! I'm not going back until this crap's over with!" He pauses. "Sorry, Dad. It just...I don't even wanna think about it. It's weird."

"To say the least. What's Sibyl up to?"

"She's going into work today. Thanks for reminding me. I need to tell her to pick up some stuff on the way home."

I tell him to do what he has to do, keep me posted, etc., and hang up. The bistro is within walking distance of the company. After settling up I top off the parking meter and stroll down the avenue to see Giselle. There are people out and about, but it's not nearly as busy as it should be for the heart of downtown Kansas City.

"You're lucky you've got your kids to take care of your wife," Giselle tells me. "I'm all my mother has, and I have to come into work."

"I'd be home too if I could help it," I say. "So how's Rob doing?"

"I don't think he has the bad kind. You don't feel like talking on the phone if you're really sick. He's sure he'll have it kicked by Friday. In the meantime, he says enjoy the city on us. How are you liking it so far?"

"I'm ready to start looking at houses."

"Great! I've got some fliers and business cards for some realtors if you want to take the time to do that. "

I do. Hell, I've got today and tomorrow to fill until Friday—assuming Rob really does get better by then.

Meanwhile, note to self: Don't get sick. Wouldn't it my luck that Rob gets better, then I'm the one too sick to interview tomorrow?

Screw it. No matter how badly I feel this interview is going to happen.

Meanwhile, I notice there are very few people out. At least they seem more or less okay. Maybe Jack was right—if we're not sick by now, we never will be.

In the evening I return to the steakhouse in the Power and Light District. There's so few people there the manager comes out and talks to the customers. He hands out coupons for free desserts the sick people back home can use when they get better. Based on the conversations I'm overhearing, most people are here because it's a break from listening to their significant others coughing and sniffling, and not being able to do a damn thing about it.

Looking at the couples scattered about the restaurant I think of the old joke: they're married, but not to each other. I'm not judging. After the last four years of waking to the terror of the same day it's not just a new city I want. Hell, I'll save the company a bunch of money and they can just keep me here. I'll find a house and buy my furniture a piece at a time, paycheck by paycheck. Sibyl's eighteen; Jack will likely move out here with me, so I won't have to sweat child support.

It's not that I hate Claire or that I'm going middle-age stupid for young pussy or anything like that. Our you-and-me-against-the-world groove has run its course. That's all. After bumping past each other in the house nearly every day for nearly four years, we're done. After 22 years I expect she'll be grateful to see me gone, too. She just doesn't know it yet.

I put away a few more tall drafts than I should. Driving back to the hotel is like driving through a deserted city. Not even a cop. Of course, it's a Wednesday night, on top of everyone else being sick.

I'm riding the elevator to my room when she calls.

"You're sounding better," I say.

"It's like being in the eye of a hurricane," Claire says. "I've got a feeling I don't have long."

My wife, the drama queen. Jesus. "You need me to come home?"

"No, no! We need this job! What's going on? Have you interviewed yet?"

"No. It turns out the boss is sick, too."

"Oh, no!"

"He wasn't as bad off as you were, from what I heard. Maybe he'll have his 'eye of the hurricane'' episode. Frankly, I think you're just depressed and freaked out from being sick. Drink lots of water, get something to eat. For all you know you've beaten this thing already."

"I hope you're right."

"I know I'm right. Just take it easy. We'll get through this."

"I know. We always have." A pause. "I love you, honey."

"I love you, Claire."

And so the scales of the evening are balanced, and I settle into my room feeling like the asshole I really am.

"Honestly, sir, I'm not sure what to do with you," Giselle says the next day. "I tried booking you a flight out but nothing's going to Colorado Springs."

"So how about Denver?"

"First thing I thought of when I couldn't get the Springs. The earliest flight I can get into Denver is Monday. Even that's not guaranteed. A lot of people are either sick or taking off to look after their sick. No telling what it'll look like then."

"Fine," I say. "I'll take it."

"Oh, no worries, I've got you booked! I'm just saying there are no guarantees. Rob sounded really bad over the phone. I know my mother is suffering. How long has your wife been sick?"

"Since Tuesday," I say. "She woke up with it."

"Just like my mother yesterday. God, it's like she's at death's door! And they say the hospitals are already strained past capacity, what with their own people sick!"

"I could get back to Colorado Springs in the rental car."

"My God, that's an all-day drive!"

"Nothing I can't handle."

"I'll need to check if I can get away with letting you do that. I'm sorry. Most people here are out, too. I'll give you a call by five, all right?"

I tell her to do what she has to do, keep me posted, etc. There's not much to do after heading out, though. The Kansas City Museum is closed. I spend the day driving around, listening to local commercial radio stations. According to the DJs, everybody's sick. Drink plenty of fluids, sleep it off! Here's a little "Peace of Mind" by Boston....

I end up eating at the bar at the steakhouse. Everyone is pleasant and chatty but I'm the only customer they have and they no doubt feel obliged. I get a growler of draft to go. I'm walking out the door when I realize Giselle was supposed to call me. I check my phone. No messages. No missed calls.

Shit.

I call Claire. It rings for a while before kicking over to voicemail so I know her phone is charged. I leave a message telling her I love her, I'll be home soon.

3

I'm not supposed to hear anything outside the windows of this state-of-the-art executive suite, and I'm sure that's what wakes me up. At 6:30 on a Friday morning in early May not one school bus chuffs down the street. Not one street sweeper, not one garbage truck hissing and banging along the curb. No commuters on their way to their 7 a.m. shift start. No cabs. No downtown joggers or dog-walkers.

I switch on the TV. Stefani Dunham of Cable Morning News talks of the unusual quiet in the Middle East, mostly due to the flu that's taken the world by storm.

She narrates the latest video of a deer wandering through the automatic doors of a supermarket, but her voice is weirdly uninflected. Her head cheerleader swagger died sometime in the night. Her hair-and-makeup crew apparently didn't show either. She actually looks beautiful. Her just-brushed-into-place hair, the dark crescents beneath her eyes betray a humanity I never expected a woman of her position to possess.

My phone chirps. Finally:

> We took Mom to the hospital
> but it was full. She's very
> sick. Don't know what else to

**do. I have to go into work.
Hope you feel okay and that
you come home soon.**

The time stamp shows this was sent hours ago. I'm only now getting this.

According to the Stefani Dunham of Cable Morning News the top story is the strain on services nationwide due to the Mayday Malaise. Hospitals are full of patients, but the hospitals can't provide adequate care because one-third to one-half of the hospital staff is sick, too. Without techs to maintain the servers and towers, cell phone service has crashed in some areas. There were storms in Georgia and the Carolinas that knocked out power two nights ago. That power is likely to stay out because too few people feel well enough to fix things. And then the unaffected people have to take off from work to take care of their sick relatives.

"And while we wait for this thing to run its course," Stefani says, "it turns out that for some people the illness is just getting worse. This is just for some people, though, the numbers are inconclusive. We're not in the business of spreading rumors. Count on our team to keep you updated with the latest." She coughs primly into a handkerchief just as they cut to commercials.

Normally you'd hear an exclamation point after that last sentence. That's because—normally—Stefani! Dunham! of Cable! Morning! News! is fully invested in what she's selling.

I power up my laptop. We still have Internet service, but the pages are slow to load. From the UK's *Guardian* to the Kremlin's own *Russia Today*, the columnists are mocking "the 'Mayday Malaise,' as the American news outlets frivolously and dismissively label it" (the Germans seem particularly pissed about "the U.S.'s non-response to the crisis").

According to the foreign press the infection isn't viral, it's bacterial—and resistant to antibiotics. *Russia Today* and *Politiken DK* report rumors that a pharmaceutical company brewed this up to contain it with its specially targeted (and patented) regime of medications. Of course, nothing can be proved.

Oh, and one more thing they're not mentioning in the U.S. information bubble:

You can go fast.

You can go slow.

You can go easy—the way our Ms. Dunham seems to be going—then all-of-a-sudden hard. Or just go hard and die hard all the way.

Some have been known to go into remission. Like Claire. This article even uses the eye-of-the-hurricane metaphor. "And like the far side of the hurricane eyewall, Round Two of the disease comes on even fiercer than the first."

However it plays out, *no one gets better from this.* That's why the English, those masters of gallows humor, dubbed it the Final Flu. It's the last thing you're ever sick of.

I pull out my phone and dial her cell. Nothing. Whatever connectivity delivered Sibyl's message to me late is down again already. I dial the land line. Ring, click. I do this again, three, maybe four more times on both.

"As brief as the remissions are, the relapses are brutally—some say 'mercifully'—short-lived. As are the patients." I think of Sybil's text. Claire.

Claire....

I'm flashing on our first Thanksgiving, eating on the quilt she spread on the floor of our unfurnished apartment. The Christmases with her parents. The Christmases we did on our own, accompanied by bright and happy Sibyl, then Jack.

I think of the greeting cards Claire would leave for me to find in the morning, for no special occasion at all. Just to tell me how "grateful" she was for me. For what? I always meant to write her a long letter for Mother's Day, letting her know all the things I noticed that I thought made us so much richer than most people with actual "disposable" income. We know how these stories always end, don't we?

I clap my laptop shut, look up at the TV. Stefani Dunham is still reading from her teleprompter. She doesn't sniffle or cough. I'm guessing she's in her remission stage.

What's really intriguing are the implications raised by the logical follow-up: What makes a multi-million dollar diva like Stefani Dunham, Queen of All Cable News, go on television, read straight-faced from the teleprompter, and pretend she hasn't heard her own personal two-minute warning?

My hot, damp pity party dries to cold, arid terror. Something is going down. The kind of something no mere citizen can do anything about but get home to the children as fast as humanly possible and brace for what's next.

I couldn't afford to kiss Claire goodbye before I left. I can't afford to mourn her now that she's gone. Sibyl and Jack are counting on me to know what to do—and to be there to do it. If I could drive out of here this instant I could make Colorado Springs before nightfall. I'd have to push it on the speed limit. Which might not be a problem. Then again, if I wreck, that's it. Better hope I die instantly....

So I won't wreck. I've got to get home! But I can't leave without checking in one last time with the company, at least see who's paying for what, if anything. The office opens at eight.

I shower, dress, and pack out quickly. I take the stairs on the north end of the hall. It's fifteen flights down but the effort tempers my anxiety. More to the point, it lets me out by the back door to the parking garage. I don't want the desk people to see me carrying my luggage out.

It's just another job interview! I can do this!

I walk around the hotel. It's so quiet I can all but hear the damp, hot sunlight pressing down upon the concrete. I'm so relieved to feel the air conditioning as I come in through the front door.

The dining area off the lobby is pitch-dark to my sun-adjusted eyes. "Sorry," says the girl behind the front desk. "The entire kitchen staff is out."

"Huh." Not that I'm particularly surprised.

"I know they're not all sick, either! Only one out of three got this, right?"

"I suppose the rest are home taking care of their people," I say.

"Must be nice. The way I see it, I don't work, I don't get paid! God knows where *those* people are getting their money!"

"Well, did someone at least pick up some doughnuts and brew some coffee?"

"As a matter of fact, I did, thank you very much! Would you like some?"

"If it's not too much trouble."

"Oh, not at all! You have no idea how good it is to have someone to talk to!"

From Angie I learn there are a dozen or so flu patients booked here in the hotel because the airlines—on orders from Homeland Security, via the TSA—are refusing to transport obviously sick people. "Talk about closing the barn door when the horses are already out!" says Angie.

A very pale and irritable looking woman wearing a prominent MANAGER tag comes in. "I don't like leaving my little boy at home the way he is but the show must go on, right?"

"Don't put yourself out on my account."

"Oh! Sorry! *Sorry!* I didn't mean it like that! This is just going to be a really hard day. We don't have a kitchen staff and now there's no one here to clean the rooms! It might be a couple of days on that, and for that we do apologize!"

"It's all right. Look, I'm going out to find some breakfast. Good meeting you all—and good luck!"

"Let us know what you find open," says Angie.

I nod, wave, and set off into the quiet city.

4

The more I think about it, the less sense it makes. Cell phone towers are designed to run on full automatic. The landline system, also designed for low-to-no-maintenance, works on batteries. Even if the lines were overwhelmed by chatty survivors you wouldn't get a dial tone, let alone a ring on the other end. Just dead air.

Then again, if four years of sporadic "customer care" temp gigs have taught me anything, it's that modern civilization runs on duct tape and good intentions. There's also the simple fact that too many people are either sick or taking care of their sick to do the most basic upkeep, let alone full-on relay station repair.

I've got to find some breakfast to help me kill time on top of hunger while waiting for the office to open. I'm already three blocks from the hotel when I catch sight of the OPEN sign beyond the blinking DON'T CROSS light I'm ignoring.

I pause in the middle and take in the full 360 degrees. Except for a lone mutt sniffing along the walk on one side, a couple of raccoons having at a trash basket on the other, there's no movement for as far as I can see. Not a soul in the street.

The door of the glass-fronted diner is open. There's a guy behind the counter. He's waving me in. God help me, I'm probably going to regret this.

"Just so you know," he says as I walk up to the counter. "We're all you're going to find open for miles."

"So what's that mean? You're charging a hundred bucks for a

cup of coffee?"

"You paying it?"

"No."

"Wait, wait! Don't worry about it!" I turn back around. "Credit card machine probably doesn't work anyway," he says.

"I was going to use one of these," I say, pulling the voucher from my pocket.

"Whoa!" he says. "You're a guest of *theirs*? Sure, whatever you want! Just give me a few minutes to scare it up."

After ten minutes or so my patience is rewarded with a heaping plate of eggs, bacon, hash browns, and grits, along with a smaller plate topped with biscuits, with options for jam or gravy. The cook/proprietor busies himself in his kitchen, giving me space to eat. Which I greatly appreciate.

He takes my plate after I'm finished. "Don't think much in the way of business is getting done today," he says, watching me try my cell.

I listen for the ring-click. The man's comment strikes me as strange until I remember I'm wearing a suit. "We'll find a way to make it happen," I say, thumbing off the phone.

"Too late for my daughter," he says.

"What?"

"This morning. She…she couldn't breathe."

"How long was she sick?"

"She went to bed right as rain Saturday night! Woke up with sniffles and a cough on Sunday, went to church, no big deal. Yesterday she got really bad, but that's the way it is sometimes, right? You get a little sick, then you get real sick…and she…." He squeezes his eyes shut. He shakes a little, then opens his eyes. Looking at nothing and no one in particular he says, "She couldn't breathe."

I get up from my seat. "My wife went to bed feeling just fine Saturday night," I tell him. "She woke up a little sick Sunday. She was too sick to drive me to the airport yesterday. It's her I can't get on the damned phone because everyone else is dying, too, and shit's falling apart."

"I'm sorry," the man says. "I just needed to tell somebody. Must be hard being so far away and nothing you can do…."

I take a deep breath, wrap it tightly about the rage I feel at this fool. "Ask yourself this," I say quietly. "Would your daughter want you to give up?"

"No. No, of course not. "

"Good. So where's your wife? Shouldn't you be making funeral arrangements?"

"Look around you! You think even the funeral homes are open?"

Shit. Hadn't thought of that. "So what are we supposed to do with our... deceased?"

"They said...the man said we should clean her up as best we can. Then wait for the announcement."

"Announcement?"

"They're picking up the bodies. They'll be doing...mass burials. In the city parks. They'll have a service."

"Huh. Usually they burn the bodies in situations like this."

"No! No! We'll bury them in the temporary place until we can put them in individual plots with their families. When things get back to normal!"

Normal. Right. I sign the voucher and slide it across the counter. He begins choking and weeping as he puts it under the tray in his register. "Sorry for your loss," I say. I turn and I'm out the open door and crossing the empty street to the far corner.

The manager has already left for home when I return the hotel. Angie's family is out of state; she has nothing better to do than mind the fort. Still, she's irritated with the manager for leaving her alone so Angie lets me use the office land line to call my house. Dial tone. Ring. Click. Dial tone. That's all. I do this three more times, then once more "just to be sure" before giving up.

"That's funny," says Angie. "I haven't had any problems calling locally."

The only person I could think to call locally would be Giselle. If she's there. Anyway, I need to talk to someone face-to-face, see what I can salvage from this. I thank Angie and walk away towards rear doors of the lobby leading to the garage.

"Where are you going?" she calls out after me.

"Gotta check one more thing," I say.

"You're coming back, right?"

"Of course!"

"Please don't leave without saying g—without checking out, okay?"

I smile. "Wouldn't dream of it, Angie."

"Seriously. You need to come back."

"This won't take long."

The look on her face makes me feel even worse for lying to her. But if whoever's left at the office can check me out of the hotel from her desk while clearing me to leave with the rental, then I'm going straight out on the road. I'm sorry you're afraid, Angie. But I've got two people 600 miles away I need to do that being-afraid stuff with. And 600 miles is one long mother of a drive....

I almost miss seeing the only other car on the road. It's going so fast on I-70 east it's there and gone. Warp Factor Fuck the Police. I smile for the sheer give-a-shit ballsiness of this guy.

Then I realize what it means and the bottom falls out of my stomach.

There are all of three cars on my level in the parking garage. The door is unlocked. I take the elevator to my floor. Breathe. Breathe....

The doors open on a darkened lobby.

"Who—what?" I hear Giselle say as I come out of the shadows. "You're still here?"

As with Stefani Dunham, something has aged my Hot Librarian by ten years overnight. The sweat glistens on her pale, not-so-apple cheeks where the rims of her glasses rest. "Nice to see you, too, Giselle."

"Oh! I'm – look, it's just me and Don and Chris performing last rites here."

"Last—? Did this company just close down under me?"

"I don't know how permanent it is but those were the exact words from the acting CEO: 'Close and secure all operations until further notice.' Then the networks went down. We don't even have phones. So how we're going to get that 'further notice' is something of a mystery."

If the bottom had fallen out of my stomach at the sight at that car, the ground dissolves beneath my feet at the sight of the box behind her desk, packed with Giselle's framed photos and knick-knacks. "Yes," Giselle says, "we're *all* out of work now." She sniffs loudly, draws herself up. "Look, I don't mean to be short with you but—" Giselle pulls a stack of vouchers from beside her desk. "Take all of these! Get out of town while you still can! Just take the rental and go!"

"Did you get authorization for that? I waited for your call yesterday."

Giselle freezes. Her Hot Librarian face is awful to behold: "I don't know where you've been getting your information," she says, "but people started dying *yesterday*, my mother among them. I know you're tired of hearing me apologize but I was *distracted*."

"Of course," is all I can think to say.

"I'm sure your teenagers would want you there to help them bury their mother. I'm burying mine tonight. They're picking her up from the house. They'll bury her in some mass grave. Like in some awful Third World country!"

Her eyes squeeze shut. Fortunately, I only have to endure a moment of this before a sandy-haired young man leans out the door behind Giselle. "You the guy from Colorado Springs? Supposed to interview with Rob?"

"That's me."

"Rob's dead. His wife called in this morning."

"Oh."

"I'm sorry," says Giselle, weakly. "I probably should have mentioned that."

"Figures,'" I say, but not to Giselle. It seems everyone's dropping dead these last 24 hours. Which means Claire....

The sandy-haired young man shrugs. "I don't know if you've been listening to the radio but it might be a while before you can get home. The acting governors of Kansas and Missouri have activated their National Guards. They're closing the borders and sealing off the cities against looters. Anyone not in an official capacity working downtown has to go home and stay there until further notice."

"Shit!"

"We'll give you a call once things are up and running," says Giselle.

"Giselle, look, I'm sorry. Thanks for—"

"No! No....it's okay. Seriously, I'll call you. We'll need everyone who's willing to come in to work. Good luck." Giselle gives me a game smile. Bless her never-before-broken heart, she's going through every letter in her emotional alphabet, looking for an attitude to sustain her.

"We got to go," the young man says. "All of us. Now."

"Good luck to you, too." I take the vouchers from the counter and walk to the elevator.

The doors close and I realize I'm not getting paid. My family is doomed to homelessness. In the middle of a freakin' plague.

Will it matter? Will anyone notice we still haven't paid our mortgage payment? Maybe Giselle was right, maybe she wasn't just blowing smoke. Maybe she meant that about calling in everyone who was willing to work. It stands to reason that if this many people are out they'll need people to help run things once this all settles....

I'm pulling out into the street when the military Humvee blocks my path. Hard-faced bastards in cammies carrying M4s surround me. I roll down the window.

"State the nature of your business," barks someone with staff sergeant stripes.

"I just checked in with the people at my office," I say. "I'm on my way back to the hotel."

"You're going *straight* back to the hotel."

"Yes, I am."

A 2nd lieutenant steps up and whispers something in the sergeant's ear. He walks away.

"Go to your hotel," says the sergeant. "Stay there. In half an hour we're locking down these streets. If you don't have a reason to be out, you will be shot. Understood?"

"Got it," I say through clenched teeth. "Thanks, Sergeant."

I see Guard patrols at the entrance ramps. They're likely up and down the Interstate and not all sergeants and 2nd lieutenants are going to respect the suit and the executive SUV. I request an alternate route back to the hotel on the GPS and thread my way through the city.

5

My heart sinks as the hotel comes into view. My luxury prison. I was hoping to see the wide-open Interstate by now but here I am, by orders of the National Guard. So who's paying for this? What if Giselle has already checked me out?

God only knows what's going on in Colorado Springs. It's just as well I don't know because there ain't shit I can do about it....

Goddamn it, not right now. One thing at time.

The parking garage is nearly empty. I get the spot closest to the door. I take my luggage through the back to the elevator bank faced away from the desk.

I park my luggage in my room but leave off unpacking it. I wash my face, freshen up from too much time spent in the hot and humid Kansas City morning. I dry myself over the air conditioning unit beneath the window.

I consider changing into comfortable clothes but I'm thinking about the Guardsmen. They didn't ask for my ID. I could have spent the better part of an hour explaining why I'm here from Colorado, the nature of the job I was interviewing for and what the hell I'm still doing here when the manager hiring me is dead, etc. Sure, the sergeant's tone might have been more pleasant, but in the end it was my suit and the Luxury Tank, combined with my aloof, preoccupied manner that got me back here to the hotel. It's not the open road but I've got a bathroom, air conditioning, and a lot more freedom of movement than I'd have under guard. Or shot.

I go over myself with the lint roller, do a round of breathing exercises. Then I head out for the elevator.

Angie's face lights up as I step out. "When did you get back?"

"A few minutes ago," I said.

"How was it at the company?"

"They said they'd be in touch."

"I'll bet. You checking out?"

"I can't. The National Guard is locking down the streets."

"Yeah, I heard," said Angie. "Well, for what it's worth, no one from the company called to check you out. So you're still good to go on their dime."

"Nice to know," I try to say as blandly as possible, while my inner Poor Worried Bastard whoops with joy.

"Not that it matters. I can't check anyone in or out with the network down. I mean, I could do it old school with a big wide book, but it's no good until we can process the company credit card. We don't have Internet, so...."

I can't take my eyes off the bandage on her arm. She didn't have it when I left earlier. I'm about to ask when there's a loud roar, then the steady clatter of heavy diesel machinery getting underway. "I guess that's the first trench," I say.

"Yeah. Every park in the city. They're having a televised service at six o'clock. Did you see the trucks?"

"One, the way I was coming. 'Bring out your deceased.' Not something you want to hear from a loudspeaker on top of a truck. Not in this century."

"Yeah."

I nod towards her bandage. "What happened there? You all right?"

"No."

"I'm sorry."

"I was bitten by the guy in 604."

"What?"

"I thought he was going to try and kiss me the way he came at me with his mouth open. His tongue and the inside of his mouth— God! He's making these 'unnnnh!' noises like he's retarded or something and I put my arm out to push him back and he grabs it and—oh, *gross!*"

"Where did this happen?"

"Officer Dalton came by to look in on us and I asked if he'd come with me to check on the sick people. To see if they…anyway, we hadn't seen or heard from Mr. Devereaux in days so we wanted to look in on him first." Angie looks out the glass front windows to the empty street. "Whatever you do, don't go up on the sixth floor. It stinks! We're gonna have to call in a crew for that."

"Officer Dalton? There's police out here?"

"This hotel, you better believe it! We got people taking care of us! Thank God, I think I would have died from just looking at what that creep did to my arm. Officer Dalton got the EMTs up here to clean and dress this. Still, it took out a chunk! He was *chewing* on it when Officer Dalton shot him in the head!"

"I take it they gave you something for the pain."

"Yeah. I'd enjoy it more if my arm didn't hurt so much. It's keeping me more sober than I'd like. Still got that damn gun ringing in my ear, too. Guns are loud, you know? Not like on the TV…."

"The TV. Yeah, I think I'll go see what the latest propaganda is."

"No!" Angie says. She seizes my wrist. "I mean, we can watch it here, okay? Please stay! I'm kinda freaked out right now."

"I dunno…."

"We've got all kinds of stuff we can cook in the kitchen! Mix something up for yourself from the bar! I'll let you do whatever you want, just don't leave me alone!"

"Ah—what the hell. All right." As the words leave my lips I hear something like distant fireworks. Like firecrackers on a string, if the string had lengths which allowed for pauses between bursts.

She doesn't seem to hear what I'm sure was gunfire. I follow Angie into the kitchen. "Uh, so what did they give you for the pain?"

"Straight-up morphine. Yeah, I know, it makes me kinda loopy. I still feel that skin being…torn…."

"All right," I say, turning the knobs on the fry vats. "I see we've got cheese sticks here. Let's fry 'em up."

Angie finds some chicken tenders and brings the bag to me. "I'm sorry," she says. "I don't know anything about this kind of equipment."

"It's all right," I tell her. I take off my jacket and hand it to her.

"You're in experienced hands, here." I roll up my shirt sleeves, tuck my tie in between the buttons.

"You used to work fast food?"

"Does this look like a fast food kitchen to you?"

"No, no! I didn't mean to offend!"

"Pass me that stack of baskets and liners, please."

She does. "I'll hang this up for you," she says.

"Find a place to do it in here. I want it handy."

"What for?"

"My wallet and keys are in there."

"Oh."

Not that I'll need them for anything. I just want my jacket close. I drop the baskets into the oil, set the timers. Before long, we've got more than we can eat. Angie fills the little containers with honey mustard and marinara sauce. I click the fryers off and we enjoy our snack.

The bell rings at the desk. Angie freezes, afraid to go out without me. I nod at her to wait as I roll down my sleeves. She rushes away to bring me my jacket, which she put on a hanger and hung from the kitchen employee's coat rack. It's less than a minute but the bell rings again as I'm walking with Angie to the front desk, where a police officer in full urban paramilitary gear stands with a guy in tennis shorts and matching polo shirt.

"This one says he belongs to you," says the cop.

Angie laughs. "Oh, good!" She looks at me. "I thought it'd be good if you and Mr. Tanner got to meet each other. You're both smart. You could help me hold down the fort!"

"We'd appreciate the help," says the cop. "We're spread really thin. I've got another three blocks to worry about besides this one. You the guy from room 1510?"

"Yes."

"I'm sorry you can't get back to your family—um, Mr. Grace?"

"Yes."

"You're not planning on breaking out are you?"

"No. I got the memo."

"Sir, please trust me when I say I'm not telling you this to scare you. Everything is locked down until we can get going with the burial of the dead. Once the people in charge are satisfied most of them are under then we'll open the roads back up and things can start getting back to normal. But not until then. You try and make a run for it on the roads they will light your—they will light you up. Trust me, sir."

"Well, then, I'm with Angie holding down the fort. So what do we do?"

"Not much to it, really. You just have the authorization of the police department to do what it takes to protect life and property here."

"Will we be issued weapons?"

"Do you have a permit?"

"Not on me."

"Well, Mr. Tanner here had his concealed carry permit from Colorado. It means he has training. Sorry, but at least he'll have a sidearm."

"I'll make do."

"Really, it's not gonna be a problem. They're going to try and make this as quick as they can. They'll be running coverage on the local channels if you want to watch."

"Sounds like a plan."

"All right, well, I gotta go. Just stay put. You might want to go easy on your food, too. Even with the roads open we don't know when deliveries are gonna start again." The cop looks at Angie. "How you holdin' up, Angie?"

"Mr. Grace stuffed me full of chicken tenders. I just wanna lie down now."

"Well, with Mr. Grace on board you can probably do that. What I want to know is how you're doing with the pain."

"I'm okay so long as I don't think about it," Angie says.

"I'll try and bring an EMT when I check back on you all tonight." Officer Dalton turns to Tanner and me. "Lock these doors after dark, or if you decide to go to your rooms. We've only got so many locking down these streets. Believe me when I tell ya, though—if we see it moving we're shooting first and gathering data for the report later! Don't go outside looking for trouble. Don't go outside looking for *anything*."

"Understood," I say.

The cop pulls a card from his top pocket. "Give me a call if things get out of hand. I can't promise I'll respond right away, what with everything going on. So try not to let it get out of hand."

"I don't see us having any problems," I say, taking the card. "Thanks, though."

"Like I said, I've got four more blocks to check up on. Keep an eye on Angie for me."

"Will do."

Officer Dalton turns and pushes his way out the glass front doors. He turns back to us as he's halfway through. "And don't forget to lock these things! In fact, you might want to do that right now."

I turn to look at Angie. "I'll get the keys," she says.

Officer Dalton looks as Angie retreats into the office to the side of the front desk. He nods at us and takes off across the front plaza, almost out of sight before the door falls shut.

6

Angie comes forward with the keys and begins locking the doors. I turn to the guy in the tennis shorts and polo shirt. Tanner. "Is this all of us?"

"Most everyone in this hotel left last night. I have to wonder how many of them made it back to where they're from, though. Most of the airlines weren't operational this morning. Now the roads are closed."

"I'd be over halfway there by now if I'd started first thing."

"You still might as well be on the far side of the moon. My kids are with their mother in Highlands Ranch, not too far from you. I look at it this way, getting myself killed trying to get through all those bandits out there, let alone the National Guard, won't do them any favors."

"Bandits?"

"Ever see the bumper sticker, 'If It Weren't for Physics & Law Enforcement I'd Be Unstoppable'? A lot of people don't have their normal routine of going to work or whatever it is they do during the day to stop them, either. Not much on TV, and no Internet for the most part. If they're not holed up in a basement somewhere eating all the chips and junk food they could carry from the nearest store then they're out messing with people."

"I suppose it's all up to physics, then."

"The city police were talking about how the state patrol pulled this one guy and his car out of a tree. But what ought to worry you and me are the ones shooting at cars on the highway for no other reason that because they can."

"So what are you doing out of Colorado?"

"I'm a security consultant. I give presentations to company boards about doing business in depressed markets. I advise them how to brand themselves so they don't appear part of the problem, how employees should and should not talk about what they do, and so on."

"Then I guess you're all we need. I don't have a gun."

"I've got to sleep sometime. You can use the one they issued me."

"I'm going to need some training."

"I thought you told Officer—oh! Okay! Well, we've got plenty of time between now and when the burials start. Probably ought to clean this thing first, anyway. Good time to get you acquainted with the basics."

Which we do. I've always meant to get a gun, but the general commitment involved with owning one put me off. You don't just buy one of these things, load it and leave it in the nightstand drawer, hoping you'll never use it. For my part, that's just it: I knew I'd use it. Especially throughout these last four years when my general mood has been swinging somewhere between animal rage and oh-God-why-bother despair.

I go over and over taking apart the piece, reassembling the parts. Meanwhile, Tanner talks about himself, his five-star wonderful family living the Good Ol' American Dream. To people like him the Great Recession is an attitude problem. Everything is onwards and upwards, the good getting better all the time.

As much as his prattling annoys me I'm grateful he's not asking me any questions about my own family. Claire is dead. That's my grief and mine alone. She couldn't even kiss me goodbye because we couldn't afford it. *Couldn't afford it.* Seriously.

Well, honey, I didn't get sick. Now what? Just think, poor Giselle has to bury her mother like icky poor people do in their icky poor countries. How could we be so selfish, thinking only of ourselves!

I'd wondered at the rage boiling up in me this morning when that guy told me about his daughter. Now I know. That sad sack of guts didn't have anything I would have called a problem until his daughter fell ill last weekend. For the last four years I've been living in terror of leaking pipes, brake jobs, breakdowns—the One Catastrophe that would put us all out on the streets—and he expects me to feel sorry for *him*?

I've watched honest, hard-working people losing their minds, their pride and dignity eroding one dashed hope at a time in a hollowed-out professional job market, and all these Good People safe in their jobs—excuse me, *careers*—could say was, "You'll just have to work harder at getting a job. I've worked hard *all* my life!" Which translates as, "I've taken full advantage of my strong, socially established family and its wealth of resources and connections. You weren't born like me? Must be because you're *lazy!*"

I don't want anyone's sympathy now that we're "bonded" by this common tragedy—we're not—and they sure as hell aren't getting any from me. So your daughter got sick and died? Maybe you should have worked harder. Asshole.

God help me, Tanner is all about his wife and how she got the pink Mary Kay Cadillac for making x number of sales, and his son plays varsity hockey and is thinking about wrestling next year but all of his friends are into lacrosse. His daughter "dabbles" in modeling but her boyfriend is graduating from the Air Force Academy in another year so all that's up in the air. He and his wife want to move but you just can't sell a house in this market. There are all kinds of opportunities overseas, though, and his wife has always wanted to live in London so….

It comes off as quite the magnanimous gesture when Tanner pauses in his litany of First World problems to let Angie know he's thinking about her: "Why don't you find an empty room and go to sleep for a while?"

"I feel better out here with you guys," she croaks at us.

"So long as you're comfortable," he says.

"Fine. Thanks."

I get up and walk to the sofa we've dragged behind the front desk for her. Angie's skin is covered in a greasy sheen. I touch the back of my hand to her head. "Ow!" she cries out.

"I'm just seeing if you have a fever."

"It hurts!"

"What's going on over there?" says Tanner.

"She's got an infection!" I snap, annoyed at the accusatory tone in his voice. I look down at Angie. "Can I get you to drink some water?"

"I just want to sleep…."

I go into the back and fill a glass with crushed ice and water. "I'm setting this here," I tell her when I get back. "Don't be shy. Believe it or not, you need this."

I'm aware of Tanner looking at me as I return to my seat at the bar. I pointedly ignore him.

"There are a lot of germs in the human mouth," he says. "In fact, a bite from a human is one of the worst you can get."

He says this oh-so casually. Never mind the young woman burning up with fever on the couch. Just when I think I'm the most bitter-twisted, soul-numbed waste of skin in the house, here comes Mr. Cool-Head All-Is-Well Security Consultant.

"You need to rest for a while?"

"No, I want to see the service. We still have some cheese sticks and chicken wings here. Might as well make supper out of it."

"I like the way you think!" says Tanner.

Thank God for small favors.

The coordination of the media is impressive. Each of the local stations has their assigned neighborhoods and their parks to cover. They have their separate theme music, even separate logos and titles but the narrative is the same: a straight-out-of-nowhere summer cold somehow became the Final Flu and now the world takes historic pause to bury their first wave of dead from this once-in-a-century epidemic. "Like in the days of the 1918 Spanish Flu we all look forward to getting back to more-or-less normal," I hear people on two different channels say word for word. "Of course, the new normal will take some getting used to!"

The other satellite channels show documentaries on the Spanish Flu, with nods to plagues past. I suppose if you watched some of that for long enough you might come to accept that one out of three people dropping dead is perfectly natural.

Of course there's the usual corny-phony scenes of prayer among the surviving members of Congress and the Senate on the Capitol steps. "We encourage everyone watching to tune into their own local channels for coverage of what's happening in their own areas," says the voiceover. "We know it seems out of the ordinary to ask viewers to turn away but it is imperative we stay in touch with our local communities and do what has to be done to normalize issues specific to our respective localities. Every community has its own issues with the Flu, and its own requirements for taking care of the remains of the deceased. Meanwhile, we take you to scenes of faith from around the globe...."

The clips they're showing from inside churches could just as well have come from coverage of Easter services in any given year. The voiceover repeats the script.

So, good citizens that we are, we click on to the coverage on the parks closest to our area. The solemn bumper music plays as they come back from break—the break being a list of the stations to call to have your deceased removed for you, based on ZIP code, school district, etc.

"Worldwide catastrophe" is a phrase that turns up now and again. We're coming together, of course. Americans *always* come together in Times of Crisis. (Unlike those snooty French, I suppose.) And so we will gather to mourn our dead and carry on...shopping, or whatever.

The narration is hushed as the camera follows a soldier/Guardsman pulling a little bundle in a sheet from the back of a canvas-covered truck. "The flu was extremely random in its selection of victims," says a male narrator. "Whereas the Spanish Flu of nearly a hundred years ago targeted young, healthy adults and spared the very old and very young, this flu took infants, the elderly, the young, middle-aged—everyone. Every family has been affected. My family, my co-host Andrea's family, Jeff the cameraman's family, our producer, Jean, in the van. *Your* family, too."

"Balls!" I say. "Let's open up the bar."

"Let's wait until all this is over," says Tanner. "Then the first one's on me."

This pompous ass is hardly dressed to be in charge of anything but a country club tennis court and I wouldn't recognize his authority there, either. I'm sliding off my stool to pour myself a beer when I hear the firecrackers again. I go to the plate glass doors and try to make out where it's coming from.

"Sound to me like its coming from one of the problem areas,"

Tanner says.

"Problem areas? How is anything a problem with damn near everybody dead and the National Guard on the streets?"

I'm aware of Tanner looking me over, weighing my capacity for frankness: "There are certain cultures that resist having their deceased taken away from them without a proper viewing period."

"The blacks aren't giving up their dead so the National Guard is shooting them?"

"Ah! You're aware of the practice."

"Of the long vigils, yes. Shooting people for it, no."

"We're in the midst of an epidemiological emergency. Two days ago it was a bunch of people with colds. Now people are dead. A lot of people." Tanner gestures toward the TV. "This is about getting a biohazard good and buried before we lose what's left of us."

We see shots of the canvas-covered flatbeds pulling to the curb in various neighborhoods. The volunteers in their Day-Glo yellow vests walk up to the doors on either side of the street. They don't use gurneys but stretchers. Once they have the body they jog to the back of the waiting truck.

The survivor fills out the paperwork on the clipboard held out by one of the government volunteers. Name, age, sex, approximate time of death. They get a numbered receipt for the body in lieu of an official death certificate.

The narration is excruciating to listen to. Platitudes, benedictions, soothing words: tasteless frosting on an unspeakable cake. I think of Sibyl and Jack having to deal with their mother's lifeless body. And I'm not there. I keep telling myself they're capable and mature enough. Which they are. Still....

The scene cuts to a park. There's a long trench and yellow police tape all around.

"This is just three blocks over," Tanner says.

"Yeah, we heard the backhoe earlier." I'm looking at all the people behind the yellow tape. Even from the screen you can feel the tension of the crowd. They want to see their loved ones covered, even if it is with a backhoe.

Tanner frowns. "This isn't good."

"Why not?"

He doesn't take his eyes from the TV. "They've had some issues at some of these burials."

"I thought this was the first wave."

"The first wave here. Burials have been going on pretty much all day everywhere."

"So, aside from the logistics of burying so many people at once, what issues have they been having?"

"There!" Tanner says.

Most of the bodies are wrapped in sheets; the ones that aren't are wrapped there at the park before being lowered into the ditch.

One of the bodies is apparently resisting being wrapped up. A pale little girl kicks and flails at the sheet. The two wrapping her are knocked back on their rears as the girl sits up.

"The hell?"

"Watch!" says Tanner. He leans eagerly towards the image on the screen.

A woman runs screaming to the girl but is blocked by a Guardsman and his M4. He pushes the little girl's mother so hard she falls backwards. Another Guardsman runs forward as the little girl falls atop one of the volunteers trying to wrap her up. It's the volunteer's turn to kick and flail now that the girl has her head nuzzled into her neck. Crimson spray erupts along either side of the girl's head. The second Guardsman shoots twice, once into the girl's head and again into the head of the injured volunteer.

"Holy shit! Tanner, what do you know about this?"

"It's been a busy 12 to 18 hours. No one knows what to make of it. I've been reading messages from my sources overseas but I picked up a lot of intel just walking around with Officer Dalton. The cops and the Guard know all about this."

"*This*?"

Two Guardsmen hold the screaming, kicking woman while two others pull the little girl from the body of the volunteer. Her face is blotted out with red. Bits of pale matter dot the clot of scarlet clenched between her tiny teeth. After some deliberation they toss the volunteer into the trench as well.

I can't believe what they're showing next. The bodies of the little girl and the volunteer are lying on top of what looks like giant writhing maggots—the corpses struggling against their shrouds in the trench.

"Yeah," says Tanner. "They're gonna have to close that up fast.

Weird how so many of them will come back at once like that. It's like that first one woke them up."

"What the blue screaming hell is going on here?"

Tanner nods at the screen. A reporter is speaking urgently to the camera: "What we're seeing here is a post-mortem reaction to the Final Flu. These are not your loved ones all of a sudden getting better. These are—"

We hear the automatic gunfire echoing loudly among the buildings outside before hearing it on the TV. The camera swings away from the reporter to down the street from the park. A figure falls forward, a broad stripe of blood plastered from his mouth to his groin. As that one falls we see another man behind him, comically barefoot in his Sunday best suit. He's clasping a woman to him. You can see the woman's screaming face over his shoulder as he chews into her. A bloom of red appears on the back of the man's head and he falls, pulling the woman with him. The Guardsman runs over, points his rifle down and fires.

"As you can see over here," we hear the reporter's voice over the image, "victims of bites from these reanimated bodies need to be put down, too. No matter how slight or severe the wound, the person bitten will sicken, die, and rise to bite someone himself. Reports of this phenomenon in other cities have indicated that the lower brain stem must be destroyed to drop the reanimated ones."

The air crackles with the *pop-pop-pop* of gunfire. "It's not just here in this park!" the reporter yells over the blasts.

"This is happening with the burials at other parks! This is why everyone was supposed *to stay home!*" The camera finds the reporter at last. He's got his back to the trench, where one can see hands waving over the lip of it. There were other bodies wrapped in sheets waiting to be put into the trench. They writhe and twist like oversized grubs. Legs begin kicking free, arms thrust stiffly out. "Many of the dead are getting free," says the reporter, "either from the sheets or from loved ones who think their deceased have miraculously recovered. The ones in the trench aren't likely to get out, as it was dug a solid six feet. The dead are utterly mindless on top of very uncoordinated. They don't—"

A scream close by cuts the reporter off this time. The camera pans right to show a Guardsman taken down from behind by a big woman in a pink muu-muu and a pale, thin teenager dressed in what must have been his prom tuxedo. They each have an arm upon which they batten down. They gnaw and tear furiously at the tough cammie sleeves. The Guardsman is young and fairly robust yet he can't break the grip these people have on him. The fat paws of the big woman close so tightly you can see the Guardsman's flesh bulging white between her fingers.

The camera turns back to the reporter in time to show two dirty figures shambling up behind him. There's this animal *hnnnnnnnh!* and the camera's image is jerked backwards. It bounces once, rocks, then settles for a view of the clear blue sky. The screams are so loud and close the mic is distorting. Beyond the screams the background is filling with the sounds of weird moans, a low growling. And more screams. A dog yelps and cries over and over....

The slurping and smacking noises are the worst. And the hungry *mmmmmm!* you hear as they tear into another bite.

God knows what took them so long to switch back to the studio. It's just one man at the news desk, no spiffed-up female counterpart. He eventually looks at the camera, his forehead creased as if weighing what he's about to say next.

Finally:

"Homeland Security told us to make sure no one was frightened or otherwise led to believe that this situation was out of control. Well, you all saw what we saw. If you have Flu sufferers in your house, you have a decision to make. How do you want to remember them? You can either finish it now and put your loved ones out of their misery—or you can try and finish it while fighting for your life. Fighting against what has to be the devil's cruelest trick on humanity since—"

The anchor swallows hard. "For our viewers, however many are left out there, please stay indoors like they're telling everyone now—but *don't* trust the authorities to get this under control anytime soon, if ever. Not only are people still dying from the Final Flu, a lot have died already—and not all of those bodies made it to those burial sites. As you could see from the live feed we had earlier, most of these wandered in from—"

The screen goes to a generic blue "Loss of Satellite Feed" page.

"I can't believe it took them that long to cut him off," Tanner says. "This is looking to be much worse than anyone thought."

"The people you talked to knew about all of this and thought they could contain it?"

"How hard could it be? One in every three caught the Final Flu. Not everyone died at once. Even if they did, it's still two-to-one. You'll notice they don't move very fast, either...oh, and speaking of which, could you get off your chair and move behind me as fast as possible?"

I look over in time to see Angie. Her eyes are dry and unfocused but I'm sitting closest to her and she's stumbling straight towards me. I jump away from my chair and Tanner bangs a slug between her eyes. She falls, her arms still reaching out to take me. Her teeth are still showing from under her lips as she sprawls across the floor.

Tanner slides off from his chair to stand over her. "Look at the color of her skin," he says. "She wasn't dead all that long. Her lividity would have changed over time but looking at her you'd think she was just fine, if a little pale. Feel her skin, though!"

"Er, no thanks. Her eyes were all I needed."

"Hmm...well, yes. They can't produce tears or blink anymore. Good catch! Hadn't considered that one!"

"Goddamn it, it's obvious this has been going on everywhere else. Why aren't people being warned about this?"

"Actually, the reanimation phenomenon started just last night Stateside. People have been dying of the Flu in Europe and Asia all last week but this business with walking, flesh-eating cadavers is a new development. I must admit, though, I'm curious. How would *you* explain this?"

"How about we start with the truth?"

"Who would believe it? That's why they were encouraging people to see it for themselves on their local channels. People can deal with it that way. Or so they thought. The National Guard here certainly wasn't ready for it. They didn't fill in that trench like they were supposed to once those things started stirring." Tanner glances towards the plate glass entrance. "We might want to get out of sight of the doors."

The first shadows are stumbling forth into the street from between the buildings across the avenue. They're far enough away; we're buffered by a wide, brick plaza anchored by a center fountain. Still....

"We should kill the lights," I say, but Tanner has them off before I'm halfway through saying it.

Just as I'm turned to walk back to the desk the elevator door dings and opens. The light in the elevator is blocked by one, two, now five figures stumbling hesitantly into the lobby.

"Tanner!" I spring for the front desk.

"Nnnnh-*waaaaah!*" They key in on my voice and movement and shuffle in my general direction.

"Can anyone here say his or her name?" Tanner asks.

"Unnnh!"

"Mmmmmgh!"

"All right, then. Good night!"

This gray, big-bellied old man wearing nothing but boxer shorts with his wedding tackle hanging out goes down, a red-black hole misting open between his eyes and exploding out the back of his skull. The man in the soiled and stinking flannel pajamas springs backward, as does the one in the gray track suit. God help us, the next one sweated out his last fever nude, his final death-shit moist about the backs of his thighs. Tanner drops him.

"Okay," says Tanner, still grinning. "The last one's yours."

"What? You're kidding, right?"

"No. You're taking her down."

She's a slight, bird-boned thing with expensive hair poofed into a cloud behind her head from lying feverish in bed. She dressed in pink silk pajamas but like all God's children, male and female, rich and poor, she voided her bowels at point of death.

"Look around you!" says Tanner. "Find something you can use!"

The shit-stench is eye-watering. I don't see anything around me but various pieces of furniture.

"Come on! She's just a woman! Not even a big one!"

I pick up the single big upholstered chair—lighter than you'd think, really—and throw it. It knocks the woman onto her back. I pick up the seat cushion, which had flown loose, and put it over the woman's grunting, snapping face. She bites the cushion. The force of her contracting jaw deforms the cushion from the other side. Like it's being pulled into a black hole.

Putting all of my weight into my heel I stomp down upon the woman's head. I feel teeth break, then her jaw. But I can't quite kill her. I start jumping up and down on her head. I lose my balance and fall backwards.

The pillow tumbles from her face as she rises. Rage flares in her undead eyes, standing one on top of the other as her broken-necked head rests with one ear flat upon her shoulder. Her face is black and blue, her teeth bloodied, but there's enough of them left to inflict damage.

"Goddamn it, Tanner, shoot the bitch!"

"You sure?"

"Fucking positive!"

"You don't have to curse."

"Are you fucking *serious?*" I roll to my feet, the woman between me and Tanner. I put my heel into her solar plexus and kick her towards him. He's startled so the first shot misses her head. His second shot drops her.

"Are you all right?" Tanner says over the ringing in our ears.

"You mind telling me the point of this?"

"I was curious to see how you would react in extreme crisis. You handled it in a manner…quite unorthodox."

"I finally got you to shoot it, didn't I?"

"Yes, and thanks to your rage issues, it's not pretty."

"Whatever works."

"The question is, should we trust you with a weapon?"

"Is that really up to you?"

"In a sense, yes."

"In your dreams."

I look at him, he at me. He holds the Glock up just so. I turn and walk back to the bar. Shoot me in the back while I'm going for a beer. I can think of worse ways to go.

"Okay, let's stop this!" Tanner says. "We'll find you a weapon, if only to double our firepower! There's this one thing, though."

"What?"

"Guns seem to attract them."

I look out the front. The shadows of a dozen or so once-living people lean against the glass by their foreheads. Most of the men are dressed in suits, but barefoot. The women are in nightgowns or simple dresses. Some have dirt down their fronts where they clambered over the other bodies to get out of their trench. Maybe half have that wide streak of red-brown blood around the mouths and down their middles.

"We need to get out of this lobby," says Tanner.

"Ya think?"

It's not like they can really see us, with those drying and unfocused eyes. But their slackjawed heads follow us as we back slowly into the darkened lobby. "I'd suggest the stairs," I say as I reach Tanner's position behind the desk.

"Aren't you on the 15th floor?"

"What if five of these things are waiting at the door on the 14th? Even if I had a gun I'm not sure I could get enough shots off at once before I got bitten."

"No, what I'm saying is I have a card for the express elevator to the presidential suite. You could walk down five flights instead of climbing 15."

"Oh. That's what we'll do, then."

We walk to the express elevator and get in. "I expect the presidential suite is fairly large. Why don't we just move our stuff up there?"

"Until when?" says Tanner. "Until all those police and National Guard we're not seeing get all those carnivorous walking corpses under control?"

"Point. So what do we do, Mr. Security Consultant?"

"I don't know about you but I'm going home to Colorado."

"Tonight?"

"Oh no. First thing tomorrow I need to scout the area. Make sure the National Guard is really down. Then we make a run for it."

"We?"

"Sure. I thought you might wanna come with."

Come with? Right. "What about those bandits you were talking about?"

"Nothing the two of us can't handle. If we leave early enough we should be able to blow through the worst areas without incident."

"Of course."

"See you at breakfast, then."

The doors open. I can tell he's already made camp here. Sly bastard.

"The emergency exit stairs are here," Tanner says.

I raise my hand in acknowledgment as I push through the door.

"Make sure you're wearing sensible clothes in case we have to abandon the vehicle," he calls after me. "We have to be ready for anything."

Going down the stairs I realize I never did get my beer. I should probably just raid the fridge in my room. If I ever see a bill I'll laugh until I stop.

7

On my way down the hall to my room I'm startled by the *whump!* of a body throwing itself at the other side of a door, roaring and snarling like a frustrated predator behind the glass at the zoo. Thank God that thing hasn't figured out how to work the latch. Thanks again for being many doors down from mine. I don't want to have to try and sleep with that thing's angry, hungry yowling in my ears.

I open the door to my room, this same room I woke up in this morning. The same room on another planet, where the hotel staff is dead or food for the same. I close the door behind me and secure the latch.

The sun edges below the horizon, its orange-yellow beams blazing like a silent scream through the window. I look down onto streets that were completely empty this morning. Still no cars or trucks rolling about. Just...people?

It's like Mardi Gras, wall-to-wall bodies and not one of them walks a straight line. I see no cars or trucks, armored or otherwise. No muzzle flashes of rifles or sidearms. All you see are these erratic, atomized little blotches, every one a stone killer.

I could get a view of the park from the other side of the building, see if the National Guard vehicles are still there, what the police are doing, if anything—that is, if I had the master key. I could take a quick trip downstairs and look. Run down the stairs, find a weapon I could use...no. Couldn't find one in the lobby to save my life earlier.

But in the kitchen? All those knives and tools!

Christ, it's a long way down. Why not wait for the morning? We're leaving then, anyway. Me and Tanner. He's got that Glock…

…with how many bullets left in it? Besides, the blasts attract others.

And Tanner?

I'm pounding down the fire stairs, the heavy base of a floor lamp cradled in one hand. Going round and around down the concrete and steel flights, the reality slams home: I'm in a 20-story convention hotel with absolutely no staff on duty. The only traffic on the street are mobs of flesh-eating pedestrians. Law enforcement and the military have been neutralized, if not eliminated altogether. There's no one left alive but people with severely morbid Irish luck—like me—and smooth-talking psychopaths like Tanner. And I expect the rest are plain psychopaths who don't have Word One to say whatsoever.

The 15 flights go quickly. I take deep breaths to steady myself at the door into the lobby.

I push it open.

Cool, damp stench washes over me in a wave of climate-controlled air. God only knows how bad this would be if the power were out. I listen for movement while my eyes adjust to the darkness. I notice the curious dead have left the windows and doors about the hotel. Most of the traffic is concentrated on the streets and sidewalks. Our fountain-centered plaza outside of the front doors gives us a good buffer.

I hear noises from the back area. I spare a glance at the bodies on the floor so I can step around them. The old man in the boxers is on his back, his junk still hanging out the flap. Mercifully, all I see of the woman whose face I'd ruined are her pale, blood-and shit-streaked legs. I walk past the front desk and Angie's still on the floor. Poor Angie. I step behind the desk, stop short when I see her face.

God!

There's no way Angie could have made a face like that when she was alive. Not on tequila, not on angel dust, not on a dare. Her teeth are dry like her eyes; they don't glisten so much as glow with pure menace. This is a monster's face. I realize now the worst wasn't leaving her on the floor like a pair of dirty socks. It was letting this dutiful, sweet daughter of the paved-over prairies to turn into *this*.

The light outside is fading. I edge around the front desk to the lounge area. The TV is still on. The screen shows a stock loop of landmark shots from around the world, implying that the SOS is going out to all the powers that matter, so remain calm (and feel free to join in the prayers if you need something to do while cowering in your shelters-in-place). There is no news on what is happening in the individual countries, let alone here in town. Just shots of large congregations, close-ups of supplicants on their knees, mumbling into their clasped hands. I'd try the other channels but that noise in the kitchen....

With the *mmmm!* and *hnnnnn!* sounds over the slurping and smacking there's no doubt as to what it is. The question is, who is that thing eating? Did Tanner come down ahead of me and get caught?

(Goddamnit I don't want to do this I don't want to do this *I don't want to do this!*)

I push through the swinging doors.

I see the dark mass on the floor before me. The creature—Jesus, what do we call these things?—doesn't look up until I turn on the light. She was a woman once, younger and somewhat more attractive than the scrawny cougar I defaced earlier. She looks up at me from where she sits carelessly on the floor, like a toddler plopped on her butt to play with something. She doesn't see me, of course, but she knows I'm there. She sniffs. Smell must be a major factor in how they register living flesh.

This lady's problem is she's got a scabby VanDyke around her mouth from feasting on the cooling remains of Officer Dalton. Registering new scent is difficult with her current meal literally under her nose.

I stand as still as possible. After a while she resumes noshing from a rip she's torn through Officer Dalton's exposed man-boob. I take a step back.

With a triumphant roar she rises quickly, facing me as if she really sees me. Her arms thrust forward, fingers clawing. I swing the floor lamp stand and she grabs it with blood-freezing force, the metal support pole warping in her grip.

I let go of the stand and duck behind the hot table. She slings the stand away, stumbling over Dalton's body as she comes for me. I'm casting about the room, looking for the—there! The chef's station.

A heavy, cleated meat tenderizer. A cleaver.

She has animal sense enough to brace one arm against the hot table to hold herself upright as she takes large strides to close the distance between us, her blue-gray hand gliding along the brushed steel of the grill table. But I have two working legs and a righteous fear for my life.

The cleaver is in my left hand, the meat hammer in my right. She rounds the edge of the table. Her arms stretch to take me, her flesh-clotted teeth bared to her blue-black gums as she moans in anticipation of fresh meat. I bring my left arm across my body and swing out.

One arm falls just below the elbow; the other dangles by a strip of flesh. The woman yelps, more in rage than pain, and lunges at me with her legs. My right arm comes up, around, and brings the hammer square between her eyes.

I can't tell if she's truly down or just stunned. Recalling the reporter's admonition that the lower brain must be destroyed I bury the cleaver in the back of her skull where she lies face-down on the floor. If that doesn't do the job I don't know what will.

"Unnnnh?" says Officer Dalton, and I'm so glad he spoke up or I wouldn't have seen him. I pull at the cleaver.

It's stuck. I step out of the way and end up tripping over the woman's body. Officer Dalton reaches down for me and I roll away just in time. He falls across the woman, his hand pushing at the blade in the back of the woman's skull. With a sklutch-squish it bends to one side, prying up a section of bone. Best of all, it's loose.

I can't reach it without being grabbed. Dalton's hands flail and grasp at me across the remains of the woman who turned him. I think of how that Guardsman's flesh bulged in the grip of that fat woman, of the lampstand in that girl's hands. Once those things have a hold on you, that's it. You're done for.

It's probably what happened to Dalton. No telling what he was doing with this woman in the first place but it's a safe bet he didn't think something so inconsequential as a woman could take his fat Trained Professional ass down. All she needed was a couple of handfuls of clothing and flesh and her jaws did the rest.

I scramble to my feet. Knives of varying lengths hang from the wall behind the chef's station but they're not long or thick enough to sever hands. Not as fast as I need to do it. The world's largest iron skillet sits to one side. I swipe at it with one hand and nearly dislocate my shoulder. I grab at it two-handed and swing as hard as I can at Dalton's hands. I hit one; with luck I broke the bones in it.

Like the woman before him, though, mere injury only enrages him. He lunges for me. I sidestep. Dalton's foot catches between the woman's ankles and he goes down face-first. The muscles in my chest and arms sing as I raise the skillet, dropping the broad black iron on the back of his skull as hard as I can. The shock buzzes clear through my elbows. Between the tile floor and the swift impact of broad, flat, heavy-as-hell iron skillet, his head is…okay, we're done.

I stand over the stilled bodies, fighting my gag reflex. I'm aware of a terrible shit-and-spoiled-meat odor and it's not helping my adrenaline hangover. I marvel at how readily—and with a force I didn't even know I had—I slashed at other humans with sharp blades and swung blunt objects into their skulls.

I barely make it to the sink. The projectile force of my vomit covers the distance for me. I turn on the spigot and work the spray hose to rinse my mouth and clear the sink.

I turn to face the bodies. Of course, they're not human; their drive to eat living flesh is fucking nasty, fuck them! Still. This came so easy. Not that I'm ungrateful for this opportunity to second guess my own success. Still, rage issues? Was Tanner right?

Tanner. Christ. The only living person I know and he's running his own game. Lucky me, though, I have a minor gold mine at my feet. Officer Dalton, and his full urban paramilitary battle-rattle, bleeding between my shoes.

The stick? Jesus, that's hilarious! I think it's a safe bet everyone who's surviving this so far—especially the ones who will make it through until morning—has guns. There are more than a few chewed-over National Guardsmen and police to pick over once someone drops their turned carcasses. If I can forget my squeamishness long enough to drop a zombie cop there's a good chance someone else—someone with no squeamishness to forget—is doing it even better.

The Taser? No. The only thing I can really use is the 9mm and the holster. Three shells in the magazine, but an extra full mag on the belt. Loud, but definitely lethal. I've got a flashlight, too. I take the cleaver and hammer to the sink to rinse them off and it occurs to me I might not have access to running water for a while. Might as well make use of it.

I find the blade sharpener. It's one of the better ones, as befits a chef who works at a hotel important enough to rate its own police officer. I stuff it in my pocket as I walk around the back of the kitchen, looking for the back door where deliveries are taken. I'm guessing he came in this way, but I can't be sure, no more than I know what he was doing with that young woman. A rape in progress? Or maybe he really was playing hero to some scared young thing hurt by one of the monsters.

Yeah, right. Seriously, though, didn't this Trained Professional see the same things I did on TV, only much worse, and up close and in person? After watching Guardsmen with body armor and M4s go down, what made him think his XXL uniform would shield him?

I'm no detective, I can't tell if they came through this way. The door is closed, and (should be) locked from the outside. I put my ear against the metal. Then, cleaver in one hand, hammer in the other, I lift my foot and push the door open at the bar with my leg.

Clear. Even better, the dumpster at the far edge of the loading dock is open. I let the door fall closed. I make sure it's latched and locked before I run back to drag what's left of Dalton and his lady friend here.

The door braces open with a hinged foot at the bottom, enabling me to half-carry, drag the bodies out and sling them into the dumpster. The dumpster lid leans against the lip of the dock so I don't have to go down to street level to close it. I find the mop and bucket, fill up the bucket and clean the gore from the tile.

I'd rather not look at the bodies in the lobby, let alone manhandle them outside, but they won't smell any better come morning and I'm going to want breakfast. I find a luggage dolly and start rolling the bodies two at a time to the dock. Then I find some disinfectant and get the blood and shit up as best I can. Poor

Angie….

In any event Tanner doesn't need to know what I just learned I'm capable of. Not while I'm still trying to make sense of it myself.

God help me, this is actually kind of thrilling.

8

Tanner gamely pretends he didn't get punked this morning. "I thought you'd gone ahead and left," he says.

"I figured I'd sleep in," I say, walking past him to the kitchen behind the bar. The look on his face when I came around the corner behind the stairs was priceless. At least he's not wearing those silly tennis shorts.

"You realize it's a long way to Colorado from here." says Tanner, following after. "We've got a lot of Kansas to cross. Six hundred miles!"

"I'd allow for some leeway on our ETA. You said it yourself; we don't know who's waiting out there for us on the road. Or what."

"Okay," he says. "You're right about that. That's why I was hoping we could go scouting on foot. I suggested that last night, too, if you'll remember."

"I remember. And since this is the last place we'll have ready access to food for a while I suggest eating the biggest, heartiest breakfast we can come up with. Right now."

I bang through the swinging doors behind the bar into the kitchen. He bangs through after me. "We don't have the time for that!"

"*You* don't have time for that. Me, I figure I've got the rest of my life to starve to death." I take off my suit jacket, hang it up where Angie had put it yesterday. "For however long that is."

"We can find food on the way!"

"Oh, you'll let me stop to eat? When?"

"I thought you'd want to see your family tonight!"

I laugh. "You were honestly going to let me see my family first? My apologies, Mr. Tanner. All this time I'd presumed you were passive-aggressively carjacking me."

"All I'd asked was whether or not you want to come with me to Highlands Ranch. I've got guns and supplies there. I thought I was doing you a *favor*."

"That's what you want the man with the rental vehicle to think while he does all the driving, puts all the gas on his credit card, and takes nothing from you but orders." I'm turning the dials on the fryer and grill. "By the way, how were you getting around while you were in town? Didn't you have a rental of your own?"

"I had a driver."

"You'll want to call him up, then. I'm running my own itinerary here."

I go into the fridge for eggs. Tanner is still standing by the grill when I come out. "You gonna eat all that?" he says, watching me crack eggs on the grill.

"Not right now. I need to find something to carry the rest with me."

"Look, I understand if you don't trust me," Tanner says as I check the fry vats. "I imagine you figure you had a pretty good reason to move from your room."

"How did you know I'd *moved*?" I say.

"You weren't answering; what else was I going to do? I had the master key. I looked in. Everything was gone; I figured you'd left already!"

I go to the freezer and get some breaded chicken tenders. I wish I'd thought to put these in the refrigerator to defrost last night but moving all those twisted-faced corpses turned me off all thoughts of food. I was too happy to grab my new gear and get out. Last night was no good until I got a fresh, non-corpse-carrying luggage carrier up to my room and moved everything down to the second floor. Then I could finally work on my growler of high-end draft before passing out.

"Look," Tanner says. "Like it or not we need each other. Our best chance for surviving is to have someone on shotgun at all times. Alone, we don't stand much of a chance. We have to sleep. Those things don't."

I pull my large oval plate close for the eggs. Something's missing. Orange juice? I drop the first round of chicken tenders into one fry vat, a bag of onion rings into the other. The crackling and steam causes Tanner to step back.

"There's probably an optimal number of people who could expect to make it safely through the swarms of dead and the occasional bands of marauders," Tanner says as the racket dies down. "Right now it's just you and me. But we need to build on this. We've got to trust each other!"

"It doesn't occur to you that trust might have gone out the window when you let that zombie cougar have at me last night?"

"What? You're going to hold *that* against me?"

"Unreasonable as it sounds to an arrogant, sociopathic fuck like you, Tanner, yes."

"Okay, okay! Look, I don't know what you're talking about but I obviously crossed a line somewhere. I'm sorry! It won't happen again. Will you accept my apology?"

"No."

"You're not accepting my apology, then."

"I just said I wasn't. That you don't know what you're apologizing for renders it invalid."

"All I heard was cursing and my name."

"Then we're done! Look, this might be the last time any of us will see eggs, bread, and fried cheese sticks, and I'd like to say a proper goodbye! So—" I jerk my head in the direction of the door.

Tanner opens his mouth to say something but shuts up. He turns and leaves the kitchen. I hear the TV come on in the lobby.

I'll give him credit. He could have pulled his gun. And the more I think about it—goddamnit, he's right. We both need a wingman. The hell of it is someone like him won't entirely have my back. And you could fill a fleet of Luxury Tanks with the fucks I don't give for him.

Which brings home how long it might be until I have eggs again. The monsters were eating the family dogs at the mass burial; will chickens survive this? Cows?

All of a sudden I flash on my wife. My son and daughter. Our cats.

I feel the heaviness upon me. Just as it was when I woke up, writhing within the constricting black coils of an anxious pre-dawn hour before I managed to fling my legs over the edge of the mattress. I try telling myself I would have left my wife well cared for before I began furnishing my new house in Kansas City.

Right. I was still leaving her to grow old and die in that crumbling little starter cottage in that crumbling old neighborhood in crumbling north Colorado Springs.

Which she did anyway.

My wife of 22 years.

My son. My daughter.

Goddamn, and those poor fucking cats! (Yes, the cats!)

The timer beeps over the fry vat. I pull up the basket, bang it to the side to knock the oil off, and hook it to drain. The snap-clicks as I shut off the fryer and the grill—I wish I had something less trite than "sounds like the slamming of coffin lids" but it's all I got.

I hear the TV outside in the bar. I look around the kitchen. The bright overhead lights. The fry vats and electric grills. Humming. Buzzing. Functioning.

Like regular TV programming, this is all going away.

I doubt there was even an evening shift to relieve at the power plants this a.m. How about the water and sewage treatment plants? How many of those workers were straining against the yellow tape when the dead kicked out of their winding sheets and clambered out of the trenches on each other's backs?

I pull up a stool. I could sit outside at the bar but I need to take all this in without the distractions of Tanner, the TV, and whatever might be pawing at the front plate glass in the lobby.

I'm working the knife and fork when I realize what I've been missing. Good Lord, the PTSD must be making me lose my mind already....

I go to the fridge and bring out all the bacon that will fit on the grills. Breakfast tastes so much better as I take my bites in between laying out the strips and cleaning as I go. I use the time before the first turning of the meat to secure the insulated bags used to carry up room service dinners. Once the bacon is turned it's less than a minute before they're draining on the paper towels I've laid out for them.

I'm laying out the rest of the bacon along and a box of sausage patties when Tanner comes through the door. He's a smidge paler than when I last saw him. "There's nothing on the TV but pre-recorded loops," he says. "Nothing. Not even local stuff."

"It was like that since before dawn," I say.

"It's just—well, this was to be expected." Tanner pulls himself up a little. He chuckles nervously. "Crazy as it sounds I half-expected someone to pop in with a weather report."

"Weather's gonna be what it's gonna be," I say, breaking down the boxes the bacon and sausage patties came in. I put them in the lined trash barrel behind me. "Hot, with a chance of afternoon thundershowers. What about it?"

"That's just it," Tanner says as if he'd heard something else entirely. "The sky looked good from the roof but these things can blow in anytime. If nothing else, we need to be in the air well before afternoon."

I stop and look at Tanner.

"What?" says Tanner. "I pretty sure these things didn't eat the Cessnas and Pipers. If we can find one of those and gas it up we're out of here."

"You can *fly*?"

"Well, it's something I just thought of, really. I didn't want to make a big deal of it. It's been so long…."

"Tanner, you are a piece of goddamned work. I swear, if you're making this up—"

"I've only flown these things on the computer, all right?" Tanner says. "Are you willing to take that chance? Because whether or not I want to chance it myself is what's got me in knots right now!"

"How many hours did you put in on the flight simulator game?"

"Enough for my wife to comment on it."

"Enough that you're seriously willing to try it?"

"Various stretches of hours over the years. Just haven't had the time for lessons and licensing. It's been on my bucket list."

"Here's your chance to prove to your wife you weren't wasting time."

"Really? Are you trying to talk me into this? You didn't strike me as that desperate to get back!"

"In the best of conditions it takes all day to drive across Kansas. And that's assuming we're starting at dawn, and that nothing and no one stops us."

"Even without interruptions we'd never get home in time," Tanner says, as if speaking to himself.

"No interruptions in the air. We'll be in Colorado well before dark."

"I don't have to take it too high."

"We can just follow I-70."

"That'll work until Denver."

"Where you'll follow I-25 south towards Highlands Ranch. At least until we're in the open country outside Lone Tree."

"Where'll we land?"

"Any open stretch of Interstate should do."

"Huh. Yes. They were actually designed for that." Tanner pauses. "Thing is, we have to assume Highlands Ranch and Colorado Springs look a lot like this. If they're not broadcasting out of New York, Atlanta, or Los Angeles, it's Game Over across the board. Which is why I'd like it if you came along. Safety in numbers."

"We'll need food."

"Yes, I understand that better now. You think you could spare me a plate of what you've got left?"

"Take the leftover eggs and French toast. The bacon and sausage will keep if I cook it thoroughly."

"Protein and fat. Yeah, this might be the last we see of it."

I hand him an oval plate. "Let's worry about that when we get to wherever we're going."

I expect him to take it outside to the bar but he straddles the stool I was using and eats where I was just minutes before. I'm under the impression that this is all coming home to him, and he'd rather not be left alone with it.

This shit is getting weirder by the minute.

I've sealed the bacon and sausage, the chicken tenders, the onion rings and cheese sticks in large freezer bags. I sucked the air out of the bags before sealing them; they'll have to keep until I can find a cooler—and room in a vehicle to carry that cooler in. And ice....

I take my vacuum sealed goodies to hide in my luggage. I've had my stuff—all of one suitcase and my laptop bag—packed and staged and ready to go since showering this morning. Tanner is so busy tearing into the French toast and scrambled eggs he doesn't look up as I bang out of the swinging doors.

He's finished when I get back from bringing my luggage down from my room on the mezzanine. "We ready?" he asks.

"Soon as you stage your gear."

It's already downstairs, bless his heart. All we have to do is bring the Luxury Tank around and load out. Tanner insists on going with me. "Just keep that gun holstered unless we have no choice but to blast our way out," I tell him. I show him the hammer and blade on the belt I'd liberated from Officer Dalton.

"Where'd you get the gun?" If he shows any surprise I miss it. He's as cool as the other side of the pillow.

"Officer Dalton stopped by while I was cleaning up."

"He did? Why didn't you tell me?"

"Because we have trust issues, Tanner."

"It—I was mainly curious if he had anything to say."

"Just, 'take this, it's really bad, you're on your own.'"

"Oh."

We turn the key in the glass door and push it open. Like stepping into the hot beating heart of rotting garbage, the damp, parboiled stench fouls our skin and clothes on contact. Just when you think you've adjusted to the smell of walking corpses and their shit-soiled legs, a fresh wave of humid stink rolls over like a fat ocean swell. Our mouths are tightly shut; it's all we can do to keep our eyes open as we cross the brick-paved roundabout the valets used to bring the cars around.

Clear, so far. No—in the street. I tap Tanner's arm with the back of my hand and point. We stop behind the fountain and watch him walk.

He's a heavyset middle-aged guy, big-shouldered and silver-haired. I'd rather not think about who was there by the bed when he woke up and whose blood that is down the front of his blue silk pajamas. As for what he's doing on this street in front of the hotel, I'm guessing he got out of the other major hotel one block over.

The wet brown stain in the back of his pajamas is one thing but there's something pale, white, with pink and yellow trailing down his leg. It tumbles out his pants cuff in gloopy, lumpy clumps like some horrible cottage cheese. The stench is beyond mere shit.

Tanner and I both have our hands over our mouths. We don't even wait for this thing to pass, shaking his left leg along the way to let more pale pink-yellow matter loose. We take quick breaths behind our hands and make a run for the garage.

That smell is even worse in the garage. Like it's been cooking in here. Our watering eyes aren't yet adjusted to the dim yellow light when a skinny white wannabe gangbanger rises from the shadows in the near corner behind us. It doesn't cry out until we turn to face it. If it hadn't been for all the scraping and shuffling as it got to its feet it might have snuck up on us.

Tanner reaches for his gun. I hold up my hand and walk towards the boy, the meat tenderizer in one hand, the butcher's blade in the other. The boy raises his arms to grab at me.

I swing the blade and one hand falls away mid-forearm. He drops his other arm before I can hit it. His angry bellow echoes throughout the parking garage. He swings his remaining arm around but I've switched out the blade for the meat tenderizer. The boy falls sideways. I step quickly behind his head. I remember something about how some fighters can kill you instantly by shoving your nose bone into your brain and I angle my next blow to do just that.

That should settle it but Tanner and I are in the not-so-sweet spot of surround-sound *hrrrrrrn!* echoing throughout the concrete cave of the garage. The Luxury Tank is just ahead in the first space beyond the handicapped spaces. I click the remote lock and we both run to the vehicle.

I start the engine and as I turn around to check my rear I see a stocky girl in a gore-blackened XXL sleep-shirt stumbling towards the Tank. I shift into reverse and slam into her. She falls backwards, her skull cracking loudly on the pavement. I hear the snapping of bones as my left rear tire rolls over her.

It's a short roll out from the garage to the doors of the hotel. I wish it was further. Apparently a bunch of these things have been using the garage to keep out of the sun. It won't take them long. I screech to a halt before the glass doors.

A buzzer squawks against my trying to pop the hatch while we're still in gear. Tanner takes this as a signal to jump out of the Tank before I can get it stopped. He's already at the doors, pulling them open as I throw the shifter in park. The hatch opens without complaint, but it's slow. I open my door and jump out. The walkers from the garage are staggering out into the sunlight and headed our way. I see two more coming across the plaza from the street.

Tanner puts my luggage out first. I wedge my gear between the rear seats. I turn and Tanner is already handing me his large suitcase. Now his suitbag….

I turn and look up. "Behind you!"

Tanner has just enough time to duck out under the grasp of the rotund man in the stained gray track suit. This seems to surprise him. He senses my presence, though. With loud crowing noise, he leans in towards me for the kill. I'm reaching for a hammer I'll never pull loose in time when there's a deafening *bang!* and the man in the stained gray tracksuit falls over.

And then Tanner tosses me his golf clubs.

Golf clubs?

"Goddamnit!"

"Just close the hatch, let's go!"

For a split second I want to throw them at the family of three, mom, dad and Junior toddling up behind us. Instead I toss the bag of clubs atop Tanner's other gear, slam the hatch, and run for the driver's side door—

—where I'm met by a petite, late-middle-aged woman in a pink nightgown. I see her rage-and-hunger-twisted face and punch her in her gut. She folds. I open the door, throw myself in, slam!

Tanner is already inside. "Why didn't you leave the keys in the vehicle?"

"Force of habit." I've got the Luxury Tank cranked, I'm in gear. A thump of hands and arms across my driver's side window tells me the woman has found her feet just before I bolt across the brick plaza.

The dead are massing in the street to intercept us. Normally I'd turn left to get to the Interstate but the swarm is too thick. I might as well drive into a wall. Or a mound of pale, carnivorous ants. I turn right, hoping I can round the block. Wherever these things were hiding as the sun came up, they're out, drawn to the hum of our engine, the roar of Tanner's gunfire, the cries of their fellow walkers. I see them coming out from around the buildings, stumbling down the streets I'm crossing, ambling towards us down the otherwise empty avenues.

I glance over to see Tanner trying to figure out the GPS over the bouncing and swerving. "Kansas City International Airport!" I say while pulling hard right to avoid a group of three lunging for us. I avoid overcorrecting and hitting the lamp post by jumping the curb at the corner. That was my first right turn. Fortunately this street is clear. I sprint down this block and skid into my next right, knowing full well I won't be as lucky on this last run.

"Keep straight," the GPS says.

All of Kansas City seems to be pouring out of the side streets to swarm us. Three or more will be bold enough to punch through the glass to get at us. I imagine the rest tearing at the sheets of safety glass, heedless of injury (hell, it just pisses them off more), reaching in with lacerated hands and pulling us out by whatever those hands grab first. How many mouths, how many sets of teeth will cover our bodies, from our faces, eyes, ears, arms, legs? How much will we actually suffer, our beings torn away a single mouthful at a time, before death takes mercy on us?

"You strapped in?" I ask Tanner.

"I recommend picking up the pace, if you don't mind," he says.

"All right, then. We're going to hit some people."

I press hard on the accelerator and I'm good for the first half of the first block. A man in a suit with his bloodied shirttails hanging comically over his slacks steps out to meet the Tank. He thumps off the front quarter panel, shaking the frame of the SUV as it rolls along the sunny, stinking street.

"Keep straight," the GPS reminds us. "Prepare to turn right."

I swerve left but hit two more with the right quarter panel. One spins away, the other goes under the tire. The moaning of the massing dead is like one long sustained shout we can hear even in the nearly airtight cabin of the luxury SUV. We're halfway through the second block but the mob is thick in front of us now. I can't see where to turn.

"Turn right, one hundred yards," the GPS says.

"Don't slow down!" Tanner says.

If I hit these things full force I'll trigger the airbags. I cut my speed just enough to bring the ones in front under. The automatic all-wheel drive kicks in and we're grinding and squishing and breaking the bodies beneath (God, they'd better be) run-flat tires. We rise up on one corner, then fall. We roll up, sag down as we pulverize select pockets of flesh and bone, then roll up another, plunging nose down again over the uneven terrain of howling corpses.

The interior of the Luxury Tank is dark for all the diseased once-people slapping and pounding at the glass. I can barely see over the hood for all the angry cadavers clawing at the front of the vehicle. I hear the strain like cracking ice in the driver's side window in the rear. I press just a little further on the accelerator. We lurch forward. But only a little. Then we're pushed back again.

The sound of moaning, snarling dead people grows louder in the near-airtight space of the cab, humming in our very teeth. The side windows are bloody from the fists pounding on them. It won't be long.

I floor it.

They back away at the roar of the engine enough for me to lurch forward again. The nose of the vehicle dips as we clear the latest mound of bodies. One of the tires is spinning but the rest are working. This angles us to the left a little.

"Turn *right*," scolds the GPS.

I cut the wheels left and right. The snarling once-people back away from either corner. They seem to have thought they were safe where they were but now they can't predict how I'm going. The ones directly up front are crazed with hunger, rage, God-knows, and still go under—except one bad boy with a neck tattoo who has thrown himself up on the hood. I brake hard. He slides back but holds on. I throw the shifter into reverse.

"What are you doing?" says Tanner.

I stomp the pedal again but the crowd behind me is like a wall. All four tires spin uselessly on the slick, ruined flesh beneath us. I hear a sharp crack over the sound of whirring tires. I look back and the window on the other side is crazed with tiny lines. The only thing keeping the rear window intact is all those hunger-mad dead people pressing in from behind. The sheer force and mass of all their bodies make it harder for the ones closest to us to hammer at it with their fists.

"Just get us out of this!" Tanner says. "We'll shake him when we're clear!"

"Yes, *sir*," I say. I put the shifter back into drive and floor it again. I see what looks to be a slight break to the right and cut the wheel that way.

We jolt away just in time for another loud crack. A wide, jagged shard of the rear window on the driver's side bows in. An arm thrusts through the gap, working at the wedge of safety glass, peeling it back.

9

The crumbling edge of the safety glass runs red from all the lacerated wrists and hands pushing their way in. The thumping at the other windows becomes heavier, louder. I'm working the wheel, all but standing on the pedal. Three out of the four tires are spinning; the rear shimmies from one side to another. Just not so fast or forceful enough to shake the mob pressing in on us….

Suddenly we jackrabbit away so fast we're thrown back into our seats. The arms and hands rip and snap backwards out the crumbling shards of safety glass.

Inertia makes up for our lack of traction and our front end goes up again. The kid with the neck tattoo who's been sliding towards me across the hood is slammed face-first against the windshield. We come down the other side, bearing down on one last quartet of living dead. The kid tumbles over, knocking them backwards. Flesh is crushed, bones are snapped.

There's the freeway entrance ramp, free and clear. We fishtail one last time in the gore before shooting up onto the Interstate. Sunlight pours into the cab like a blessing as we rise into the wide-open lanes of I-70.

"That was close," says Tanner, looking back over his seat.

"Christ!" I'd go faster but the handling feels funny on the Tank. The tires sound weird, too, making a low, but distinct roaring as we fly over the white slab concrete.

"Sounds like a run-flat tire running flat," Tanner says. "Might want to slow down in case one of them starts coming apart."

"So much for the Luxury Tank," I say, letting my foot relax on the pedal. Only a bit, though. I've got my eyes on the sides of the highway, looking down at the throngs milling about the city streets below us.

"I can see how something like this would give you the illusion of safety," Tanner says. "What you really need, though, is something high off the ground. A truck with a lift-kit and really big, fat tires. The kind you have to climb up into. Even then, you don't want to let yourself be slowed down by a mob. Of course, you'd be freer to move with those big tires, so that wouldn't be an issue."

"So let's land by a truck dealership," I say.

"Arapahoe Road by Centennial Airport has dealerships. Anyway, that's not a bad idea. I'll have to rely on you to look for places like that while we're in the air."

I'm sarcastic; he's serious. Holy shit, this just might work.

We ride in silence, just the low roar of the left front and right rear tires riding on their reinforced sidewalls, the bluster of the wind in the back where the window is ripped halfway out. It's all I can do not to collapse into a shivering mess thinking of the different ways this could have gone.

Staying in the city would have been a mistake, I see that now. We were damned lucky the hotel didn't get swarmed. It would have happened eventually. And with that many of them crowding the lobby and the lower floors (the glass wouldn't have lasted long) we would never have gotten away. We'd have stayed trapped in the upper floors until we starved to death.

I can only imagine how it's been going on our side of Colorado Springs. When Claire died. What happened when she came back. I can't help feeling that even if we could beam ourselves over sci-fi style in the next five minutes, it's already over. We'll be lucky if we can save ourselves.

After a while Tanner cuts on the radio. The few stations he finds are on automatic, music and commercials running without intermittent DJ commentary. We catch two stations looping the same Civil Defense bulletin telling us all to stay indoors until otherwise notified. I laugh at that one, but only the first time.

It gets old fast, all of it. There's a sense we're not only wasting time, we're endangering ourselves listening to these old, obsolete messages. Even the music. Tanner cuts the radio off.

We pull onto the exit for the airport. It's looking good until we start down the main road there. We see the dead walking along the sides of the road, reaching out to us as we drive through. Two here, three there, six walking single file on the left side. All going our way.

"They've figured out there's people here," said Tanner. "This isn't going to be safe for long."

"Is it safe *now*?" I'm driving as fast as I dare down the middle of the road, praying these things don't work up the nerve to step in front of us. So far they turn and look and keep walking.

"Let's see," Tanner says. "No, that's the edge of the first wave there. Depending where we're going here I'd say we've got a good half hour before we're in real trouble."

"Great," I say. Thirty minutes to find a plane, make sure it's airworthy, load it up, gas it up and go. Shit!

"Apparently someone got here just ahead of us. The stumblers we're seeing here are following the sound of their vehicle."

"This just keeps getting better."

"Don't get discouraged. We've gotten this far. I don't see why we can't find a plane and get up in the air before we have to fight our way out."

To find the airfield on roads designed to take passengers to and from their flights…eventually I come across a closed access gate. I get out of the truck. I pull the chain the lock's attached to and see it's already been shot apart. I hold it up for Tanner to see before sliding open the gate.

"These things really key in on gunfire," Tanner says as I climb back in. "Explains the size of the herd coming towards us down the road."

"Our more immediate problem is inside this gate," I say, pulling ahead slowly.

"If we steer clear of them we should have no problem. They just want to get out of here same as—."

A slug explodes through the left rear window behind me and out through the right. I turn the wheel and stomp the gas pedal. I try driving in an irregular zigzag pattern to elude further shots but the handling is difficult, as if the power steering was out. We've got a wide expanse of runway to cross and I can hear where the rubber is coming off one of the rims.

"It's all right," says Tanner, looking back. "The guy seems satisfied we're not trying to steal his little Piper. Assuming that's his, of course."

We come to a row of hangars. Tanner seems encouraged that someone thought to close them up. Still, that means we have to tap out locks. Tanner almost used his gun but it occurred to me to use the hammer. Which, as it turns out, is almost as loud. Sound carries across the tarmac, across the remains of the prairie, to all that hear in this dead quiet world.

We open the overhead door only to see the aircraft's starboard engine in pieces on the floor. So we roll over to the next hangar. It's a Gulfstream IV. "I don't know anything about jets," Tanner says. "A shame, because we'd be in Colorado in an hour."

I'm hoping the third time is the charm but it's the fifth that gifts us with the dual-prop commuter plane built to take a dozen passengers and their gear. It doesn't belong to an airline; for all I know some rich Mormon kept it so he could fly his largish family to wherever they cared to go. Bottom line: no grease-blackened parts lying around the hangar. The plane looks clean and well-taken care of. We can only hope it's gassed up and good to go.

You can see them now outside, lumbering dark and graceless through the stately blonde grasses stretching behind our hangar. Even if the Luxury Tank had all its tires and windows intact I'm not sure I could get us out.

A shriek rises from the hangar on the other side of the tarmac. Gunfire. More gunfire.

Our thirty minutes are up.

"I was really hoping to taxi her up and down the runway so I could listen to the engine," Tanner says. "Topping off the tank would be nice, too."

"Screw it! Let's see if the engine starts!"

We kick away the chocks on the wheels and scramble up the ladder. Tanner doesn't waste time strapping in. The twin props roar into life, the wash knocking the tool chests and other items about the hangar. Tanner lets the plane roll out of the hangar into the sunlight. He pulls up alongside the remains of the Luxury Tank. I've popped the hatch with the remote; we jump down the ladder and run to pull out our luggage. I'm able to carry all of mine up the ladder and into the cabin. I take Tanner's gear as he hands it up to me.

I figure I'm doing pretty good at not making a face when he brings over his golf clubs but Tanner's own expression startles me. He's looking at something, something I can't hear over the roaring props. He throws bag of clubs at me and the force nearly knocks me back into the cabin. He's clambering up the ladder two steps at a time. "Pull that thing up NOW!" he shouts, throwing himself into the pilot's seat." Over his shoulder I see the big SUV bearing down on us from across the runway. From the hangar where they were shooting at us.

From where the dead were attacking.

Tanner has the plane rolling as I pull the ladder up. I slam the door just as he brakes hard, throwing me forward.

I pick myself up to see the big SUV has parked athwart our front wheel. A woman with a bright red headband and big sunglasses is jumping out the driver's side, waving her hands in front of her as if to say *Don't shoot*. Tanner and I both have our nines in hand when we go to meet her at the hatch.

"Good! Good!" she says. "Look, I'm glad I caught you! Our plane's been—we've been overwhelmed. We need to go with you."

"We?"

"My son and I weren't the ones shooting at you, okay? That was my husband. He's dead now, are you satisfied? Just let us on the plane! They're all going to be here soon!"

"You're fucking kidding me," I say.

"No, I am *not* 'fucking' kidding you! We need a ride! And I'll thank you to watch your language around my son. He tends to repeat things. Especially if it's something you'd rather not hear."

A tall, pudgy boy of maybe eleven or twelve staggers up behind the woman. Tanner and I raise our nines.

"Oh!" the woman laughs. "My husband said this was going to be a problem. I figure I keep Michael clean enough, but the way he is I suppose it's easy to mistake him for one of those things."

"Ay-uh-pwain!" Michael says, pointing at us. "People wide ay-uh-pwain!"

"Yes, honey. We will, too, in a minute. Let me finish talking to these people."

Tanner bristles at the sight of the boy. "You're not coming with us," he says.

"Listen, I'm not some silly yuppie soccer mom with a special-needs child! I'm Lieutenant Colonel Sheryl Handler of the United States Air Force! My husband was Colonel Handler, and we were…look, even if I could talk, we don't have time! Let us aboard!"

"The bullshit thickens," I say, just loud enough for Tanner to hear over the props.

She must have read my lips. "What I can tell you is that we were on our way to a classified location. I'm pretty sure if you take me there they'll let you in, too. I don't see them turning away pilots handy with guns. Seriously, forget my husband, I've got my own connections! We can work something out!"

Tanner looks at me. I shake my head.

"Okay, I know I'm not in uniform but I've got my ID and copies of the invita—uh, orders! Look, let me show them to you on the way! You don't believe me, set me down somewhere! Those things are already on their way!"

I look past Tanner to the cockpit windows. Already half a dozen are shambling towards us from her hangar. And those are just the ones I can see.

"We've got just over a quarter tank of fuel and we're wasting it talking to you," Tanner says. "I'm going to ask you once to move your vehicle and let us by."

"You're kidding, right? A woman and her child, you're just going to leave us here?"

Tanner thumbs the hammer on his nine. "You have your vehicle. Get in it and go. If I have to come down and move it myself you will *not* like the way this ends!"

The woman lifts her chin. "No," she says. "No. I think we'll just stand here until we're *all* surrounded. If a woman and her child can't get away it's not fair for you two heartless cowards to, either!"

Tanner raises his nine at the boy. I pull a pack of crackers from my inside jacket pocket: "Hey, kid!"

The boy lights up. "Kwack-kuhs!"

The woman's eyes are wide with fear. "Those look like they have peanut butter in them! He can't have peanut butter; he's allergic!"

"Even better!" says Tanner. He snatches the crackers from my hand, leans out the door. "Here, boy! Kwack-kuhs! Fetch!" Tanner throws the pack of crackers over the wing and well behind the plane. The woman grabs at her son's arm but he jerks away.

"You bastards!" she says, chasing after.

Tanner drops the ladder. "Stand ready to pull this up when I get back!"

Tanner jumps to the tarmac and runs to the front of the plane. I see the front end of the SUV pulling back out of sight. Seconds later I'm stepping away from the hatch as Tanner huffs back through.

"Drop the ladder if you have to! Get that closed we gotta *go!*" Tanner drops into the pilot's seat and we're rolling forward. I hear Lt. Col. Handler shriek as I pull the ladder. The last I see of her she's struggling to pull her son along with her after the plane. The boy is intent on opening the crackers while three walkers approach from behind our hangar.

Tanner has already got the plane near take-off speed by the time I'm able to reach out and grab the door. I'm looking down as I'm leaning back with all my weight to pull the hatch shut and I see their faces. So many faces showing us their teeth, roaring their hunger at us as we climb into the late morning sky....

10

"Is it secure?" he says as I crouch-walk to my seat in the cockpit.

"Oh yeah."

"We almost didn't make it," says Tanner.

"Well, we did. Think we can make it to Colorado?"

"Not with this much fuel. We're going to have to set down somewhere."

"Well, this'll save some time. How far can we go on the fuel we've got?"

"I honestly don't know." Tanner's gaze flits between the windshield and the instruments. "I am curious as to how it worked out with the good lieutenant colonel's SUV. I had pointed it at the thickest part of the herd and let it roll away in drive."

"Holy shit! You let their one means of escape drive away?"

"My friend, my accomplice, whatever you are, *there was no escape!* They were coming in thick from all sides! Children in pajamas, mothers in their gowns. And then the ones who didn't obviously die of the Flu first—God! You have no idea how close I came to colliding with that bunch on the runway!"

"I saw 'em. Did we find I-70?"

"We're headed due west right over it. Not hard to find, considering how we got to the airport."

"Good." I go into the back cabin and open my suitcase. I pull out some sausage patties and bacon, bring them to the front.

"After all we've been through, we're going to eat?" says Tanner.

"Figured we could use a little comfort food right now."

"Are you bothered by what we did back there?"

I take a bite from a sausage patty, savoring the soon-to-be-extinct flavor. "No," I say after a while. "If I'm bothered, it's that that I'm not bothered." I'm about to take another bite when it occurs to me: "Although, frankly, that doesn't bother me either."

"Funny how we're obliged to feel a certain way about things, in spite of the rational outcome." Tanner glances over. "How did you know the boy would go for the crackers?"

"My wife did a stint at a daycare. One of the before-and-after school kids was autistic. One of the things you had to watch out for was he was always hungry. It was the medication he was on. He was always on the hunt for the after-school group's cracker stash. Once he found those there was nothing left for the other kids to eat. He'd lock himself in a closet or a bathroom and stuff every last one into his face."

"In *school*," Tanner says, his face darkening. "Believe me, I know you think I'm stuck up, but I would never have put my children in a private school were it not for that law insisting my daughter share the classroom with one of those monsters. Disrupting the class, exposing himself—and of course everything has to revolve around that parasite's 'special needs' while 20 or 30 normal kids do without!"

Tanner glowers out the window. "As much as I wanted to shoot that filth I'm glad I didn't waste a bullet. What I wonder now is if precious Michael managed to die of peanut poisoning before the stumblers got him."

"I understand the reaction is pretty quick. Of course, his mother might have had an Epipen handy. Probably brought him around just in time to realize he was being eaten alive." I ponder this for a moment. "I suppose it would have been far kinder to have just shot them both."

Tanner glances from the window to the indicators. "No. She got the same mercy she was offering us. That woman was more than willing to let us all get swarmed and die if we didn't give in to her."

"Mm-hmm," I say, finishing off my patty.

"To think that bossy old cow felt entitled all because she crapped eight pounds of defective waste from her vagina! My God, she would have just taken over! We'd have to put up with him bouncing around the plane and oh, by the way, get rid of anything that has peanuts in it because her worthless offspring's need to breathe supersedes the nutritional needs of rational, able-bodied men!"

"Here," I say, handing him a sausage patty. From one able-bodied man to another."

"Thanks," he says, taking the patty. "I don't know about you but I welcome a world in which such ideas can be refuted. It's one thing when you've got a non-productive person, but someone who's disruptive as well? Way things are going now, people are going to have to take a more realistic approach to 'compassion.' Put it towards people who give *back*, for a change!"

"I hear you. Look, how far out are we now?

"Look down. What do you see?"

"Looks like we're coming up fast on Topeka."

"We'd be past Topeka already if we weren't so low on gas. I figure I've got just enough airspeed to keep us up."

"We still made better time than driving. When do you see it getting critical?"

"I honestly can't say. I don't know this plane. I'm just conserving as best I know how. The needle's going down, that's all."

"Would it hurt to bring us lower? I'm curious as to what's going on."

"Once we get on the other side of town let's look for a truck stop or something. If we're going to make it to Colorado we've got to gas up sooner than later."

My ears pop as we descend, a little more steeply than I'd like before leveling out. Tanner steers us a little to the left. We jolt from the change in heat radiant from the surface below but I can see the Interstate a lot more clearly now. And the nature of the black dots along the parallel strips of white....

"Shit."

"What?"

"Well, maybe we're a little too close to the city," I say.

"A bunch of abandoned cars?"

"No. Everyone here went home to die, too. Thing is...."

"What?"

"The westbound people are headed west, the eastbound east. It's the damnedest thing. It's like they're commuting!"

"Well, can I land the plane?"

"No."

"No?"

"You could look for yourself."

Tanner snaps on the auto-pilot. After a second and third glance at his instruments he unbuckles and leans towards my side of the cockpit. He takes his look, curses under his breath before thumping back into his seat and buckling up.

Tanner disengages the autopilot. "We've got to get on the other side of this city," he says, as we ascend. We fly between a couple of hi-rises on either side of the Interstate before Tanner takes us sharply up. I look down. Traffic's thick. Where do these things think they're going?

Goddamn, this all started with a fucking flu!

"Tanner, what the hell do you think happened here?"

"What do you mean? I've got to land this thing and soon!"

"Never mind."

We cross the narrow squiggle of the Kansas River, buzz the western half of the crowded city. In another minute we're out over the rolling grassland. Still a lot of deaders out here, but their numbers are thinning the further we go.

"My best guess," Tanner says, taking us over the northern edge of the Interstate, "is that one of the pharmaceutical companies came up with this by way of having a vaccine and a cure for it. The sloppy way everyone's been doing business over the last decade or so neither their vaccine nor their cure worked."

"They were making a big deal of everyone getting that flu shot last winter," I say. "A lot bigger than usual, it seems."

Tanner doesn't seem to have heard me. His attention is fixed on the Interstate. He takes us lower, edging carefully over the narrow white strips below. I look nervously at the wind turbines we're passing between, their huge blades chopping the air so close to the wing it rocks the plane.

"Between you and me," says Tanner, "I don't think there's much that hasn't happened on purpose in last twenty years. For all we know this is all about thinning out the herd. I wouldn't be surprised at all if Lt. Col. What'sername really was trying to get to a pre-arranged location for the elites and their favored servants. It stands to reason those elites would arrange transport for everyone they wanted to save. That the retard and his family had to arrange their own transportation makes me wonder if they were really invited."

The sudden silence of the props hits like a physical blow. Tanner and I look at each other.

"Ready or not," says Tanner.

He brings us over the eastbound lanes. Tanner is slowing us as best as he can with the flaps, his hands white-knuckled on the tiller. We're coming in fast. We bump onto the white slab asphalt of I-70 and it's all we can do to hold steady at 90 mph. Tanner works the brakes and we've slowed to 60 mph when our wheels explode beneath us. The nose is tilting sharply down and the last thing I'm thinking before impact is....

TWO

CRASH

11

I feel the hands gripping me. Fingers tightening about my limbs. Terror rises—and sinks again. My conscious—what? Can't make myself stay. Not that I want to be "here" when the teeth tear into my flesh, feeling their cold, dry tongues working in, scraping across my bones....

"He's coming around!" I hear someone say. "Think we can bring him back for good this time?"

I feel a stinging on my face. My head is knocked back and forth. I can't do anything about this so I let myself fall. Back where there's no "here." I don't want to be here. There's nothing here. No one here. They're gone. My people. Gone.

(They got sick.)

(Who?) (Everybody.)

(Sibyl and Jack didn't get sick.)

My chest hurts. As with the stinging on my face, I let go and try to fall backwards into the Great White Nothing. I can't fall as far, though. The pain in my chest, my left side. The hands again, moving me.

"Derek? Derek, are you there?"

A woman's voice. Not Claire. Giselle?

(Giselle was pretty.)

No. Working class accent.

"I don't know how much longer we can justify this." A man's voice. "If he doesn't come around soon...."

"Look, I know I prob'ly put too much painkiller in him but the way I see it he's got a better chance of healin' those cracked ribs if he stays out. You wanted to see how we could learn to take care of people with the hospitals out. Here you go, first case!"

"Let's hope we don't have to duck out of here fast. He's gonna slow us down."

"Brandon an' me can get 'im in the back of my truck in less'n a minute!"

"All right, then. He's your dog, Charlie Brown." I sense him leaving the—room? It's warm but dark. I can't focus my eyes yet but I can tell it's dark.

"Mr. Derek Samuel Grace of Colorado Springs. You in there? You hear me?"

I don't know how to make words. I sound like one of them. (Who?) Those people with the bloody bibs all the way down their fronts....

"You're tryin', I see it! Come on, baby, I know you can do it!"

Derek. Mr. Grace. Derek Samuel Grace.

That's *me!*

"Hey."

"Is that what I thought it was?" She's so happy, I couldn't bear to disappoint her....

"Who—?"

"Who?" she says.

"Who're you?"

"Me? I'm Krystal! Krystal with a 'K'!"

"Krys...."

"Yes, some people call me that. I prefer 'Krystal,' though."

"'Kay, Krys...."

I'm aware of her shouting after me as I fall back again. It's different this time, though. Now I just want to *sleep.*

It feels good so I'm going with it.

I awaken to a pounding headache and the sensation of being drowned. Someone is trying to pour water down my throat.

"It's a miracle he ain't died from dehydration. If I knew how to set up a drip, I would!" the woman says.

"Well, he's still here," says another woman. "He's swallowing."

Gulping and gasping is more like it. I find myself scrambling out of the Nothing trying to breathe. The inevitable gulp brings the water down the wrong pipe and now I see green and purple bursts in the Nothing as I try and cough it out.

"Oops. Looks like he aspirated that one."

"Ass-per-*what?*"

"I thought you said you went to nursing school!"

"I went to community college to become a medical assistant!"

"Don't matter, the terminology's the same!"

"You mean all those silly-assed spellin' words and shit we had to learn? God, I felt like I was in fourth grade again!"

"And still flunkin' out!"

"Well, if you're so smart, why don't *you* hook him up to a drip!"

"Because I didn't go to school at all! And I still know what 'aspirate' means!"

The pain in my chest is bad enough with my coughing. Now I feel a weight pushing in on my middle. The white overcomes the burst of color with each push.

"What the hell are you doing?"

"Chest compressions! I'm trying to push the water out!"

"Chest compressions on a man with cracked ribs? That's it, move over! God! Just 'cause you know a buncha words don't mean you know shit!"

Water comes up, hot from my lungs. I instinctively gulp it down, along with some air. My hands find the surface I'm on, push.

"He's trying to push himself up!"

"Well, it's probably better for him if he's swallowing water. C'mon, help me with him here."

"He looks like he's doing fine on his own."

"Look at his arms shaking! He hasn't eaten solid food in a week! C'mon, help him up!"

I feel their fingers stabbing into my armpits. My eyes are open but all I see are shapes moving against a dark background. I look towards the voices, blink, shake my—no. I can't shake my head. Skull hurting.

The first thing I see is the glass with the water in it. On a metal table. It's a little higher than my bed.

"Oh, no!" A shape swoops into my field of vision. A young, heavyset woman takes the glass in one hand while wheeling the table back with her other. "You're too weak to hold anything on your own. Let me hold the glass while you're sitting up. Hannah, you think you can get him some food?"

"Like what? He's gonna need it mashed up until he remembers how to digest it."

"Bring 'im that beef jerky we got! He can learn how to work his jaw again and get what he needs from the juices."

"Huh!" I look across my bed (I'm on a smallish, single bed) towards the door where a dirty-blonde young woman scowls at me before leaving. "Better rest up!" she says. "Mr. Evans gonna put you to work as soon as you can stand!" She turns and is gone.

"What? Oh!" The young woman with me is broad shouldered, somewhat heavyset. She has a pleasant face, though. She smiles as she sees me focus on her. "Here you go," she says, holding the cup to my lips. "Very gentle-like. Sip, don't gulp. You're not quite out of the woods. If you can't hold anything down I don't know what I can do for you."

I sip, holding my hand up to get her to pull the glass back. I want to feel this cool water in my mouth, soaking the cracked sandpaper that took the place of healthy flesh.

I hold up my hand again and nod. She brings the glass to my mouth.

I'm grateful for the water on my stomach while I'm chewing the small bites I've taken from the jerky stick. I take sips while I chew. I can feel the lights coming on throughout my body with all I take in. Salt, fat, and protein. It's exactly what I need right now.

Hannah leaves after it's clear I won't choke to death. In the end I'm one jerky stick and done. I manage to say as much.

"Yeah, comin' back fast now, aren't you! You know your name?"

"Derek Grace. I was on my way—my kids...."

Krystal puts her hand to my arm. "Okay, okay! Look, I don't want to upset you but you've been out for some time now."

I draw a breath, remember the breathing exercises I did to steady my nerves, get my inner game where it needs to be. I also have to steady myself physically where I sit on the edge of the bed. My feet are touching the floor but I know I can't trust my legs to hold my weight. I'll need more than a few jerky sticks to do that. After a few breaths, once I'm more or less centered: "How long?"

"You crashed on Saturday. Today is Wednesday."

"Huh."

"Which is long enough if you've been too out of it to eat, with just a little to drink."

"Where are we?"

"East Natalia High School. In the nurse's office."

"Natalia? We made it to the middle of the state?"

"Just about. You made it, anyway. Your pilot wasn't so lucky."

"What happened?"

"We saw your plane comin' down on I-70. Your tires blew out and the plane spun around hard into the drainage off the side of the road. It bashed in where the pilot was, pretty much killin' him right there. We had to climb over him to pull you out. Two of our people were workin' on pulling your luggage out when the fuel tank exploded. We didn't have much time to hang around. You could tell the noise was bringin' the...people over, so we threw you in the back of the truck and got the hell outta there."

I resist the urge to scoot back, lean against the wall where the bed is set. "It started Friday evening in Kansas City. Is that when it started here?"

"There were stories of strange shit happenin' at County Hospital as far back as last Tuesday. People gettin' out of their beds, all weirded out like they had rabies and tryin' to bite people. This guy I used to date who works there, he swears CDC showed up and was talkin' to the head guys in their offices but they didn't stay long— they had other places to go. Cody's a bit of a bullshitter so it was all just background noise to me."

Krystal seems focused on a fold in the crumpled sheet on my bed. Looking off into the distance at the same time: "So many people starting gettin' sick last week, though. I think they had it under control until—until they didn't. They didn't even get around to pickin' up the dead on Friday like they said they were going to do. By that point the ones that had already died were out walkin' around, with what's left of their own people drippin' down the front of their pajamas or whatever."

I have a feeling she's waiting on me to ask the obvious. I'll have to, eventually. "I know Natalia's by the Interstate, but it seems weird you got all these fatalities before it really set into the big city.

"Lot of trucks stop around here. We've got an airfield, too. We're not all that remote. Who knows? Does it matter?"

"I suppose not. I gotta get back on my feet. How are we for food and water? Why are we here in a high school, anyway? What happened where you live?"

Krystal shakes her head slowly. "You really don't want to be in the neighborhoods."

"Okay, now I have to ask. What happened to your people?"

Krystal looks up at me. "My dad shot my mom as she was coming back. Then he shot himself."

"Shit."

"Pretty much what I said. Yeah."

"So what are we doing here? I mean, aside from you don't want to stay in the family home anymore. Who's this Mr. Evans?"

Krystal brightens. "He was a major in the Army! He was somethin' of a figure in the church, although I stopped going when I got old enough. He's got some smart boys. Two of them survived the Flu. His sister's boy Keith makes up the third leg of the three-legged stool, like he likes to say. As soon as things started going bad he and his boys started putting down the ones roaming the neighborhood. Got everyone that was left and moved us out here. It's kinda off the beaten path, though we had to spend a couple of days puttin' down former teachers and office staff—turns out dead people like to come back to where they were used to going. Anyway, we got all we need here. We got rooms for everybody and beds and the cafeteria was working until a couple of days ago. But Mr. Evans made sure we were ready for that."

"So what's this about Mr. Evans putting me to work?"

"Mr. Evans is trying to build a community. He says everybody has to pull their weight. Tell you the truth he was a little put-out we rescued you. We can only build our community with people we know."

"Don't get me wrong, Mr. Grace," booms a male voice from the door. "We'll do the Christian thing. But as I'm sure you and your pilot friend figured out, resources are scarce. I'd rather feed only those people who are working to feed all of us."

"Mr. Evans, I presume," I say.

"You go by Derek, right?"

"What do I call you?"

"I go by 'Mr. Evans.' I think it's good we have a little respect for people in charge."

"Then I'm Mr. Grace."

"Funny name for a guy wearing a granny gown, don'tcha think?"

I look down. I hadn't realized. I look at Krystal. She shrugs as if to say, *It was all we had.*

I look back at Evans. "Make 'em feel guilty, make 'em feel small. Standard Cult Initiation 101. Is that what they're teaching you desk jockeys in the Army now?"

A shadow passes over his face. He's not used to backtalk, but he's too polished to show irritation. "I'm just having a little fun with you, but if you're clearly the *sensitive* type—"

"Just let me get my clothes and I'll leave you to your community organizing. I just want to get home to my family. That's all." I slide off the bed and force myself to stand (one hand towards the mattress to catch me). "As soon as I get strength to walk, I'm walking."

"Take your time, Mr. Grace," he says. "We'll look after you." He pushes himself up from the doorjamb. "There's really no point in being in a hurry. Given the amount of time you've lost it's safe to say your family is long gone now. That ship has sailed."

"I'll be the judge of that."

"With respect, Mr. Grace, you haven't seen what we've seen these last four or five days. Law enforcement and public safety infrastructure are non-operative. Those people who died get up. They're phenomenally strong, and what they do to any living thing, from a grown man to a litter of puppies, is beyond rational description. They have us on strength and force of terror. They outnumber us. That you have to destroy a particular part of their brain to even stop them makes them a formidable enemy."

"Sounds like nothing's changed since I've been out," I say. "Anything new at all going on?"

"We've got a lot of shell-shocked survivors out there who look at the end of the world as license to raise hell and hurt people, shoot them for fun. The other day my boys came across some yahoos who'd shot someone walking along the state road. They'd taken his legs out so the dead could catch and eat him alive. Then they'd shoot the deaders. Just a game to them! We knew those young men, too. They weren't from the best of families, but they weren't trash, either. At least not 'til this happened.

"You go walking alone into the open country that's the kind of thing you'll be walking into. I'm sorry, you might have misheard things and we've gotten off on the wrong foot. I'll accept responsibility for that. You just get well and we'll talk later. Think about what I said."

I nod and smile. "Will do, Mr. Evans. Thanks."

He spends another moment looking me over. Finally he turns and leaves. I wait one more moment before falling back to the bed.

Krystal glances towards the door before coming over to straighten me out. "Set me against the wall," I tell her. "I want another strip of jerky and some water."

"All that dick-waving give you an appetite?"

"The quicker I get my strength back I can get out your hair, your food supply, whatever."

"All right, calm down!" She brings me the jerky and the water. "Glad to see you taking an interest in things. Think you'll be able to go to the bathroom by yourself soon?"

"Show me where the toilet is."

"This day just keeps getting better," says Krystal.

I wish I could say the same. I need my clothes, my strength, and to get as far away from here as I can. But my head is pounding and my joints are on fire. I've got gauze wrapping my chest to keep my busted ribs in place. What I need to happen won't happen today.

The hell of it is I'm at the mercy of strangers for my safety. I can only hope Mr. Evans and his boys are as good as they think they are. And that when the time comes I'm good enough to get by them.

12

Krystal swears it's for old times' sake and good luck when she pulls me to her, her hands cupping either side of my face as she kisses me square on the lips before leaving me. "Been doin' it every night since you got here," she says. "People gotta know they're loved in this life. Otherwise it ain't no point. See, *you* came around, didn't you?"

She's smiling like it's the cutest thing. I smile back, I hope not too crookedly. Because I feel cheated. Tricked back into this life, where I'm no good at all to the people who'd really loved and depended on me. That Evans bastard knew he had a solid blade to stick in my guts when he told me of the time I'd lost. It's five days after everything's gone to shit and here I am holed up in the nurse's office of a high school somewhere in the middle of fucking Kansas. Weak, tired, broken bones mending, at the mercy of twitchy strangers. Feeling more alone than I've ever known in my life.

On top of that I have no clothes. This big-woman's granny gown would break any man's spirit. The medicinal stink of the perfume worn by its previous owner is sharp in my nose. At least I'm not wearing the adult diaper anymore. Nope, I get to be naked under this thing. Jesus!

Krystal leaves me with the extra bag of beef jerky she was able to sneak away. I'm getting steadier with the water glass. Getting steadier. It's the only thing I can do, so I do it. Until I can stand it no more, and then back to bed.

I wake up feeling much better. I can stand for longer periods of time as the burning leaves my joints. Krystal brings me orange juice. It's warm, but not yet turned. "When did you lose power?" I ask.

"Not until yesterday morning, actually. We were doing good until just before you came out of it. So we're not in trouble. Not yet. We're gonna need to make a run sometime soon, get some more canned goods. I think some of the boys are going out today, come to think of it. Sooner the better, I say."

"I need to get some clothes," I say.

"You willing to go get 'em yourself?"

"Give me directions. Better yet, can I have the clothes I crashed in?"

"Right here in this bag, hon. I even managed to wash the underwear. Dry cleaner's closed, so the rest won't be lookin' so hot. Also got your wallet and keys, for what good they'll do ya."

I take the bag. My things look small and alien. But they're mine. What I was.

"If you're lucky, Dr. Hearn might have a look at you. See how well I did taking care of you."

"Eeew!" says Hannah, shuddering.

I look at Krystal. Krystal shrugs. "Dr. Hearn freaks some people out."

"He experimented on his own family members when they died!" says Hannah. "Had 'em tied up in the basement! Then he had Evans take him into town to find other bodies he could play with!"

"Hannah, you don't know that."

"Your own boyfriend told you that!"

"Brandon tells me lots of things. God knows I love him dearly but I've learned not to pay attention to half the shit he says."

"Excuse me, Krystal," I say. "Can I get a shower here while I'm at it?"

"Good Lord, I never thought you'd ask!" laughs Krystal. "Let's get you to the gym!"

Hannah is too petite for me to even consider leaning on but Krystal is of sturdy build and just the right height to put my arm across her shoulders. I curse myself for needing that sturdiness halfway down the hall. Krystal reminds me once again I've been off my feet for five days with nothing to eat, and very little to drink.

This will make six days out. I'm not even leaving tomorrow. Nor the day after that.

I peel out of the gown, resolved never to wear anything remotely resembling (or smelling) like this ever again. I turn on the hot water and soap up without any self-consciousness at all in front of these women. They've already seen it all.

"Don't use up all the hot water! We only got so much of it left, remember!"

I take my time. The water is just too damned life-affirming. Good water pressure will do that for you.

Without air conditioning the showers are so steamed we can hardly see each other. The steam wasn't enough to take the creases out of my trousers and suit jacket, though. I'm impressed it isn't torn to shreds.

But it hangs falsely on me. It's not just taking the belt in two more notches, though that sure as hell doesn't help. I wipe a mirror clear. Aside from the five-days growth of beard, I can't imagine this was the man taking thousands of dollars in vouchers out on the town in Kansas City, planning a life away from four years of poverty—and the people he'd lived through it with. Who had bluffed his way past trigger-happy National Guardsmen.

Christ, I really did that, didn't I? Bantered with a cop, then fought that same cop in his undead form. I played and won the alpha-dog game with Tanner, escaped a zombie swarm, flew away from another just in time. That is, after using a pack of crackers to lure a retarded child and his insistent mother away from our plane, to a death as messy as it was certain.

I look at myself. My family is gone. I couldn't save them. Can't save them. Not now, not even two days from now.

And with them gone I realize I have no idea who the fuck I am. What I am. What to do.

"Let's get some more food into you and get you walking up and down the hall."

"Yeah."

We walk out of the shower room into the gym. Krystal frowns at my suit. "That is so not you," she says.

"Yeah."

I can feel Krystal looking at me. Bless her overworked peasant heart, she wisely keeps her questions and comments to herself.

I make it all the way through the gym, down the hall to our wing of the school, all the way back to the nurse's office without having to lean on Krystal. "Doin' good, hon. You wanna rest a bit before we go walking some more."

"I want to lie down and sleep."

"What? Already? Well, at least you're clean. Can I change your sheets first?"

"Make it fast. I'm fading."

I hang my suit as she works. Later, slipping between the sheets I close my eyes and think over and over to myself, *I will get out of here. I will get out of here. I will not give up....*

Krystal wakes me for lunch. A TV dinner heated on a grill. Still, I've got to get my strength. She talks me into walking up and down the length of the hall after I eat. The pain in my knee joints is considerably better. I don't tire quite as quickly. I can't exactly go running out of the building towards Colorado yet. But I know I can. Eventually.

I'm left blessedly alone in the evening. I hear the others in the large building, but never see them. I wonder if Evans has this wing of the school off-limits. I'm guessing he does and for that I'm grateful. While there's still light I remove my suit and hang it up. I begin attempts at pushups. I do balancing exercises, rudimentary yoga poses I learned when we were doing that interactive fitness disc on the TV years back.

That had been fun; I wonder why I'd quit that. Then I remember it was because my wife and I were both home. She liked to watch her six-ugly-old-hens-around-a-table daytime chat show shit. I could never watch anything because she'd come in and start talking right in the middle of it. Never felt like I had my space to do it.

Well, I've got that space and more, now. Thank you, Mr. Evans, for keeping the curious away. I'm not in the mood to tell my life story to righteous idiots looking for something in my story to fixate on. ("You were outta work how long? I couldn't do *that!*") Or listen to them boast of their empty, meaningless lives as if I should be proud of their church attendance, or however many kids they have.

Or even what they lost. We weren't bonded when we had families. We aren't bonding now that we don't. Don't even think about it, you empty-headed pukes.

I check my rage. I haven't even met these people yet. And it's a fair guess they'd see my suit and get an idea I think I'm better than them (yeah, I know) and I'll end up wasting precious time trying to convince them I don't care enough one way or another, I just want—

I lose my balance doing a one-legged stand. I carom off the door jamb and somehow find myself facedown on the bed, having landed so hard into it the coarse sheet burns my cheekbone.

Shit. What the hell. While I'm here....

"Huh," says Krystal when she arrives in the morning. "Seems the better you get, the lazier you get."

"Yeah," I say, rubbing the sleep from my eyes.

She plops down on the bed next to me as I sit up. "Oh, I'm just pickin' on ya!" she says, rubbing my back. "You're still workin' on getting better. I'm still not crazy about the idea of you going out with us tomorrow."

"If it looks for a second like I'll slow you down—you can see for yourself today. I want to get out and look around at stuff. Where we are, where we're going, what's all around here."

Hannah is standing in the doorway; she looks apprehensively at Krystal.

"Oh," I say. "I take it the Great and Powerful Mr. Evans disapproves of my moving around freely.

"No, no," says Krystal. "We can take you outside."

"He didn't want him talkin' to people," says Hannah.

"There's only so many people here," says Krystal. She turns to me. "We've been gettin' newcomers every day. Mr. Evans thought it'd be best if everyone got settled in before people started swappin' How I Escaped the Apocalypse stories. All the people we'll be workin' with are fair game, though. We can get your tools, too."

"I'd wondered what happened to my belt."

"Well, Mr. Evans is hangin' on to your gun—but only for the time bein'! He just wants to see how trustworthy you are before you start packin'."

"Well, whaddya know. Gun control comes to America at last."

Hannah looks confused. Krystal shoots Hannah an irritated glance while putting her arm across my shoulders. "He just wants to protect everybody the best he knows how. I'm sure you'll get your gun back after tomorrow." She pats me on the back. "All right now, up! Let's give you the tour!"

I'd take a shower but I'm under the impression that's off the table for whatever reason. Hannah slaps a pack of baby wipes into my hand. I wipe under my armpits and dress. Deodorant would be nice but it's the post-apocalypse. Gotta loot that shit for myself.

If I thought it was warm inside I never knew how good I had it until my first taste of sunshine in seven days. I don't know what hits me harder, really—the summer sun, or that it's been seven days. I stagger out the door, my hand up to shield my face.

"You gonna be all right?" says Krystal.

"I'll adjust."

"Krystal, do I need to be here?" says Hannah.

"Oh, go find your boyfriend, Hannah! Yes, we'll get by fine without you!"

"Like you're not taking him to see your own!"

"Makes sense when we're the ones goin' on the raid to Wally World tomorrow," don'tcha think?"

Hannah sniffs and turns away.

Krystal grabs my arm, squeezes. "Good!" she half-whispers up into my ear. "We might actually get to talk for a minute." She pulls me along. I stumble after, my arm held against the punishing sun.

13

This being Kansas, there's no shade except inside the buildings. I would ask why we can't walk through the main building to the exit closest to the vocational building but I'm guessing there's a reason for this, a big one being that the windows are shaded on this side. Smart. Christ, it's hot, though.

I hear hammering and banging, the sizzle of welding, the hiss of cutting torches. After what seems an interminable hike beneath a sun that hates us and wants us dead we enter the vocational building, its every door and window open for ventilation. Generators work the industrial upright fans, and the equipment. At least they have fans, if all they do is re-circulate the hot air. Young men and older men are instructing children and each other on the use of the tools. I see women standing to the side, shy about stepping up though it's clear they're students, too.

"Evans wants everybody to know about everything. We try to keep busy during the day, anyway. Since I was an almost-medical assistant, I got to experiment on a plane crash survivor."

"What about Hannah?"

"Her?" Krystal laughs. "She wanted to be a nurse. That's her only qualification. She's not good for anything but complainin'. I just got stuck with her."

A young man steps out of one the rooms. Krystal lights up at the sight of him but he puts his finger to his lips and we follow him down the hall out the other side of the building. We push through the doors and I'm no sooner out when Krystal throws herself into the young man's arms and they're kissing.

I make a point of looking for something else to look at but this is a large high school in the middle of Kansas. I notice the flags on the flagpole are still looking good. I wonder if Evans has them taken down every evening and raised in the morning. Wouldn't surprise me....

There's a tugging at my sleeve. "Oh, hey, Derek, this is Brandon!"

I turn and shake the hand of the tall blonde youth in the standard young working man's uniform of jeans and T-shirt, with a cotton shirt hanging untucked and unbuttoned over it, a pack of smokes in the breast pocket. "Good to meet you."

"Krystal says they found you with a meat cleaver and a hammer with blood on it. You've killed deaders?"

"Yep."

"So, how do you like it here so far?"

"I dunno. I haven't seen anything but the inside of the school since I crashed."

"Well, it's time you saw some shit, then!" He looks around. "Keep quiet." He begins walking away to the adjacent parking lot.

He's walking fast and I almost have to jog to keep up. Krystal holds out her hand for me but I pretend I don't see it. Brandon is already around the driver's side of a brown, dented-up warhorse of a pickup truck. Krystal pulls open the door and climbs in. By the time I pull myself up on the runner the truck's already started, and I'm pulling the door closed as he backs out of his space and drives off.

"Evans doesn't like us driving around," Brandon says as I pull my shoulder belt across and click it into the buckle. Krystal looks at me like I'm crazy. Neither she nor her boyfriend are strapped in.

"Force of habit?" Krystal says.

"Force of body crashing through safety glass. Fuck Johnny Law, it's the laws of physics I'm respecting here."

Brandon hits the brakes. Krystal shrieks and puts her hands out to the dashboard. Brandon grins. "Fuck Johnny Law. I like that." He pulls his own shoulder belt over, looks at Krystal. "Whatever you wanna do, babe. Free country and all that shit."

"Hold on!" she says, twisting from one side to another to find her belt. But Brandon has already taken off again.

When Krystal finally digs the buckle and clasp out of the seat she looks up through the windshield and says, "Oh."

"What?" All I see are flat, browned-out fields of wheat and corn.

"We're headed towards where we found you," says Krystal.

"We gotta be careful, though," says Brandon. "They're watchin' that area a little more closely now."

"How many people does Evans have now?"

"Right now it's mainly him and his boys. Maybe a couple more people over the last couple of days. Quite a few people up there in the rich section of town, though. They don't come out, neither. Hell, they don't have to! They got their people goin' back and forth. Shit, more I think about it, I'm not even sure that Evans fucker is really in charge."

"Aw, he's not all that bad," says Krystal. "But, yeah, he's got his people he answers to. He don't like people to think that but he does. There's too many people back in that nice neighborhood street there. It's like he says, they're all holed up in there. They're not just hidin' from the dead people, either."

"Still," I say, "some puff-chested ex-Army major with two teenage boys and a nephew are calling the shots for how many people? I gotta say, I don't get this."

"Evans has some others in town goin' along with him. Not everybody's at the high school, either. Just the refugees he's pullin' off the road. He uses the principal's office during the day sometimes to play administrator, but just the other day he got someone else in to do his pissant wranglin' for him. Most of the time he's out tryin' a round up survivors in town. There were 50,000 or so used to live here, which wasn't a lot as of week ago. I imagine it takes some time goin' through the whole town, talkin' people out of their hidin' places, decidin' where they should go...."

Brandon pulls a cigarette from his shirt pocket. He lights it, stares ahead. Krystal glowers at him.

"Of course," says Brandon, "there's people him an' his kind ain't got any use for."

"You don't know that, Brandon!"

Brandon blows a volley of smoke at the windshield. "You know how these flim-flam men'll tell ya, give us your money now, get in on the ground floor or you'll miss your chance? The way I see it with Evans and his people, you get out while there's just a ground floor. The longer we stick around, the harder it's gonna be to get away. Evans is gonna get' more an' more people to carry guns for him. He's gonna build that little community of his. Basically one big work camp while he an' his kids an' his rich buddies live easy. He's gonna have shit locked down so tight out here you got just as good a chance as bustin' out of prison."

"Pretty much the way it was before," I say.

"Yeah, 'cept there ain't gonna be no welfare or disability for those who can't or won't cut it. You just won't show up for dinner that night. Or maybe you'll turn up missin' come breakfast."

"Now you don't know that's what happened to Marcus!" says Krystal. "He'd been talkin' about cuttin' out ever since Evans got everyone together at the school!"

"Correction: ever since Evans put *people like us* into the school. You know, for our own good and shit." Brandon looks at me. "Marcus woulda come and got me. He an' I were tight from way back. Krystal here's too sweet to wanna wrap her head around it but those fuckers took Marcus' poor white ass out!"

"I thought it wasn't safe in town. With all the deaders, that is."

"Back when you were alive, you didn't have no business in a place, you didn't go there. Just like that now that everyone's dead. That's the way it is in the rich people's section. Reckon it didn't take 'em all mornin' to clear the dead outta there. Shit, Krystal, I showed you this! They're out there runnin' their generators and sprinklers and everything like they don't care! It's a miracle all them stinkin' mobs ain't all come in to check 'em out. I'm guessin' it's all those nice shade trees they got growin' over the streets soakin' up the sound. Hell, most of these former citizens see a tree they know they don't belong there. Just graded-off dirt and heat stroke for the rest of us."

"So we ring a louder dinner bell. Or just draw 'em in, like with bait."

Brandon nods. "Yeah. You could do that."

Krystal looks from her boyfriend to me as if she'd just found herself among total strangers. It's all I can do not to crack up.

"Fuck!" says Brandon.

Krystal squeals and reaches out for the dashboard.

Brandon backs the truck up. Through his window I can see a

man in overalls sitting outside the rows of corn, chomping away at a snake. The snake's fishbone-thin rib bones are sticking in his teeth and the soft parts of his mouth and the man has to pause to pick out the slivers, sucking the meat off of them as he goes. By some reflex the snake begins slithering away, even with its midsection chewed out. The man's large, pale hand falls upon its tail. He's still picking the bones out of his mouth with one hand as the snake coils back and bites furiously at the other.

"That's Mr. Sanderson, isn't it?" says Krystal.

Brandon looks over at me. "Help me with this, will ya?"

We both jump out of the truck. My heart jumps as Brandon turns his back to the man in the overalls to look through the items scattered in his flatbed. "Shit, there it is!" he says, pointing to my side of the truck. I pick up the demo bar and run around the front of the truck.

The former Mr. Sanderson is looking in our general direction, sniffing the air. "*Nnnnnyahhr?*" he seems to ask Brandon. He lets the snake go and gets to his feet. The snake flops around in the dirt, bleeding out.

"Mr. Sanderson, oh man! I'm sorry, sir! Mr. Grace, toss me that bar!"

Sanderson is already on his feet and moving towards Brandon. Once his back is to me I bring the curved end of the bar hard down on the back of his skull. It stuns him; he's just about to turn around after me when I club him one, two, three more times. He falls to his knees and I step around to the front and club him three more times on that side. I get a crack going in the skull and hammer at that until his head opens up.

At last he is still.

Krystal has both hands to her mouth. I turn to Brandon, hold up the demo bar. "I'm sorry, you wanted this?"

Brandon looks at the dusty, bloodied form face down in the dirt. "He used to pull the hay wagon for us in the fall when we were little. I made extra money helping him bring in hay when I got older. He was one of the few decent motherf—he was a decent man."

"I don't know what to tell you, Brandon. Except you're going to need something better than this. I know I'm weak, but it shouldn't have taken me more than a couple of strikes to crease his skull."

Brandon looks at me like he might explode on me in rage or tears. "Brandon," I tell him, "I'm sorry you lost somebody. Everybody's lost somebody, all right? Besides, this was not Mr. Sanderson. It's some fucked-up thing eating a corn snake by the side of the road because nobody else was walking by out here. All right?"

Brandon's eyes are fixed angrily on the remains of the monster that was once Mr. Sanderson.

"So what do we do with the body?" I say. "Do we leave it out here or do you want to take him back for proper burial?"

"We're supposed to burn 'em," Krystal says.

Brandon shrugs violently, like he's trying to get something off his back. "Help me get 'im into the truck," he says through his teeth.

"He's gonna stink to high heaven in this heat!" Krystal says. "You don't think we oughta leave him here and come back for 'im later?"

I've made a point of grabbing for the armpits; let Brandon have the shit-stained legs. "Krystal, hush," I say.

"What! I—!"

"*Quiet!*" I lay Mr. Sanderson's shoulders and head on the gate of the flatbed and haul myself up. With Brandon pushing at the legs I'm able to drag Mr. Sanderson's remains to lay on their back in a clear space among the tools, empty potato chip bags and beer cans.

Brandon slams the gate shut and I jump over the side. We climb back into the truck in silence. He puts it into gear and we scratch away down the road.

"Just so you know," Krystal says, "I remember ridin' on that hay wagon, too."

"Woman," says Brandon, "*shut up!*"

We ride along at a reasonable speed—hell, almost slow. I expected the exact opposite but now I realize this is Brandon's way of showing deference to one of the few adults who was ever kind to him.

After a while Brandon turns on the radio. He runs through the stations—where they used to be, anyway.

"Yep, that one's gone. Was up yesterday." He comes across another repeating the Civil Defense script over and over. "I reckon that one'll be up 'til the end of time," he says.

"It's already on past Doomsday," I say.

"Shit. When was that?"

"Friday, where I was. I heard it came a little earlier here."

"Things were going to shit all week long," Brandon says. "There wasn't no Doomsday. More like Doomsweek. Rome wasn't built in a day. Shit man, where you been? I thought you been around!"

"It was different in Kansas City," I say, knowing that's not the whole truth. I was in an air conditioned bubble of leather upholstery and tailored suits and free passes to the most fashionable places in the Big City, where you sweat from working out, but never while working. Far from the concerns of people who dirty themselves handling oil pans, bed pans—of course, at least they had jobs, however shitty, and saw things going on around me.

I realize now I'd have been fatally clueless if I'd stayed home. If I'd just been there in my basement office, never encountering the sick cabbie, all the sick people at the airports and on the plane. Seen Giselle break down. Seen Angie transform. It would have been just me and Claire.

What would I have done there, with no frame of reference save the worry and helplessness of watching Claire die? When I see the dead rise and it's not strangers on a TV over a bar in a securely locked hotel, it's my wife of 22 years and I'm not saving anyone because I'm the first one going down....

"Well, here we are." Brandon pulls off the road towards one of the many drainage/irrigation canals that run between properties in rural Kansas. These are among the few places you find trees out here. He parks under a thick, gnarly looking specimen with crazy limbs and thorned twigs. "Watch where you step," says Brandon. "These fuckers'll go right through those shoes of yours."

I stand just inside the shade line while he goes down to the black, stagnant water at the lowest part of the ravine. Krystal looks at me. "You feelin' all right? Color's gone out of your face!"

"Just thinkin' about things."

"Your family?"

"Yeah."

"Aw. Bless your heart!"

The rustle of leaves and debris shoved aside draws our attention downhill. "Hey, Mr. Grace," Brandon calls up, "you hear anything before you crashed?"

"There was an explosion beneath us. I figure it was the tires on the landing gear. Either we were going too fast or we hit something, I don't know."

"You hit something, all right," says Brandon. He pulls it from its hiding place.

I see the spike strip dangling from his hand and then I remember. The last thing I thought I saw before the bang and the nose going down. A line across the asphalt.

"Brandon, you can't be sure of that!"

"You saw me pull it out of the landing gear yourself!"

"You don't know who put it there, though!"

"Who the hell else is out here, Krystal! Who?" Brandon looks at me. "I got three more in here that I pulled off the roads comin' past town. I figure they musta pulled these out of the back of the cars at the sheriff's substation close to here. After the crash me and Marcus went out lookin' for 'em. We took 'em and hid 'em. I try and get back to see if they're puttin' any more down. So far, they don't seem to have to, at least as far as I-70 is concerned."

"How do you figure?"

"They left your burned-out plane by the side of the road. It's practically a goddamned tourist attraction now, with a burned-up body in the cockpit an' everything! They just kinda pop up out of nowhere when they see people they want, invite 'em to dinner, give 'em the tour. A lot of people are so damn happy to get a square meal on an actual plate they'll give up their freedom for the promise of another helpin' of mash-potato flakes outta the box." Brandon smirks. "But it's on a *plate*, see, so it's all good!"

"And the people they don't like?"

"Well, if they look white enough, they'll let 'em go. Niggers an' beaners an' other colored folk, not so much. They end up where Mr. Sanderson up there is gonna end up. In an ash pit, with hot tar poured on 'em and set ablaze."

"You hear somethin'?" says Krystal.

It's the unmistakable sound of an approaching engine. Two of them. Brandon puts the spike strip back in its hiding place and strides up the embankment. "No sense trying to run," he says. "Just stand here and be cool. We'll tell 'em we stopped to take a leak."

"How do we explain being out here in the first place?"

"New guy wanted the tour. Just let me do the talkin', all right?"

A shiny black pickup the size of a small building breezes in front of Brandon's truck and scrapes hard to a halt, blocking our way out. Pulling up behind us is a bright yellow beauty of a truck, tall off the ground, a beautiful chrome job.

Of course, it could only belong to Mr. Evans. "What are we doing out here?" he says grinning behind black aviator sunglasses. A tall bruiser of a man with a bandolier across his huge chest and a Smokey Beat hat comes out of the black truck to join him. I see a blonde kid in the big yellow truck looking like he wants to come out. I gather Dad doesn't approve of the risk.

"Just givin' him the tour, sir."

"I'll bet. Who's that in your flatbed?"

"Mr. Sanderson, sir." I wince to hear Brandon say *sir*. He thinks this shows Good Upbringing, and it does—an upbringing as a disposable peasant.

"Where'd you find him?"

"Out on the east side of his field, sir."

"What was he eating?"

"A corn snake, sir."

"All right, then. You better get him up to the processing area. Mr. Grace?"

I look at Evans.

"You all right?"

"I'm good."

"I'd like you to take the rest of the tour with me."

"That's all right. Brandon and Krystal had it covered."

"No, they don't. They got work to do when they get back to the school. That right, Brandon?"

"Yes, sir." Brandon looks at me. "Good to know you, Mr. Grace."

"You, too, Brandon."

Krystal stands next to him, stricken. I nod at her, smile. *I'll be all right* when we both know that ain't at all so.

"Oh, stop it!" says Evans. "You're all going to see each other tomorrow on the box store run! Now go take Mr. Sanderson up to the processing place and get yourselves back to the school before you draw every last former citizen of Natalia down on us! Go!"

Brandon and Krystal take one last frightened look at me before the brute with the bandolier and Smokey Bear hat turns in their direction, and their sense of self-preservation overwhelms their morbid instinct to have one last look at the condemned man, maybe watch him die.

The brute walks past the battered brown truck towards his own. He moves his truck over just enough for Brandon's comparatively puny rustbucket toy to get by. Brandon zooms away down the frontage road. I see him make his first left way down the road, driving back up into the general area of where we came from all of 45 minutes ago.

Evans nods his head towards the black truck and the man backs it up close, parks it and gets out. "Brick," says Evans. "Check out that area down there where they were when we were coming up. Unless, that is, Mr. Grace cares to tell us what's down there."

"I'd hate to spoil anything for anybody."

"Indulge us."

"No."

I can sense the big man bristling but Evans nods towards the wooded ravine and with one final look at me Brick turns and walks down the slope.

"Come," says Evans. "There's much you need to see."

It's a long walk to anywhere from here. If I'm going to get killed, I might as well enjoy a final ride in air conditioning. I follow Evans back to his truck.

14

The blonde-haired kid—I'm guessing he's at least as old as my son, Jack—slips into the rear cab as I pull myself up into Evans' big yellow truck. The new car smell is almost overpowering, bringing back fond memories of the Luxury Tank. Of course, this is a far more practical vehicle for the Batshit New World we're coming into now.

"You like my truck?" Evans says as he climbs into the driver's seat.

"Yes, it's nice," I say. I note the low double-digit on the odometer as he starts the engine. "Just picked it up at the dealership?"

"Believe it or not, I'd custom-ordered this just three weeks ago. I was scheduled to go in and sign for it the day everything started shutting down around here." Evans puts the truck in gear and we pull away. "I'd made a substantial down payment on it so it's not a 100% post-apocalypse discount. Though Nelson back there and me did have to take out the salesman in order to take delivery, so to speak. Turns out my man Bud had wandered into work from his deathbed. Still in his pajamas and everything."

"Huh."

"Yeah. Bud was a good man. I'd been getting a new truck from him every year for the last ten years since I retired from the Army."

I think of my 11-year-old beater back home, and how grateful I'd been it only needed minor repairs every year because a car payment would have been out of the question even in the best of times. "I guess this is the last year they'll be making new trucks, then." It's a stupid thing to say but then I'd rather not have to explain my first thought: *Must be nice.* My second thought—that I need to find that dealership—is also best unsaid.

"Sobering, isn't it?" says Evans. "It's why I'm trying to round up mechanics like Brandon. We're going to have to learn to fix what we have, because this is it."

"Well, I'm glad to know you'll be keeping Brandon alive a little longer," I say. "He seems like a good kid."

"Of course the ultimate would be to get some body-work men. Just imagine, we could keep everything running and looking good at the same time! We didn't lose that many people. All we need to do is gather the scattered masses unto us, so to speak. It could even be better than before!"

"So that's what the spike strips are for. Glad to know my pilot buddy didn't die for nothing."

"That's what Brick's gonna find down in that ravine?"

"What if he does?"

"We'll put them away. Those weren't supposed to be out there."

"Why were they?"

It's a small spot of silence, but I can hear Evans' son shift a little in the backseat. He's probably armed. I'd sure as hell have armed Jack if he was with me.

Finally: "Mr. Grace, as leader of this community I accept responsibility for the errors in judgment that brought you to us. But I also want it understood that those spike strips were procured and deployed without my knowledge or authorization. Your boy Brandon there was hiding evidence of his own wrongdoing. His friend Marcus had already fled the shelter in fears of punishment for that."

"So you and your people didn't kill Marcus?"

"Contrary to what you may have been told, people are free to leave whenever they please. All we ask is that they do their supplying outside of Natalia. We need everything we've got to rebuild here, let alone take care of the people here willing to help us with that."

"So I'm free to leave, too, then."

"Absolutely. But let me try to talk you out of that. I think you might do well for yourself here."

"Really?"

"I know it doesn't look like much but you only see so much from the Interstate. The land is good here. We can get things growing."

"It's just not my part of the country. Not enough trees."

"Funny you should mention that."

We come upon a dark green wall of trees along one of the many short ridges that ripple through central Kansas. We cross a small bridge over a creek before turning down a side road. We turn down another road and the temperature drops noticeably where these trees touch over the street. Large, old houses on wide, raised lots sit comfortably out of the direct sun, sprinklers watering the gracefully rounded knolls of Kentucky bluegrass in some of the large front yards.

The old money "Good Families" would have been here a week ago while the real money ruled from their hundred-acre-plus farms and ranches outside of town. Now we're back to the old neighborhoods. It makes sense, though, at least for the time it will take to train the peasants bunked in the high school to serve the New (Old) Paradigm.

"You like it here, huh?" says Evans.

"Made in the shade," I say.

Evans pulls into the driveway of a large, 19th-century manse. When did it suddenly become impossible for modern builders to include rounded towers with conical roofs? So beautiful, unlike the tacky, blocky McMansions our century's managing classes accept as "luxury living"—what I was drooling over in Kansas City barely a week ago. I'm guessing the swells lived here during Natalia's wild western cowtown days. That these magnificent structures still stand after well over a hundred years....

"What do you think?" Evans says.

"I'll take it."

"It's yours if you want it. I used to know the owner. You remind me a lot of him. I think you might even be the same size. Anyway, the generator's hooked up. It's been running for a while so you can take a hot shower and see if those clothes fit."

"So what do you need from me?"

"We'll talk about that over dinner."

"Oh. When and where?"

Evans holds out a familiar object. "My house. Dinner itself is at six. Cocktails at 5:30 if you're so inclined."

I take the object. It's my phone.

"Fully charged," says Evans. "Here's your charger, too, by the way. Mr. Riley two houses over and across the street had a spare to fit it."

"I'll be damned," I say, taking the neatly wrapped bundle of wire-and-plug.

"I took the liberty of putting my number in your Contacts list."

"Great."

"We can at least talk to each other here. Of course, if we really get going we can get some of these other cell towers operational. Expand our sphere of influence, as it were."

"All right," I say, nodding.

"Let's get inside, get you started. Got air conditioning in there. Get cleaned up; maybe you can get in a nap before cocktail hour."

He pops his door, I pop mine. No one's under gunpoint. So far, so good.

Evans nods at his boy and he runs down the driveway to the street, presumably to their own house along the shady lane. I follow Evans up the front steps of the house to the wide front porch. Mr. Evans makes a mini-ceremony of handing me the keys to unlock the door. I push the door open into a cool, dark space. The smells of hardwood floors, old furniture swirl around me.

This is the kind of place you live in, not at. You don't step into a living area right away; we're in a foyer. If I had a coat or boots this is where they'd come off before going into the first sitting area, just off the dining room.

"There's one room in particular you may be interested in," Evans says.

I follow him up the steep hardwood stairs. We emerge into a wide, dark hall, lit only by the faint light through the trees outside the windows of the many rooms. It's so delightfully cool, even in this upstairs, I could lie down on the floor and sleep.

"We had to air it out," Evans says. "I think it worked, but I was a little too close to the project, in and out while they were scrubbing. We had the mattresses hauled out, of course. We've yet to liberate replacements for the master bedroom and the daughter's room so you might want to stay in the guest bedroom until we get that deep into town." Evans stops and turns to look at me. "Just so you know this is a problem in every house on this block."

"Who lived here?"

"The Tellers. Carol and Kaylee. Husband Nick supposedly got called away last week and frankly I don't look for him to come back. If he does we'll get you another place. This is the nicest one that's vacant, though."

"I appreciate that."

"Speaking of things appreciated, we noticed you had a butcher's meat ax and a meat tenderizer on your belt. They looked very much used. Not like in a kitchen, either."

"What about it?"

"I saw you with Mr. Sanderson today. You're not afraid to approach these things."

"Assuming you really saw me with Sanderson, you'd know I came at him from behind, after his attention was drawn by Brandon."

"I do know that, because I was watching with the binoculars. We knew you'd left." He adds quickly, "You're honest. You're not a braggart. That speaks to your character. I just thought you might be interested in seeing this room. Nick Teller was something of a collector."

Evans takes a few steps forward and left and we're in a windowless room full of glass cases. He had to have known the one that would catch my eye. "What am I supposed to do with this?" I say.

"You're going out with us on the expedition tomorrow, right?"

"I can use this?"

"It's not doing us any good in here."

"All right, then. I can't help but notice, though…."

"You'll be surrounded by my people. Until we come to an understanding, they'll have the guns."

Because we have trust issues, Tanner. I catch myself smiling at the memory. Christ, I almost miss that shifty bastard. "Fair enough," I say.

"You see the belt over there. That ought to go well with the clothes we have for you. Luckily we had enough old-school hunters on this street for a match."

"Don't take this the wrong way, I love it and all but—this isn't what you expect me wearing to the dinner party, right?"

Evans laughs. "No, no! I've got those laid out in your room. I just wanted you to see this. We'll talk about what we're going to do after dinner! You like this, though, right?"

"I can do a lot with that one blade I saw."

"I'll bet! Let me show you to your room!"

It's still a pretty good size for a guestroom. It has its own bathroom, which is really the only thing I care about in these matters. Evans leaves me with a reminder of the cocktail hour time, and he lets himself out. I look among the clothes on the bed, and realize—well, what could have been done? No one thinks to stock up on underwear in the bag for the apocalypse. I'll have to wash what I have on, either in the sink or in the laundry.

But only this one time. I'll have to make a personal shopping list for tomorrow's adventure. Underwear, shaving, and deodorant. I'll look for a suitcase in the house. For right now, it's a bathrobe, a shower, and hell, I just might take that nap. The more I rest, the better I heal. The quicker I heal, the quicker I'm on my way to what's next.

Slipping between the sheets, squeaky clean and commando, I'm asleep before I can think to chant mission focus to myself. Just about the time I'm supposed to get up I'm awakened by something that doesn't sound like my phone alarm. It's my phone's ringer. The one for calls outside my area code. I'm thinking Rob or Giselle until my eyes snap open and I realize where I am.

"Yeah?"

"Sorry to wake you, Mr. Grace. We have walkers in the neighborhood, just wanted to give you a heads up."

"Where are they? That is, in relation to where I am."

"They're headed west on the avenue. Right down the middle of the street. We figure they'll be out of here in about half an hour."

"Where?"

"You're not thinking of going out to meet them are you?"

"I'm just asking."

"It's just three of them. Five blocks east from you by now."

"That's all I need to know."

"Just let them clear the area before you come over. I probably shouldn't have called but I didn't want to take the chance of you coming over early and running into them. We're trying to get a system going for situations like this."

"I appreciate that. Thanks."

"All right. Just wanted to keep you in the loop. This shouldn't affect our schedule."

"Good to know. Thanks."

How long would it take three stumblers to cover five blocks? I figure I've got just enough time to get dressed. The hunting khakis it is, then. Wouldn't want to mess up my dinner clothes. I make a note to get jeans—fuck these glorified cargo pants—and steel-toed work boots.

I'm dressed and out the door before it occurs to me to wonder where the neon blue hell my enthusiasm for killing zombies has come from. The answer is gripped in my right hand. A walnut grip large enough for two-handed action. The business end is a 20-inch blade that widens and curves upward at the tip. The tempered steel is coated in black carbon. This is a panga, kissing cousin of the legendary scimitars used by the Barbary pirates. Chief instrument of the Rwandan genocide. Shorter, non-coated versions are used to cut sugarcane. This one was meant to separate people from their appendages.

The people I have in mind had no trouble covering four blocks while I fussed with the blousing over my boots. Assistant liberal arts professors from K-State Natalia? At least one of them has that standard-issue smug, begging-to-be-punched face wrapped in a wispy beard and standard-issue wire rim glasses. Apparently attacked in their offices—I see broad rips in the flesh of one of their hands, rips in the blood-stiffened forearms of their suits—I can't imagine they're coming home. Apparently they feel welcome enough here, though. A memory of fundraiser parties past?

A tall hedge screens me but the street is wide. I'm going to risk them doing the loud moan that brings on their fellows from wherever else they may be lurking. I'll just have to move fast.

I need to know that I can do this.

Those assholes cringing behind the curtains in their houses need to know it, too.

I'm listening for the scrape-slide of their feet. Instead, it's a near-normal tread. I'm guessing these are fresh as these things go.

The footsteps slow. Do they scent me? I peek around the hedge. They're still halfway down my block, they're heads swiveling over their torn, ill-fitting blazers. They're looking for something....

"Over here, gentlemen!" I say, stepping out behind the hedge. Their heads quit their back-and-forth, their scabbed noses bird-dogging on my voice. All of them have the gore-stripe down their Oxford shirts. Apparently they stopped to eat on their way out of Natalia, that's why it took them so long to get here.

I jog up towards Smug Face. He's got dried blood all over his glasses. Not that he needs to see me; his senses of smell and hearing are at maximum capacity. He staggers forward, mounting the closest thing he can to a charge.

I've got two hands on the walnut grip. I wait until his arms come up. The blade hums through the air as I swing left. His forearms thud to the asphalt. I step back lest I get sprayed but after the initial pressure squirt the blood merely oozes from the stumps.

Stumpy bellows angrily at me. I'd bury the blade in his skull but his companions are close behind and I have no time to free a stuck blade. I drive a two-handed swing into his neck and send his head tumbling over his shoulder to the street.

His buddies behind him already have their arms out. The body of the first one is falling over, though, which slows them down just enough to step in position and make my move. One rightward swing carries the blade through one neck and into another. The first skull cracks loudly as it hits the pavement and is still; the other slaps to the street on one cheek, its jaw still gnashing up and down. The bodies fall over stiffly, not buckling at the knees but tilting off-balance and down. I step to the side to avoid the splatter from the neck stumps and the blood that spills slowly, endlessly, into the street. And that's the end of it.

Except it's not. Two heads are still snapping about me on the wide street. And here comes Evans and a couple of other old fucks across their bluegrass knolls. I really wish I had my meat hammer. Any kind of hammer. I use my boot to roll the one head over to face the sky (and really wishing I was wearing steel-toed boots) and bring the blade down across the eyes. I'm standing over the wispy-bearded man's face and raising my blade when an unfamiliar voice cries out, "Stop!"

Evans and the two other men arrive at the scene. Evans speaks first, "Why did you feel you had to come out here?" He's trying to sound stern but the words are coming out too fast, and his voice nearly cracks with his panic.

The look on his face, his body language among the two older men confirms what Krystal and Brandon were telling me earlier, that despite Evans' pretensions he answers to other people. And here's two of them.

So it's to these two liver-spotted old fossils—one of them wearing a cowboy hat, so help me—that I address: "You're *welcome*. Does it occur to any of you that the more of these things you drop, the fewer there will be to violate the sanctity of this Very Good Neighborhood? Or is such elementary thought too much like work for you lazy old parasites?"

The former Major Evans of the United States Army is so mortified I swear I can hear his breath catch in his throat. I keep my eyes on the two thin, bald old men, letting them feel the full weight of my contempt.

Not that old rich men feel much of anything outside their own thick little skulls. That I do not fear them, however, makes them uneasy. "This was Lenora Jefferson's grandson," says the one not wearing the cowboy hat. He has the stern carriage of someone who is accustomed to being listened to, not the other way around.

"What of it?"

"We need to treat his remains with more *respect*."

"Like he respected the victim he spilled all the way down his front? Well, since you're the obvious expert, why don't you show me how it's done?" With the tip of my boot I give hard nudge of the still-snapping head of Beloved Grandson towards the man's feet. To his credit, he doesn't move, even as the dried, cracked eyes roll in his direction, the teeth snapping at the brown leather tips of his old rich man shoes. "Maybe you can put it in a box and give it to her." I nod towards Evans. "Be sure to get the glasses."

Evans looks at me, takes a step back—and the glasses go crunch beneath his heel. He stumbles back again and looks in horror and what he's done.

"Or not," I say.

Evans leans over to gather the remains of the glasses. The old man sighs, steps back. "You may finish him," he says.

"No," I say, "I 'may' not." I turn to Evans. "I'll pack my gear and get out."

Evans glances up at me from where he's picking up the glass. He's pale, and the sweat glistening on his face isn't from the heat. I turn and begin walking away.

I'm just at the foot of the driveway leading up to my place when I hear, "Mr. Grace!" I turn at the unfamiliar voice. It's the man in the cowboy hat.

"Are you sure you want to pass up drinks and dinner before you leave?" he says with an unnaturally white and expensive grin. "I'd be honored to have you as my personal guest!"

I walk back towards the men. The man in the cowboy hat looks at Evans, nods to the body. "Take care of this." As I approach Evans is crossing the street to the other side while tapping numbers into his phone. No, he sure as hell isn't touching those bodies. We still have superior feudalism through telephony. Call the poor bastard tasked with the cleanups on Aisle 7 and git 'er done.

The man with the cowboy hat seems to have lit up in the last minute; I see his blue eyes glinting even in the shade. He holds his hand out to me. "Emory Kerch," he says. "This gentleman over here is the former police chief of our fair city, Duane Paulson."

I take Kerch's hand, shake it. "Derek Grace." I look at the man named Paulson. He's got nothing more than a hard-faced scowl for me, his hands firm by his side. I smile and nod at Paulson and turn back to Kerch. Who still has my hand....

"So it's 'Derek'" then. I wondered if you might not go by your middle name 'Samuel.' My father's name, a fine name!"

"I wouldn't disagree on that account. If you're buying the drinks, call me whatever you want. But only for the drinks."

The man guffaws loudly. "My great and merciful God, we have a flesh and blood American man in our midst! Derek, my good man, let's do something with that messy blade of yours and get started on those drinks!"

"If it's all right with you, Emory, I'd like to get into some more appropriate attire."

"All right, now!" says Emory. "Just don't take too long! You like beer, right?"

"I've been known to drink one or two."

"You like it on tap?"

"Love it."

"I got the finest pale ale from the local microbrewery. Frosty cold in the keg!"

"I'd change right here in the street if I could. Where's this all happening?"

Emory points to a side street coming off this avenue. "Turn there, then the first house on the right. You'll know it when you see it. I can send someone to pick you up if you need me to."

"I appreciate that. I need to get my strength back, though. I was out for a while. I won't say no to a ride back, though."

"If any of us are fit to keep it on the pavement! All right, now, we'll be lookin' for ya!"

"Be out and on my way in ten!"

All this time Emory and I were talking the man complaining about Mrs. Jefferson's grandson was looking away and around like I did when Brandon and Krystal were kissing. Nice to be getting a feel for the real hierarchy around here. I walk up the driveway, knowing full well it's all about taking out the dead and taking the city. And my new friend Emory is going to count on me to do the first part for him. As for how the second part shakes out, it's probably best I'm somewhere else when that comes up.

For right now, it's all about the beer. Pale ale? Goddamn it, Emory had better be shooting straight with me. I can handle being lied to about anything else. Hell, I expect it. But for God's sake, let me have that cold beer!

15

Seriously, fuck these boots. These cammie pants aren't cutting it, either. A good, tough pair of jeans is what I need. Something I can run in without a bunch of crap clanking about my legs in the cargo pockets, which I know I'll be stupid enough to use.

I change out quickly. These dressy-casual khakis aren't bad. Even the shoes are more comfortable than they look, but that's what money will get you.

At least I don't have to worry about money anymore. I'd say Thank God for small favors, but that wouldn't be right. It's not a small favor. It's an epic blessing.

One I traded the wife and kids in for.

Goddamn it, Emory Kerch better not be lying about that beer. It's been a while since I got my drink on.

I hear loud talk over rushing water as I start down the driveway. The bodies have been removed from the street. Two men aim a fire hose at the residual gore while another stands by, an empty bottle of bleach in each hand.

How much blood is in the human body? We had three bleeding out through open necks here. All that dead-person blood full of Final Flu and Christ knows what. Good idea on the bleach, but I'm not sure two gallons was enough.

The cleanup crew looks up at me as I pass along the lower edges of the knolls beneath the houses. I look back at them and their gaze returns to where the force of the water pushes waves of brown-red ichor towards the storm drain. They just want to get this disgusting detail over with and get the hell out.

I'm not even halfway down the block when Evans' Big Yellow Truck pulls up. Evans leans out the window. "Mr. Kerch isn't in the mood to wait the half-hour or 45 minutes it'll take you to get to his place."

"Really? Sorry to hear that."

Evans rolls alongside as I continue walking. "Look, what if I told you there's a doctor Mr. Kerch called up to look at you?"

"Carrots first, Evans. Sticks when you run out of options. Don't tell me Army OCS taught you backwards." Not that it would surprise me.

"Mr. Grace, I admire your attitude. But you need to understand who you're dealing with."

"Yeah, yeah, you've got the guns. Use 'em, then! I've lost everything and everyone I ever gave a shit about. You're threatening me? Fuck you!"

"No, no! Shit! All right, so I'm no diplomat! What I'm trying to tell you is you're valuable to them. They want you to clean out Natalia for them. But it's not a good idea to piss them off!"

"It kinda goes without saying in most relationships."

"Look. Please. Get in the truck. We'll be there in two minutes." Evans pauses. "The beer does look good. He's got frosted mugs."

"They're already drinking?"

"It's a fine day."

"Hm. All right. Goddamn it." Whatever the hell this is, let's get it over with.

I walk around the back of the truck to the other side of the cab. "You might want to watch it with the language," Evans says as I climb in.

"Yeah." I'm looking into the backseat. Clear. We're moving the moment I close the door behind me. I pull the seatbelt on while keeping an eye on Evans.

"Look," says Evans. "Like I said, I admire your attitude. I lost my wife, too. My ex-wife really but—look, we all lost someone, all right?"

"Evans, I lost everyone. So don't take it too harshly if I insist you shut the fuck up about this and just *drive*."

We arrive at the side road. He's making the turn. To the house?

I'm told I'd know it when I saw it.

Okay. I see it.

I can't even guess how many acres this is. The grounds are enormous; it would have taken me forever to walk this twin-rutted path up to the mansion wrapped in its own vast and thick copse of trees. "Wasn't this party supposed to be at your house?"

"I live in the house on the back of the grounds. Right on the edge of the golf course."

"Oh."

"For what it's worth—and I'm not trying to put you down, now—this change of plans has nothing to do with your work with Mrs. Jefferson's grandson and his friends."

"So long as I'm not a victim of my own success."

"Look, I don't know how else to tell you this—this isn't Mr. Kerch's house. Last week this belonged to an old, good Natalia family going back generations to pioneer days. That's all I got to say about it!"

I laugh. We crest a ridge and the house looms larger before us. A solid granite monstrosity from the days when people knew how to build proper estates.

"I can't believe you find this funny," Evans says.

"I can't believe you just fell off the red-white-and-blue turnip truck. For God's sake, how do you think these assholes get to where they are in the first place? Hard work?"

Evans looks at me like I'm the first one to break it to him that the American Dream is just that. I almost feel bad for him. Still, it's that same blank-eyed naïveté that's killed us all. By this time in the 21st century we should be trick-or-treating on Mars with the ghost of Ray Bradbury. Yet here we are, earthbound with the dead.

"Just don't make them tell me to shoot you," Evans says.

"Take it easy, Evans. It'll be all right."

We ascend the ridge to the large circular parking area. We take what's apparently a reserved space for Evans around a tall, spurting fountain. It's a majestic piece of work, reminiscent of the one at the hotel last week. Except this one is three times as large and made of real polished stone, not molded concrete.

I keep close to Evans' back, avoiding eye contact with the others walking across the plaza. A large black man in a suit, sunglasses, and a Bluetooth in his ear gestures us to move towards the rear of the estate. We follow a white pea-gravel trail around the side of the massive stone house, an impossibly green, impossibly uniform lawn to our left, a wooded park to our right, the thick storybook trees shading the path.

For all the stubborn force of stone represented by the mansion, another man was shitting in the master bath as of last week. I suppress a grin, thinking of Evans' dramatic reading of this news as if such things could never happen. We're Americans, by golly, not lawless Somalians!

The grin fades as the smell of cooking meat and the sounds of a large group of people talking increase with our approach. I realize you can't mime a barbecue but if the trees surrounding the property mute the sound, they still won't entirely blunt the smell of the meat. For all our sakes I hope Kerch has some people watching his perimeter.

We reach the end of the house and are circling around to take the steps up to the wide stone balcony overlooking the back lawn. I stop to look at the revelers. All well-dressed, with "untroubled faces" as the great Bukowski observed. They're mostly young, though the leathery wannbe-young are also represented here. Some dance to the DJ, others stand and mingle and flirt with one another. Fans blow across huge blocks of ice to cool them as they pick shrimp and roast beef and God knows what else as the world dies screaming.

Hemingway had described such people in *A Moveable Feast* as those for whom "every day is a fiesta." One party after another. Nice work if you can get born into it.

"I hope to God you don't envy those people," says Evans. "You ever hear the saying, 'Fattening hogs ain't in luck?'"

"'Be careful when you're gettin' all you want. Fattenin' hogs ain't in luck!' Yes, the down-home wisdom of ex-slave Uncle Remus. As for how that relates to shiny rich young people who want for nothing but more beats per minute and a hit of Ecstasy, I have no idea what the fuck you're talking about!"

Evans is once again mortified into silence. Still, as we approach the steps and begin climbing I get the feeling he knows something. He just doesn't know how to tell me because he can't even explain it to himself.

As stumped as Evans is by basic concepts outside the narrative bubble of the Great Red, White and Blue Turnip Truck he's still a good guy to know. The big black guy we pass at the foot of the steps doesn't even glance at me as I pass; he's busy keeping the people behind us from coming up. "This is a private area," he says in deep bass voice.

"Look at him!" I hear Kerch saying just before I reach balcony level.

"He's not liking this at all!"

"I'm sure he'll like it just fine when he realizes we got it covered. Today, anyway."

I look over Evans shoulder. Sure enough, there's Kerch wearing his white Stetson like a crown on top of his long, toothy head. A squat, somewhat stooped gentleman wearing tinted bifocals stands next to Kerch.

"Doing quite well for a man with cracked ribs," the stooped gentleman says. "Come on, let's have a look at you. By the way, I'm Dr. Hearn." He holds out his hand as I follow him into the main house. I turn and look at Kerch, who smiles and waves. Apparently I'm meant to do this.

We pass through a pickup area/lounge with a window in the wall for the kitchen. We keep walking until we come to a study larger than my own master bedroom back home. Shelves and shelves of books circle the walls to the high domed ceiling.

Dr. Hearn has me strip to my boxers. He feels around my rib cage. "They said your ribs were cracked."

"That's what I was told. I've made a point of not testing the theory."

"For all I know I might see a hairline fracture somewhere in an X-ray but near as I can tell they're just badly bruised. Or, rather, they were badly bruised. You seem to be on the mend. You've apparently lost weight, but it was weight you could stand to lose. You'd make a nutritious meal."

"What?"

"The bacteria reanimating the dead can only process protein. They pass fat as waste."

"Oh."

"It's not something most people are around long enough to see. You have to have done enough time in the field to see this."

"There was this middle-aged guy in blue silk pajamas

staggering along down the street in Kansas City. Something was falling out his pants leg. It didn't look like normal…feces."

Dr. Hearn seizes my arm. "Describe it!"

Yeah, I see where Hannah gets her heebie-jeebies about this guy: "Pale yellow, with brighter spots of yellow, shot through with red and pink. It seemed to have the lumpy texture of cottage cheese, but more gelatinous. The stench was beyond description."

Dr. Hearn nods vigorously. "Yes, yes! Your subject had just eaten within six hours! The bacteria have a quicker collective metabolism than living people do, apparently. Of course, as with us, meat proteins break down easier than fat. That's why when people starve themselves trying to lose weight they lose muscle tone before anything else. In the case of the reanimated, they just pass the fat altogether. They don't even try to break it down. The bacteria lack the necessary enzymes."

"Uh, have you been able to…analyze it?"

"The zombie scat? No, I frankly can't get that close." He chuckles. "I do understand it's highly flammable, though. Which makes me wonder about what might happen if a reanimated one swallowed a bone, or something else that would stop him up. Even worse, it could rip an intestine and have all the meat and fat falling into the body cavity. It's bound to have happened somewhere already. Most just gulp their flesh down after masticating for two or three bites."

"You've gathered quite a bit of data in a little over a week."

"I talked to the senior medical officer with the Army unit that came through on Sunday. He's the son of a friend of mine from medical school. Good boy. They're on top of this all the way."

"An Army unit came through while I was out?"

"You notice they don't have any problems at the high school. Or on Oak Blossom Lane. They were here maybe 90 minutes but they cleared quite a bit of space for us. Anyway, if you see any unnaturally bloated looking specimens would you please send me pictures? I can put my e-mail address into your phone."

"I don't have a data plan."

"Sure you do. You work here, you've got data."

"Oh. Good to know." I hand him my phone.

"Any other issues you'd like to talk about?" he asks as he thumbs his information into the slide-out keyboard.

"No. Just grateful nothing's really broken."

"Well, I think you're good for the grand expedition tomorrow. Just pace yourself, take it easy."

"Trust me, I'd sit it out altogether if I could. I need underwear, though."

He smiles, hands me my phone. "Come, let's tell Emory the good news. I have to get home and rest up. I expect I'll be plenty busy tomorrow."

Emory is standing just outside the door as we leave the study. Dr. Hearn nods and his grin fills the room end to end. "I take it he can handle swinging at things with his arms?"

"He should be okay for a quick run."

"Quick is how we're doing this," Emory says, nodding at me. "We get in there, grab everything we can find and carry in two minutes, and leave in three. These things mob up quick. We're gonna be quicker. Anyway, thanks, Clyde! I'll stop by after lunch tomorrow with some liquid encouragement for ya."

"You have a detail going to the liquor store?"

Emory's grin widens. "After tonight, I don't see any way around it!"

"All right, Em. I'll be looking for you, then." Dr. Hearn turns and walks through the front of the house to show himself out.

I turn to Emory. "I appreciate the professional visit."

"He would have seen you earlier but he had his hands full, as you can imagine. Not a young guy. We need to find some doctors in town, let 'em know we have a safe place for 'em to live and work. Speaking of safe, Clyde and I were talking about you coming up. We were impressed how you were assessing the security and finding it wanting."

"This is why I don't play poker."

Emory laughs. "Well, just so you know, we've got people in the woods and on the other side of the golf course. If they see any of the former citizens looking too interested they sneak up ninja-style and take them out. We got people taking phone calls from the front. If it sounds like the former citizens are mobbing up we'll shut it down and take them out as they come through the woods."

"I stand corrected."

Emory slaps me hard on the back. "You're smart! There's a future for smart people here, just so ya know!"

"Does that future include a frosty cold pale ale?"

"Oh, no! That's the here and now! By the way, you hungry?"

"Oh, yeah."

"How do you like your steak? We got some shrimp to go with that, too!"

"Medium rare, and hell yeah on the shrimp."

Evans wasn't lying; these are frosted mugs fit for Norse gods. Now this is how you do carrots, I think as I carve into my perfectly medium-rare steak, careful not to shove my mounds of fries and jumbo shrimp off of my plate. Emory Kerch even has lobster brought out, and sees to it I get a fat claw, "For what I saw this man do today right in the middle of the street. Three at once!"

I hoist my mug to the assembled. I realize I'm eating among other would-be monster slayers and they don't appreciate the attention the alpha dog is showing me. Other men, and one old woman, are also in attendance at the patio table overlooking the back lawn where 30 to 40 sensibly dressed people are mingling, talking, dancing to the music. It's easy to imagine nothing ever happened. We're loud and smoky and I can only imagine what it's like on the perimeter.

Maybe they like it rough. You can tell by looking at them; I'm among people who have been waiting for something like this. For the world to go to shit, just so they could strut their stuff. And why not? There weren't many opportunities to shine when things were "normal." They stare holes in me as I look past their shoulders to the back lawn beyond, where others like them stalk the woods. Kerch apparently wasted no time finding people who would approach a hungry "former citizen" for the brutal pleasure of cracking its skull, stabbing its eye, making a once functional human fall to the ground.

I saw Mrs. Jefferson's once darling grandson and all I could think of was my encounters with gasbags like him back in college—years ago we had things that looked like him, wispy beards, wire-rim glasses, and convinced they knew everything because the answers were all in this one book by Hip Philosopher of the Moment. They looked down on people like me who had to work their way through school while they passed the time sneering at others for their "pedestrian tastes" in books, movies and music while they themselves indulged in "guilty pleasures" like the Hip

Popular TV Show of the Moment and whatever ethnicky subgenre of music is being played over the speakers at the swankest coffee shop near campus. I swear there's some alien mother in the basement of every liberal arts college shitting these things out fully grown, wire-rims, beard, bad suit and all, and I'm only sorry I couldn't make Mrs. Jefferson's darling little Grandson Who Teaches at the University suffer.

I think of the borderline elderly woman I gut-punched before Tanner and I drove away from the hotel. The lizard-brained rage and hunger in her face wasn't at all dissimilar to the entitled attitude things like her projected when they were alive, alternately complaining and demanding in a voice pitched somewhere between metal-on-metal and an air horn. Seeing her fold up and fall in front of me felt good.

No telling how Emory Kerch "earned" his money but it's apparent he's a student of human resentment. There was a lot of rage bubbling beneath the surface in the days before the Final Flu. I know, because I owned most of it. For disease-spreading cab drivers. For chatty nitwits whose life is an easy hustle. For pompous cops who are never around when you need them and all up in your business when you don't. For all the generic stupid fucks toddling around in the costumes of their tribe: Hip-Hop Nation, Soccer Mom, Fat Peasant Girl. McMansionland Student Athlete, Skateboard Slacker, Rich White Cause-of-the-Week Feminist Princess, Retired Old Fart in Plaid. Modern Cowboy, Indie Band Hipster. For all those smirking, laughing Untouched dancing to the DJ on the vast back lawn, protected from everything wrong with the world.

Ask Emory Kerch where he fits in and he'll laugh and tell you he's just a Guy Who Knows How to Make Money. Gaming the jealousies and resentments of his lessers is just one of the tools in his box. Of all the rich assholes in the world to work around I'm dealing with the most dangerous breed of all: that shrewd backslapper who knows how to *earn* it. All the old money aristocratic connections in the world can't save you if someone like Kerch knows someone else who's been slighted by a Good Family—and needs only a little nudge to do something about it.

Given the looks I'm getting I wonder if I'm being set up. Or maybe we're all being set up. A skinny Goth kid, with a line of rings on one nostril and the whitest skin I've ever seen on a white person glowers at me in a way I'm guessing is supposed to be menacing. There's another barely-legal-to -drink boy in a gray wife-beater who looks over from time to time, but is otherwise pretending not to acknowledge my presence. A petite blonde girl with deep brown skin who stares at me when she thinks I'm not looking.

All at once the three get up and leave their places. "Dinner break's up," says the older man next to me.

"Oh."

"So how you liking it so far?"

"The food's good. The beer's better than I hoped for. Course, it's been a while."

"You ready to be in charge of that crew?"

"What crew?"

A hand claps down on my shoulder. It's Emory Kerch. "Come on, George, you know I haven't had a chance to talk to him yet!"

"He's been here nearly a week!" says George.

"Most of it unconscious. It's been a busy week here. Anyway!" Kerch claps his hand on my shoulder. "You about done? Just wanted to take you away real quick."

"Can I bring my beer?"

"Well, hell, yeah! I was thinking of taking our meeting at the bar!"

"By God, then lead the way, good sir!"

"Wooo!" crows Kerch. "You gonna be so much more fun to take meetings with than Evans! Let's go!"

I walk with Kerch away from the table and force myself to dismiss the idea of all that steak, shrimp and lobster going to waste. Only someone in a struggling class sweats those details. Jesus, that was good stuff, though. Too bad for all the people in their hiding places all over the world, struggling with that last can of beets no one wanted a week ago....

The bar is beyond the room leading to the balcony, built around the kitchen. A smiling, buxom lady in a black tube dress steps forward to wait on us. "See, here's the thing," Kerch says as we settle into our seats. "I think you could clear out the town."

"How many lived here before the Final Flu?"

"Maybe fifty-thousand. It's a lot, I know. But if I could get enough people trained to fight like you, we could get it finished before the end of the summer. We could have a chance to live! The ones walking the freeway, we'd only take on for exercise. Just so long as we can clear the city, and make it safe for cattle in the country. We can build an old-fashioned city-state here. You know that's the future, right?"

"You know more about this that I do. I'm just looking for some clean underwear."

"See, maybe you think that's funny, but I call it practical! Practical thinking is the difference between just surviving and thriving. You like all this, right?"

"What's not to like?"

"That's just it. If we can keep the supply of meat and whatever coming until we get a grip on raising our own—without people trying to eat the steak right off the hoof!"

"What do you need me to do?"

"Just ride with Evans tomorrow. He normally wrangles our dead-people fighters, but I think you're a far better example. You'll get out there and do it with them! You know how these officer types are, they're not conditioned for real combat, you know what I mean? Hell, they get flustered over a paper jam in the printer! You're more the senior enlisted mentality. Were you in the military?"

"No, but I've spent a lot of time working with them."

"Coulda fooled me. You move like a man with training!"

"Nope. Just an older guy who knows he's only got so many moves before he wears out."

"Not into a bunch of show-offy drama, like some of these kids we're working with. They watch some movies, read some comic books, and they think they're King Shit out there. You can't tell 'em anything!"

"Well, I expect 'market forces' to take care of them in short order."

"Market forces! The way the wannabe badasses of business used to talk. Especially when they wanted to absolve themselves of responsibility for decision."

"Failing to acknowledge that they themselves were a 'market force,'" I say, finishing the thought for him.

"That's exactly what I used to tell these punks! I'd tell 'em, You screw me over and the biggest goddamn market force you ever saw is comin' down on you!"

I nod. Point taken. "So, ride along with Evans. See what he does. Take over wrangling the zombie-killing talent. Anything else?"

"Well, Clyde—that is, Dr. Hearn—was concerned you'd overdo it here."

"Yeah, I should get my rest."

"This is all shutting down before nightfall. Evans and the people out there already got their hands full taking out the curious. Hell, I oughta shut it down, now! Anyway, Denise here is getting you a growler to go! Oughta help you get to sleep."

"Thanks."

"Oh, and don't forget this!" Another attractive young blonde rocking a tight black dress and cleavage appears with a clam-shell carry-out box. She doesn't smile, though. Her face is hard, all business. "I can tell you're a man who hates waste," says Kerch. "I had 'em throw a couple more steaks in there for you. A man needs all the red meat he can eat!"

"You know it. I'll drop a couple of more zombies for you just for that."

"That's the spirit. Rebecca here'll drive you home."

I slide down from the bar stool. "Thanks, again, Emory."

"Nothin' to it. You gonna be ready to roll by seven tomorrow?"

"That was my next question. And, yes."

"All right! We'll see ya then!"

I take my growler from the bar and follow Rebecca out through the house to the front entrance. She carries my take-home clamshell, her hand holding it up just so as if it were the Christmas goose. As if by magic a chauffeur's cap appears in her free hand. She sets it atop her perfect hair as we step outside. This lady is so fluid and professional in her movement that walking behind her makes me stand that much straighter.

And there are eyes upon us as we descend the palatial stairs from the front entrance, towards the black SUV closest to the door. Yes, we're stepping down towards the Big Man's personal conveyance, but if there's any envy in the glances, it's easily missed. There's an urgency to these dozen or so couples flooding out to their vehicles parked around the fountain and along the lane.

Something's going on and we're being sent away. As close as Rebecca and I are to our vehicle the others have already started their cars and are driving as fast as they dare away up the dual-rutted road. Like frightened animals before the stampede.

16

Everyone else is in an obvious hurry but Rebecca doesn't waste a move. Rebecca unlocks the SUV with the remote and opens the rear door for me to climb in. She waits for me to straighten my legs and settle in with the growler jug before closing the door and walking around to the driver's side.

She's climbing in when a deep, nearly subsonic *THOOOM!* nearly blows the door back. Rebecca puts the take-out box on the passenger seat and closes the door. Our ears are spared the brunt of the now-pulsing bass, but we can still feel it in the soundproofed interior of Kerch's Luxury Tank. Rebecca turns the ignition, pulls the shifter into gear. We swing around the vast fountain and up the long trail to the main road. I turn to look behind us. One other car is following us out. Indeed, all the cars parked around the fountain and in front of the house are now gone.

"Where did everyone else park?" I ask.

"There's an underground lot on the south side of the estate," Rebecca says. "You can't see it from here."

"Sounds like the party's just getting started for them." I turn around in time to see Rebecca's eyes flash steel-gray at me from the rear-view mirror.

"Mr. Kerch had them move the DJ booth and bar table further down the lawn. That way they could turn it up."

"I could swear I saw the DJ leaving in front of us. He was in an awful hurry."

"He's grateful Mr. Kerch finds him useful," Rebecca says, a chilly edge to her voice. "The kids are running their own party now."

Kids? Rebecca isn't much older than the youngest back-lawn reveler I saw. I look to the rear-view, but her eyes—no laugh lines or crow's feet about them, and steely as a Navy destroyer—remain straight ahead.

"He seemed more frightened than grateful."

Rebecca says nothing. We race up the slope to the main road. Rebecca takes the turn without stopping. Despite the state-of-the-art suspension we bounce hard coming up on the narrow macadam. She all but floors it once we're straightened out.

"Jesus! What's going on?" I ask.

"If you don't know then I'm not at liberty to say."

"Balls!"

"Evans will brief you tomorrow morning when he comes to pick you up."

"Great."

Rebecca requires no direction to find my house. She brings us all the way to the front porch before parking. That she kills the engine seems strange. I almost wish Tanner was here to explain the etiquette to me. Maybe we're not supposed to smell exhaust fumes. I sit and wait for Rebecca to open my door. I know to do that much.

I hadn't realized she'd already grabbed the take-out box from the front seat. Smooth. She opens the door and I ease out of the bossman's Tank. I expect her to run ahead of me and hold the iron-grated outer door while I unlock the main. Instead I glance down to see her taking a suit-bag and an overnight bag from the back of the SUV.

I don't have long to wonder about this when the distant *thoom!* is cut by a collective scream. Quick, faint—these people are maybe two miles away—but there's no mistaking what it is.

Rebecca is up the porch steps with her luggage and my leftovers. "We have to get inside. Now!"

I work the keys and push the door open. Rebecca rushes around me into the house. She pauses long enough to stand by a window looking out on the driveway and point her remote. She winces as the horn honks in acknowledgement and I understand exactly what is going on. I lock up the front door while Rebecca draws the blinds on the windows facing the driveway.

"We'll need to shut off the generator, too," Rebecca says.

"Goddamn it!" She's right, of course. "All right, let's get the food into the fridge at least. Find a flashlight, some candles. Shit!"

As we make it to the kitchen my text ringer goes off. I set the growler down by the sink and thumb the screen.

> ATTN ALL:
> Lockdown. Herd 100, 200 or
> more coming from west side
> of town, should filter out into
> fields by dawn IF NOT GIVEN
> REASON TO STAY. No heroics
> pls. Evans.

I'm about to click out of this when my text ringer goes off again.

> This means you, Grace. Pls
> let herd pass.

I text him back:

> Laying low. Don't worry about
> me. Be safe.

I'm putting my phone back into my pocket when Rebecca says, "I found a camp lantern in the utility closet. It's full."

"Fire it up. I'll get the generator."

Outside on the back patio I almost think I can hear an *mmmmmm!* from the distance. I cut the generator off. I listen some more. Nothing but the ringing in my ears and some evening birdsong. I slip back inside, taking care to close all shutters and blinds, draw every curtain. We're still an hour and a half from sundown but the house is dark as a tomb. It takes me a minute to orient myself and find the kitchen.

"Rebecca!"

I take another few seconds to allow my eyes to adjust to the dark. I walk slowly, quietly towards the stairs. The creaking from the ceiling confirms my suspicion and I pound on up.

I can see the light coming out from beneath my bedroom door. Which turns out to be locked. I'd hate to kick this thing down; it's solid wood and probably as old as the house besides. Fortunately I have a skeleton key on my ring. So I could get into the weapons room…I decide to stop in there first, pick up a little something that had caught my eye earlier.

I have to move fast, though. Fluid, just like my girl in there. I have the key in one hand and my weapon in the other. I close and lock the weapons room. I stand still and breathe for one, two seconds. Three. I go to the door.

I have it open in a second. Rebecca stands on the other side of the room, just inside the bathroom door. Her steely eyes blaze rage and she charges me. It's only as I pull the bokken back to swing at her shins that I realize she's buck naked. Thank God. She's moving like she knows exactly what she's going to do next so I bring the flat of the wooden blade forward as I dive to the floor, out of reach of any grasping or punching moves. The Japanese practice sword clacks hard against her shin and Rebecca flies forward over me, through the door and into the hall.

I roll to my feet and I'm swinging the flat of the blade hard on her exposed ass and again on her other side, right against the side of her knee. She screams loud and high, enough to hurt my ears where I stand over her.

The scream cuts short as I've got my blade and body angled to drive the business end through her belly. She sees the look in my face. Rebecca is a cold bitch, but she's not stupid.

"Goddamn it!" she says. "I'm supposed to be fucking you!"

"You're not even supposed to be here! The plan was to come home and drink alone until I passed out. Not to entertain Frost Ho's." I glance down and see, oh for Christ's sake, she's waxed thoroughly bare. Having changed my daughter's diaper on three hundred or more occasions I can't say I'm comfortable with the sight.

Rebecca shifts to one side and I retrain my focus: "Not yet. You're going to answer some questions or I'll gut you and feed you still breathing to the stumblers." I pull back to wind up for a lunge and she brings her arms tight around her knees.

"What do you want?" she says, eyeing me for signs of pity or weakness.

I shift my balance with the wooden blade and show Rebecca my best psycho face. "Who is Kerch killing out there? And what for?"

She looks me right in my best psycho eyes when she says, "Evans will tell you everything in the morning."

I swing the flat of the blade fast and hard against the outside of each knee. She screams. I swat her ass again and bring the blade up over her soft middle.

I pull the blade back....

"Stop! No! You saw them! Excess! *Trim!*"

"I figured that. But where were they from? I haven't seen them around here before."

"They're from that big McMansionland development on the northeast edge of town. Upper-middle-manager types. We didn't invite the people we can use—the stoners and the party girls, though, there were so many! A lot of them living with one parent, and that parent died. So Mr. Kerch thought he'd kill two birds with one stone. Get rid of all the useless eaters who see the apocalypse as a long vacation."

"What's the other bird?"

"Okay, look, if I'm already telling you this, may I please get up?"

I swat her hard and fast on the backside. She yelps. I back into the room and pull Rebecca's pink silk bathrobe from the hook on the bathroom door. I toss it to her. Rebecca gets to her feet, grimacing at the aching in her knees.

Her breasts stand strong and firm over a taut belly. No tattoos or piercings. Clean and classy. She'll heal quickly. Rebecca ties on her pink bathrobe, her nipples sharp through the silk. She takes hesitant steps back into the room, making faces as she walks off the soreness.

"The other bird, Rebecca."

She stops, puts her hand out to the bed to steady herself. "Mr. Kerch and Dr. Hearn have been talking about ways to control these things. Instead of risking the lives of useful workers trying to hunt down every last one, you could draw them away. Send them somewhere else."

"To a rival city-state, maybe."

"Huh? Oh. We're all we know about out here."

"So far."

"Please. All we've got that anyone would want is land. And that's all Kansas pretty much is. Plenty for everybody."

"So why bunk all those people at that high school? Why not let them move into some of the empty houses?"

"Oh, come on! They'd just trash whatever they moved into. Living at the school, maybe we can get them into the habit of cleaning up after themselves. We can also see who works and who doesn't. Mr. Kerch isn't giving free rides here. You pull your weight, or too bad!"

I think of what Brandon said about escaping. Kerch is getting his plantation organized and locking it down tight.

"Mr. Kerch has big plans," she says. "If he sent you home with me it means he sees something in you. You don't want to piss him off beating up his favorite driver! Look, even I don't get the lobster and shrimp because he says it's fattening!"

"If you'd been a little more free with the information this wouldn't have been necessary. Also, walking off with the one and only light source and locking yourself in my room with it is damned rude."

"Well, excuse me! Where am I supposed to shower?"

"There's a room a little further down the hall and to the left. It has a classic claw-foot tub you can soak yourself in."

"On the side of the house furthest from the light. Great. So I still get the lantern, right?

"The former owner was good about putting candles in every room. You can even have this one if you want." I toss the candle from the dresser to the bed, atop her suit bag.

Rebecca zips it up into her bag, looking warily at me. "So you're just sleeping alone in here?"

"Eventually. I'll be in the front bedroom looking over the street. If there's anything to see in the dark I'll be looking at it until I'm tired of drinking warm beer. Unless things get really exciting I don't expect to be up too late. You gotta wake up early?"

"Seven is the general start of the workday here."

"Great. We'll set the alarms on our phones, then. See you in the morning."

Rebecca gathers her bags as quickly as her pain allows her and leaves. As soon as I heard her door shut down the hall I change into pajamas and a bathrobe so I can soak my one and only pair of underwear in the sink. With luck I can use the electric dryer in the morning. Assuming they've got all this under control by then.

I lock my bedroom door behind me and pad downstairs into the kitchen where my growler is. After satisfying myself that everything is locked up, blinded and secure I return upstairs to the master bedroom overlooking the front lawn and the street below. There's an ancient wingback chair in the corner with a matching ottoman. I'm settling in as the first *thoom!* reaches my ears. Followed by a *hyaaaannnnnnh* from whatever's following it.

Jesus, these assholes had better know what they're doing.

My phone rings a text alert.

> Herd calved and away from estate. Bringing them down Oak Blssm Ln sending them east. If have not done so already turn generators OFF. Remain indoors. Set phones to vibrate only, updates when we have them.

"Calved"? Like a glacier? The *thoom!* of the bass is getting louder, closer. Is this Oak Blossom Street? They can turn left instead of right, send these things back into town or south to the Interstate.

The bass is vibrating objects where they sit on level surfaces. I can just about feel it in my bowel. It's not steady—they could draw every deader for miles that way—it's as if the guy in the car, truck or whatever was manipulating the volume on the subwoofer. He only turns it up when he seems to need it.

The moans of hundreds of hungry dead buzz the windows as sure as that subwoofer bass. I can only imagine what it would sound like outside. I move to open the window then realize, no, the smell. Not just me smelling them, either. Granted, I'm up a steep knoll and there's no wind but—

I crack the cap on my growler bottle and down a gulp of tepid pale ale. The last rays of the sun angle through the tunnel of trees that is the lane where the Good Families live. As I watch the low-riding red Cadillac roll slowly down the street, I understand this guy could have turned left. He could have led that entire ghastly crew back into town, or south towards the Interstate, sent them walking down I-70 clear to Baltimore.

I wonder if it's coincidence that the Caddy stops right in front of my house. Of course, I have no idea who lives across the street. The Caddy does have to stop from time to time so its entourage can catch up. Whether or not it really needs to THOOOM! right there is subject to debate. I really fear for the windows with this one, but they hold, thank God.

I see the driver through his open window; I recognize him as one of the older teens at the high school. He's got that timeless greaser sneer going on, his arm hanging out, tapping the side of his door, the scent of his warm, living flesh another draw for his following.

I see them as they pass the privacy hedge between me and the house next door. The sun fails behind them, as if their passing drains the very light from the world. Men in suits, men in black denim and wife-beaters. Children in pajamas, mothers in their gowns. And then the ones who didn't obviously die of the Flu first…I'd never thought about what Tanner meant by that. The ones whose heads hang to one side because the meat around the collarbone is just so damned convenient. The defensive wounds on the arms. Huge chunks of flesh torn right through the cloth by jaws driven with the force of senseless rigor mortis and rage-purposed hunger. Yeah, some of those children in pajamas…blood-black-stiff pajamas…shit….

The first rows sport glistening new blood-bibs, the chin-to-crotch remains of Natalia's high-end slacker community. In Emory Kerch's Hard Workin' New World, the party really is over. It's dripping down the front of a homeschooling mom in her shift, staining the power tie of that sales rep.

That same tie is crimped from where someone had grabbed it in an attempt to steer those hungry, meat-clotted teeth away from her own face. Or his face. You can guess who those are stumbling up a couple of rows behind. They're damned hard to look at, with the skin pulled away, the muscle exposed beneath their eyes, around their mouths. I wonder if they died right away from the shock or they had to bleed out first.

Their collective moaning forms a low hum, like an epic cloud of flesh-eating flies. They reach the rear of the Cadillac, close enough to touch. The arms of the ones in front go up, they pick up speed. And just as they're about to touch, the kid lets his foot off the brake. The horde lets loose a collective *hyannnnh!* in their frustration. The kid releases a *thoom!* in response.

I get up from the chair to go to the window on the other side of the room. The driver is making a point of stopping in front of each house. Kerch is letting everyone know he's not making exceptions for anyone.

Well, good for him, I think, taking another gulp from the growler bottle. All governments rule by terror. Kerch's terror just happens to be more terrifying than most. I wonder what that Paulson guy said to Kerch to bring this on. I noticed Paulson wasn't there at the party.

It's tricky what this kid is doing, especially with the multiple stops. He's got 300 or so deaders stumbling up after his Caddy. They bunch up in the middle. So many rows deep, the ones along the edge who are just following the horde don't see the moving vehicle, don't smell the live meat dangling out the window. They can't see, but they know there are structures up on these knolls. Where people used to live.

I see some of these gray, ripped faces turned towards my window and I freeze. A shift in shadow might be enough to bring them up the driveway. Them and 300 of their friends. Oh, Jesus. I'll need to get Rebecca to kill me for sure because there is no way this is going to end well....

A large-barreled shaft suddenly appears in the middle of the curious woman's face. A few seconds later and her companion, a middle-aged old schlub in boxers and a stretched V-neck undershirt, falls backwards with something sticking out between his eyes.

The ones that are moving, keep moving. Any that look sideways are dropped by the large-barreled arrows. Any stragglers falling too far back fall over for good. Apparently Kerch company policy applies to the undead as well as the living: slackers are terminated.

As the last of the herd passes in front of my window I realize what they mean by calving the herd. Evans' crew figured a way to draw a number of deaders. As enough of them passed, or (more likely) the herd was already thin enough in the middle, they cut them down. What could be a horde of thousands is only a few hundred. A few hundred you could Pied Piper away with one smart-assed kid and his sub-woofer.

I've got to hand it to Kerch. In less than two weeks he's taken the most grotesque human catastrophe since the Black Death and made it work for him.

All I want is a change of underwear and a quiet place to hole up. After I make sure my family is really gone, that is. I need to do that much first. But that's it. I have no need to rule the world. Nor do I care to help some other alpha dog rule the world. It was bad enough when everything was "normal." Now….

I listen as the Caddy and its grisly entourage disappear into the dusk. The kid isn't wasting his time stopping in front of the empty houses towards the end of the lane. He's rolling straight out to the road leading down to Old Man Sanderson's fields. Standing there in the near perfect darkness I take another hit from my growler jug. I feel like I should have a cigarette. Can't say why. I quit smoking 20 years ago.

I turn and walk right into—Rebecca? I stumble backwards with the jug sloshing in my hand. I nearly fall into the window before I get my feet steady beneath me.

"Oh calm down, it wouldn't be fair in your condition! Look, I know you don't want to be bothered but I need a glass for my cognac. I was hoping you could get it for me. Or give me the lantern and I'll look for myself."

I look around for the lantern. She holds it out in front of her. "Here."

I take the lantern from her and walk out the door. I wait until I'm in the middle of the hall before I fire it up. Then I go downstairs. I pass quickly through to the kitchen. I'd rather no one catch so much as a flash behind these blinds.

I find the hutch with the specialty glasses. Two long-stemmed tulip glasses are clinking in my hand as I climb the stairs. Before I make the first landing my text alert goes off. I continue on up. I come to the door to my room and set the lantern down on the floor as I dig for my keys. Rebecca appears at the edge of the light.

"We're drinking in here?"

"I don't want the light in the front room. I was hoping you'd pour me a hit. We don't have to keep each other company."

"It's creepy in this old house. You mind if I hang for just a little while?"

"Fine."

"I liked this room better in the first place."

"Don't get used to it."

"I won't."

I push the door open. Rebecca picks up the lantern and follows me inside. I nod at the dresser and she puts the lantern there. She picks up the glasses from the bed and begins to pour as I check my phone.

ALL CLEAR. Pls remain indoors as crew clears bodies. Leave gens off per norm.

"I didn't know we left our generators off at night," I say.

Rebecca hands me my glass. "Only for the summer when it's tolerable. The winter is going to be something else, though. We either get tankers of fuel or get the electricity going again. Either way, we've got to get these dead people cleared out of town."

"I have no doubt our esteemed patron Mr. Kerch can make that happen." I raise my glass. "To our esteemed patron!"

"So you're really thinking of sticking around?"

"Why not? Emory laid out a nice spread at that death trap he set up this afternoon. I'll be honored to kill a few thousand zombies for him."

Rebecca looks at me suspiciously. "You lost everyone. That's what I've been hearing. You have family in Colorado and now they're gone."

"My wife is gone. I don't know what happened to my children."

"How old were they?"

"Seventeen and nineteen."

"You're not going to try and look for them?"

"Survival would mean them going where the former citizens aren't, and that means well away from our neighborhood. They could be any number of places along I-25 from Monument to Pueblo. That's a lot of area. All I can do from here is wish them well. They're smart kids. If anyone can find a way to get by it's Sybil and Jack."

"It doesn't bother you that Mr. Kerch put those dead people on those poor kids?"

"What poor kids? If they're not going to contribute, no shrimp and lobster for them! By the way, you say you can't have shrimp and lobster?"

"God, no, and I love it!"

"You can have mine from the box downstairs."

"What's this for?"

"A peace offering. Not an apology, mind you. Just peace."

Rebecca smiles icily as she lifts her glass towards me: "Let there be peace between our houses, Mr. Grace."

I hold my glass up. "Peace."

Rebecca sits on my bed. I take the chair at the foot of the bed. It's very good cognac.

After a while Rebecca says, "I lost everyone, too."

"Yeah?"

"No. I lost everyone before this all happened."

"Any advice for the newly bereaved, then?"

"No. Not really."

I laugh, hold up my glass. "To alcohol!"

Rebecca does a terrible job of suppressing a smile. "You've adapted to all this rather quickly."

"There's not a lot going on in the way of alternatives."

"No," says Rebecca, looking into the distance. "No, there isn't."

We sit in silence for a minute. Then: "You mind if I bring back some candles for the room. This lantern's a little bright."

"Do what you have to do."

Rebecca takes the lantern out of the room. I reach over and finger the blinds on the window. It's completely dark out now. The stars twinkle brightly through the humid Kansas air. The temperature would be going down in Colorado Springs, where the air is drier…speaking of dry, I should wring out my underwear and hang it up….

Rebecca returns with the candles. She lights both and turns off the lantern. The light is warmer, more intimate. "Better," she says, settling back on the bed. "Oh, how are you over there?"

I raise my glass. "Never better."

"Hm. Let me top you off."

Before I have a chance to get up she's leaning over me, the silk from her lingerie top brushing my face. I glance down to see the curves of her breasts as they push against the fabric as she fills my glass.

Rebecca's eyes meet mine. "Okay?"

"Yeah. I just remembered something, though."

"Oh?"

"If I don't wring out my underwear and hang it up I'll be going commando tomorrow. I should probably set my alarm so I can start up the generator and run the electric dryer."

Rebecca straightens, still standing very close. "You're going out into a sea of hungry dead people tomorrow and you're worried about your junk swinging free in your pants?"

"The last thing anyone needs out there is a distraction."

She puts a finger on my nose. "Stay right there."

Rebecca takes a candle from the dresser and walks to the bathroom behind me. I hear the water in the sink as she wrings it from my shorts. There's a glug as she unstops the drain, a fresh run from the spigot as she rinses the soap from the shorts and sink.

"You don't have to do that," I say.

She shuts off the water. "No, I don't," she says. I hear the rustle of the shower curtain as she drapes my shorts over the rod. I hear her dry her hands before she comes back out. "I'm leaving the candle in the bathroom on top of the toilet. I think we can get by with one in here."

"I wish I could have seen that," I say.

"Seen what?"

"You rinsing out my shorts. There's nothing sexier than watching a woman take care of basic household business."

Rebecca reaches down, runs her fingers along my ear. "How long were you married, Mr. Grace?"

"Twenty-two years."

"You ever step out on her?"

"No." I look up into her eyes. The light's behind her here, but they still seem to flash steely silver from time to time. "I'm not looking for an award. We just took it day by day."

"Until the days ran out," she says.

"Yeah. Pretty much. No kiss goodbye." I draw a long, burning swallow from the cognac. "Couldn't afford it."

She looks at me curiously. Given the kind of man a woman like Rebecca is used to, an expression like "couldn't afford it" must sound laughably strange. I smile and turn my glass up.

Rebecca reaches out, wraps her hand around mine. She takes my glass, raises it to her lips. She puts it on the dresser. Before I can protest Rebecca turns and falls into my lap. Her long fingers curl around the back of my head. "You *sip* cognac," she says, before demonstrating on my lower lip. My lip burns with the residue. "You don't *gulp*."

Her open mouth, hot and stinging, presses into mine. I feel the heat beneath her silk top as I clutch her to me. I'm drowning myself in this hard young woman, drowning the lost old married guy with near-grown kids in a baptism of saliva and premium liquor.

With a strength that might have amazed me five minutes ago I rise from the chair, Rebecca cradled in my arms. This is something I have to do. The kiss was one step over the line. It's time to commit fully to my new life. Full-body immersion, anointed in the oils of her warm, living flesh.

I cradle her in one arm while ripping down the covers with the other. She bounces lightly as I drop her, smiling lips parted, her steel-gray eyes flashing. I meet those eyes with mine, knowing they'll belong to someone else entirely when the sun finds us in the morning.

17

It's the sound of the power coming on that wakes me the first time. I feel her side of the bed. Only a hint of warmth where I'd fallen asleep spooning her sticky-wet heat. No, but Rebecca is turning on the lights on her way out, bless her heart....

I awaken again at my customary five-minutes-before-the-alarm. I'm looking around for my phone—it should be under my pillow but I was too preoccupied to do my planned pre-sleep prep. I throw my feet over the side of the bed and cast about the room. I find my phone in the chair I was sitting in before things took a turn for the animal last night. On top of the clothes I was wearing yesterday evening. Laundered, dried, and folded. My underwear, too. Right under the phone.

Rebecca turning on the generator before she left was a nice bonus, but if you'd told me she'd wash and fold my clothes, even pick up the room before leaving, I'd have said you were full of shit.

Her womanly musk lingers thickly in the air. Part of me doesn't want to shower the memory of her from me. Which is all the more reason to get it over with.

Rebecca's not stupid, I think as I turn on the water. She knows I didn't buy her invitation to white-knight her away from her professed misery here. She also knows I'm making plans of my own that don't include kowtowing to the likes of Kerch. How that's coming out in her report back to the Big Man, and what he'll do about it—well, hell. The only thing I can do is make myself look really good in the field today. Pay for last night's dinner and then some if I'm to buy myself another day's time.

The quick soap-and-rinse helps me wake up. I dress in the clothes I had laid out for hunting yesterday. Fuck it, I'll even blouse the cuffs around these boots.

I thump down the stairs. The smell of coffee flavors the downstairs air. The pot's already timed off but it's still warm enough. When was the last time I've had coffee? I'm starting to lose track of the days. Now I know my headaches and general difficulty in staying awake wasn't just dehydration and pain-killers.

I open the blinds in the kitchen, let in the morning light, green and pleasant through the leaves. Plenty of time later for the harsh unsheltered glare even the dead prefer to avoid. For now I hold this mug to my nose, draw in the bouquet of this fresh-ground coffee. If this isn't the last time, it's close enough. What beans are left here will mold and rot before we can use them. And that will be it. Hell, we're probably done with bananas already.

And everything that was made in China will stay in China and so fucking what? I won't be making red-of-fang-and-claw love to young steel-eyed blondes any time in the foreseeable future, either. Adapt and overcome, chump. 'Tis better to have indulged and lost than to never have indulged at all.

Besides, I think as I open the heavy wooden blinds one at a time, comfortable in air conditioning, a pretty house in a pretty neighborhood makes damn near anything tolerable. God, what a difference shade trees make!

I flip the blinds near the corner by the patio and a girl's dirty, mascara-streaked face looks at me from the other side of the window. She waves her hand frantically, looking towards one side, mouthing the word *Help*, her eyes squinting tears.

I expect her to meet me at the back door, but she crouches where she is, crying. I go outside to meet her. I squat beside her outstretched leg. The wound is scabbed over but blood and serum still leak out of it.

"At least it's not a bite," I say. "How'd you get this?"

The girl, barely of legal age to drink by the looks of her, looks up at me. "You don't know?"

"Would I be asking if I knew?"

"You're not, you don't—? Oh, God!" The girl begins sobbing.

"We were dancing, it was no big deal, we're out in the country, right? They told us it'd be okay. They said move closer to the golf course because old man Kerch goes to sleep at sunset. It's really nice, all that food, stuff to drink...."

She catches her breath. "Then those people-things came out of the woods. Everywhere! Like one for every tree around the golf-course, they came out of the trees; *they came out of the trees!*"

She grabs the front of my shirt. "We're running back towards the house. Okay? Someone said, Shoulda known, no DJ, the bar's half-gone, no bartender...but if they wanted to kill us they could have just shot us! *Why didn't they shoot us in our heads!*"

"That's a bullet wound, then?" It's a long, scabbed-over tear, and by the looks of it, deep. The wider exit wound is where most of her bleeding-weeping is happening. A filthy, brownish-pink sheet of dried matter cracks and flakes around her calf and ankle.

"They aimed their guns at our legs! Jeff was right next to me, he fell down. Katy and Jenny were in front of me; I think I caught the one that went through Jenny's... Jenny was all bloody in the back, she just fell—!"

The girl catches herself. She wants to scream, scream as hard and as loud as she can. She keeps looking around though, her jaw half-open and quivering.

"Did you used to live out here? Where's your family?"

"Oh, please! They're gone, okay! It was me and Jeff staying at his place. We lived in Northampton." She glances up at the house, resentment brimming in her eyes. "We were *nice* families, too!" she says. "My dad's place was bigger than most of these houses; we just didn't have the yard and all these stupid trees!"

"So what are you doing out here with us poor white trash, then? Why didn't you run home?"

"Evans sent out a text message about a herd walking through the neighborhood. I barely got away from the ones on Mr. Dougherty's back lawn! What used to be his back lawn...why didn't Mr. Kerch just shoot us all in the head? I mean, seriously, who lets someone fall to get eaten alive? You know him, why didn't he?"

"No idea. I just met him yesterday." Which is only half-true, of course.

"You didn't hear Jeff scream when they caught up to him! I turned around and one of them was chewing his arm off at the shoulder! The arm, that other one was pulling on it, it came—oh God!"

"Are you the only one who got away?"

"I don't know. They were even killing their own people! Those two big black guys who were watching the front door and the steps? They came down in the yard, waving us back with their pistols. They shot that one guy in the back of the leg. He started shooting back and that was good because I could run…." The girl's face contorts in pain.

"Honey, I don't know what to tell you except let's try and get that cleaned up."

"Can I stay here?"

"I don't know about that…."

"It won't be long! I've got relatives in Topeka!"

"I'll bet they'll love you for dinner," says Rebecca. She's maybe three steps behind me. Clean, pressed and sharp in her black dress and chauffer's hat. The touchscreen of her phone beeps beneath her thumb.

A shrill squeaking noise strains from the girl's wide mouth. "She's…that mean bitch is Kerch's driver! You—these aren't good people! They killed those guys! They kill their own! You don't think they'll kill you if they decide they don't like you anymore?"

"Mr. Grace's eyes are wide open, parasite!" Rebecca says.

The girl looks around as the sound of an approaching vehicle fills the warm, early morning air. She looks at me, frantic. "I can't run anymore on this! I think it's infected!"

"If it isn't, it's definitely getting there," I say. I feel sick. There wasn't a lot I could do for her two minutes ago; there's nothing I can do for her now. The phone in Rebecca's hand is now a small .22, and she's standing in the classic shooter's stance, legs shoulder length apart, the barrel of her gun trained just over my shoulder at the girl. I step away.

A large white pickup stops in the driveway just behind Kerch's black SUV. I hadn't thought to look and see if it was still here; I'd presumed Rebecca was long gone. I realize now she was working this straggler detail.

Two young men come up the drive around the SUV. I recognize one of them from the cleanup job yesterday. They grin as they sight the girl on the side patio, her legs splayed beneath her, no longer able to even stand. "Hey, 'Becca!" says the one I don't recognize. "I see you and your new boyfriend are on the job!"

"Shut up and take her away," Rebecca says.

"All right!" says the one from yesterday's cleanup crew. "Gonna get us some of that hot rich-girl action!"

"I'll bet she's shaved down there!" says the other. Both take an arm and pull her roughly to her feet. A fat tear rolls over the girl's cheek, smacking audibly on the concrete by her bare, bloodied feet. She looks up, meets my eyes. I look away.

"Goddamn it, bitch, stand up!" says the cleanup crew guy.

"She's definitely not gonna be able to walk when we're—"

A sharp firecracker *pop!* Rebecca lowers her arms. The girl gapes forlornly at Rebecca. The blood pools in her jaw, spills over the corners of her mouth. The young men nearly drop her. "Shit, 'Becca, what the hell!"

Rebecca's arms come up in a smooth arc. The complaining one drops, his right eye a red-black hole. He pulls the girl down with him, and the other young man on top of them.

Rebecca looks down at the survivor. "You have anything to add?"

The young man shakes his head slowly.

"You sure?"

He nods.

"Can you take these bodies to processing? No more bullshit, and keep your dick out of the dead girl?"

He nods.

"Mr. Grace!" says Rebecca.

"Yes?"

"Take out your phone. Go to the menu. Go to Tools. Click on the Clock feature. Go to Stopwatch."

I take out my phone. I get to the feature.

"Let me know when a minute is up. That's how long Brian here has to get both bodies into his truck and out of here before I call in another crew to come get his."

I click the virtual stopwatch. "Let's see what you got, son."

Brian already has the girl over his shoulder and is running with her to the truck. The blood pumping from her head soaks his backside when it's not slapping and splatting along the driveway. He shrugs hard by the truck and the girl's body flips over his shoulder, clunking into the flatbed. He's three steps into a sprint back up the driveway when he slips in the gore and bellyflops. His entire front is covered in blood and dirt; he almost looks the part of a rough-and-tumble deader just back from lunch.

Yet he still has 25 seconds to go by the time he gets back to his companion. He's halfway down the driveway in his truck when his time is up.

"I'm sorry you had to see that, Derek," Rebecca says. "I'll call the cleanup crew and get that mess taken care of."

"I just hope I have enough time for coffee before Evans gets here."

"There's a travel mug in the cupboard. Use it."

"Great. Thanks."

"I've got to get to work. Take care."

"You, too." I watch Rebecca walk away, her heels clacking smartly on the driveway around the pump-splatters from the unfortunate girl's head.

I go into the house. I pull the take-out box from the fridge. The shrimp and the lobster are gone, along with half of one steak. Well, shit. It's the least I owe her for doing the laundry.

18

Evans is running late. At least I'm able to get some coffee in me. I'm sitting with a cup on the front porch, listening to the flies buzzing over the mess in my driveway when he pulls up.

"Did you get any sleep last night?" I ask, climbing into the Big Yellow Truck.

"I'll be all right," he says.

"For the sake of everyone planning on walking away alive today you'd better be."

"It's like Mr. Kerch said yesterday. Real quick. In and out. Our job is to make sure these hammerheads we're wrangling do their jobs. Which, after the example we set last night, shouldn't be all that hard. By the way, can you tell me something?"

"What?"

"How is it we're down another man as of this morning?"

"We're down a lot more than that after last night, I imagine."

"No!" he says sternly. "I'm talking about what went on after that fugitive got captured. I want you to tell me exactly what happened."

"The fugitive? You mean that little girl barely older than my own daughter with the gunshot wound on her leg? That barefoot waif who escaped getting eaten alive only to—?"

"I'm not asking about the girl," he says angrily. "I'm asking what happened to—"

"Evans, I don't like your tone and I'm not telling you shit!"

Evans keeps his eyes on the road but it's clear he's rattled. I just want to keep pushing his buttons until his fat head explodes. He was annoying enough before but for some reason I really fucking hate this stupid, strutting rooster.

It's one thing to talk to me like I'm the minimum-wage-slave help who has no choice but to suffer for his bad day. But this is *my* bad day: I keep telling myself, God damn it, that stuck-up richie cunt would have thought nothing of throwing me under the bus for being poor and in her way. Still. What happened was fucked up. Worst of all, there wasn't a goddamned thing I could do but turn my head and look away like a common chickenshit slave who doesn't want to die either.

I knew better than express outrage in front of Rebecca and her aim with that little .22. Hell, I knew so well I didn't even *feel* that outrage until now. Which pisses me off even more. So congratulations, Evans. Your soft Veteran-of-the-Global-Tour-of-DoD-Golf-Courses ass is mine for the flogging until I can make peace with myself for being a pussy in the face of simple mean-ugly bullshit.

After a while, Evans sighs heavily and says, "I asked a simple question."

"Why don't you ask Mr. Kerch why he decided to kill his own personal security people?"

"Why don't you?"

"I already know."

"You do, huh?"

I look out the window on my side of the truck and pretend to be interested in the scenery. Seriously, I need to snap out of this. I'm getting into some serious mission creep. All I need to do is pack my bags and slip out of here. That's all.

We're taking that turn the red Caddy might have taken last night if it hadn't been so important for the Good Families of Oak Blossom Lane to see how far Kerch would go to enforce obedience. Out from the shelter of the trees I'm reminded of North Nevada Avenue in Colorado Springs where it crosses the railroad tracks from the Old North End. You go from genteel old houses and shade trees to pawn shops and crumbling motor courts in less than 100 yards. Except the houses and lawns are considerably larger here, and the trees are so thick it's like coming out of a cave. You'd never know what was back there.

A trash-strewn tallgrass lot on either side, the road ends at a commercially zoned four-lane street. Beneath the naked bulb of the sun the cool shade of Oak Blossom Lane seems an unimaginable fantasy. We're rolling through the Real America, that hellscape of fat blonde weeds pushing through sun-bleached blacktop, of litter nesting in the corners of empty storefronts. Now fully owned—by popular uprising!—by the very people who used to live and (sometimes) work in the flat-roofed buildings squatting along the stained and broken concrete.

Evans drives quickly. Given all the shadows I'm seeing assert themselves as we pass that's a good thing. I see wet trails along the sidewalks, pale pink globs to septic black stains on the concrete: zombie scat in varying stages of decay.

Evans veers right at a fork and charges up one of the many ridges in this Kansas Smoky Hills country most people mistake for "flat." You can see the Interstate from here; in turn this Wal-Mart Supercenter is well within sight of the travelers there. I see all of two of them, both walking in the westbound lane. They don't respond to the sound of our engines.

There have to be others closer by, however. So far, it's just us chickens up here in the corner of the empty parking lot. Brandon's brown rustbucket comes up, then a white pickup, then a blue. The red Caddy shows up. Another pickup, lavender with dark purple flames decaled on the side and pimped out low to the asphalt appears. I'm surprised I didn't hear it bottom out at the foot of the slope.

"Aren't we supposed to be spread out doing our thing? What's up with the convention here?"

Evans doesn't answer. Fine. As long as he's got the motor running and the air conditioning on full. Other vehicles pull in, but the answer to my question drives up soon enough. Kerch's black Luxury Tank, foreign made and worth three times the one I drove to death in Kansas City, pulls to the center.

Rebecca steps out to open the door for the boss. Kerch comes out and motions for everyone else to do the same. As we do so Kerch walks over to where we are. "Let's get up there in the flatbed, all right?" he says, clapping us on either shoulder.

Evans drops the tailgate and helps Kerch and me up. I see Brick walking among the vehicles, pointing at the ones with their engines still running to support the air conditioning. The motors shut off one by one. Only Kerch's Luxury Tank is allowed to remain running:

"We don't have a lot of time, so I'll make this quick. Last night, this crew—all of you here—killed 986 total confirmed walkers. Nine hundred eighty-six. If we can pull that number every day for forty-nine more days straight we can own this city free and clear! We can move some people into the power plant and look at getting it running again. You could be in your own houses before it starts getting cold. Would you like that?"

"Oh hell yeah!" someone hollers, and the crowd laughs.

"Every former citizen you take out is one closer to comfort and freedom. Some of you saw what they did last night. Every bit as ugly as it was tragic! You know Mr. Evans' boy Daniel got swarmed."

A low murmuring animates the crowd. I look at Evans. By this point I imagine he's too tired and drained to show any emotion. I have to give him credit for not waving his bloody shirt at me, so to speak.

"I'm taking Mr. Evans home where he's gonna take some time, get some sleep."

"Sir," Evans begins. "I don't—"

"No, no," says Kerch. "I need you to take it easy for a spell, get some rest. It's time for Mr. Derek Grace to step up to the plate." Kerch claps me on the shoulder. "You're looking fresh, Mr. Grace. You ready to get dirty?"

"Not if I can help it," I say. The crowd laughs. I pat the handles of my panga and my hammer. "These, on the other hand…."

"They'll get a workout, I'm sure! You're all going to get a workout! But we know how to cull their herd, now, don't we? Three hundred to the fields where we cut them down one by one, and six hundred here on the outside of town. In the woods, and in the dark! We lost Daniel Evans, Tyler McCracken and Jared Ledbetter. Three good men. Let's honor their memory, see to it they didn't die for nothing.

"I want you to all mind Mr. Grace here and hit our target areas. Let's get the stuff on our shopping lists—nothing more!—so we can get the hell out, restock our community supplies, and scrub another thousand biters from our city. All right?"

"Yeah!"

"All right, then. The quicker we can get this over with, the quicker we can get to that barbecue at the high school. Good luck!"

Everyone turns to go to their vehicles while the group leaders appear at the back of the Big Yellow Truck to ask the obvious question, as voiced by a Latino man whose natural expression appears to be one of perpetual worried urgency: "How do we coordinate with this Mr. Grace?"

I take out my phone and find my number in the menu. I kneel down by the side to get level with the man's face and show him the number. "Pass it on," I say. "If I can get your number I'd like to put your name with it so I'll know who's calling right away."

I hear Evans and Kerch walk to the tailgate and jump down. I hand my phone to the gentleman I now know as "Gitmo" (short for "Gutiérrez"). He'll put the others numbers in for me—I would rather have introduced myself briefly to each of the squad leaders by way of getting their numbers but I need to know what the fuck I'm doing here even worse.

"Gentlemen!" I say loudly, jumping from the truck.

Kerch doesn't indicate he's heard me. Rebecca is already out and holding the door for him. Evans turns. He's holding a set of keys up for me. As I take them, he says: "To give you an idea of how easy your job is I expect this truck back with no blood or damage on it. While your crew is loading up here you'll wait for calls from the other squad leaders to inform you when they're done.

"Now, they won't need your permission to drive to the estate when they're done. All they need to do is check in. If you don't hear from the others in a reasonable time frame you call the other squad leaders and I'll leave it to your discretion whether you'll organize a rescue and who you'll take with you to do it. If you decide to do it, that is. Were you ever military?"

"Nope. But I get the principle of bringing everyone I can home. By 'estate,' you mean Mr. Kerch's house, right?"

"Right. You'll be here at the Wal-Mart. Gitmo's taking on the liquor store, Brick is raiding the sporting goods place in the mall, Jake and Brandon are coordinating the supermarket. The people you really need to be concerned about, though, are the herders."

"Herders?"

"You're all working in a relatively small area. Billy, Russ, and Darnell will be drawing the citizens away while you work. Of course, three minutes is just a guideline. If you think you can clear out everything in those freezers and get away, do it. Those are the priority for you and the supermarket crew. Mr. Kerch has a walk-in freezer at the estate. If we can get—"

A horn honks. It's the SUV.

"I've got to go," says Evans. "Text me if you have any questions."

"Sure," I say, but he's already walking away.

I stand looking around at the people buzzing about in the parking lot. Some are grouping for a few quick words before driving off. I hear the roar and chuff of engines turning over. Some are already pulling away.

It took four years and this one very long week but it looks like I'm back in management again. I've even got the Big Yellow Truck. I think of what Evans said about fattening hogs.

Fuck it. I've got shopping to do.

19

Gitmo brings me my phone. "I'll need a little more time. The liquor store is a few blocks over and they've got it barred up seven ways to Sunday. Give me a call if you don't hear from me in 45 minutes. Everyone else should be done in about half an hour. You might want to take longer here, yourself."

"Yeah, we probably do," I say, and so much for that in and out in a minute bullshit. I figured as much, especially when it comes to all this frozen meat. Unless there are herds of deer and other wildlife roaming these Kansas fields that I don't know about, meat will be hard to come by for a while. It's this or canned food from here on out.

Gitmo and his crew are the last to pull away. It's just me and Big Yellow, a white pickup truck, and the lavender lowrider truck with the purple flames on the side. My crew includes the tall, scowly-faced Goth kid from dinner last night with the katana at his back. A shorter, compact young man with long, stringy blonde hair squeezed beneath a trilby hat carries a crossbow at his back. I almost miss the little girl between them—actually a very small young woman with her breasts mashed together beneath her too-tight black blouse in case you mistake her age; she's got a machete on her belt. The closest I've got to a normal looking kid wears a Kansas City Chiefs jersey and matching Snapback hat.

"That's expensive gear to be wearing on what's eventually turning into a bug hunt," I tell him.

"These are all the clothes I got, man!"

"I've got to pick up some threads of my own. You wanna come with?"

"Shit, man!"

"What?"

"No offense, man," he says grinning, "but I would *never* shop here!"

"Suit yourself."

"A humble leader who walks with the peasants!" smirks the Goth kid, waving his sword about his head in short loops. "He can take on *three* citizens at once!"

"So let's hear your mighty saga, then."

The kid hisses and turns away from me. The stringy-haired man in the trilby shrugs. "He was actually pretty good last night. Just so you know, Mr. Kerch's comment about seeing you take on three at once sounded pretty silly to the professionals."

"The professionals?"

"Hey, man, it's serious business! You heard what the man said about last night! We were taking on a lot more than three at once to rack up that score!"

And yet none of you are in charge of anything, I want to say. Instead: "All right, then, so what are we doing here?"

"We gotta get all the frozen stuff out of the freezers before it's all thawed out. So we back up the trucks, I reckon."

"Out front? That makes no sense. We need to be closer to where the freezers actually are."

"You the bossman," he says.

"Is this your first time doing this?"

"Individual runs. Not coordidnated-like."

"Great. Let's get these trucks over to the loading dock on the grocery side. You've got gear to break locks with, right?"

"Well, duh!"

"Let's get going, then!"

Trilby hat gets into the white truck with the guy in the Chiefs hat, who drives the white truck over. The lavender lowrider belongs to Russ, one of the herders. "Shit, I don't even know why they want us out here," he says. "We cleaned 'em out of here real good last night."

"You heard the man. He wants another thousand gone today,

another thousand tomorrow, and another thousand the day after that. We gotta clear 'em all out, no way around it."

"I saw what happened to Evans' boy yesterday. They pulled him through the busted window. He was squirtin' blood all over where he was cut up and those things had their mouths open like they were catchin' rain. Goddamn, I can't believe these were people once!"

"I dunno. They make perfect sense to me."

"Shit, you may be right," he says, starting his little truck. "Like my boy Marcus used to say, 'Humanity two-point-motherfuckin'-*Oh!*' People minus the polite civilized bullshit. They just step right up and bite your fucking face off." Russ puts his truck in gear. "Take care, man." He drives off.

I climb into the Big Yellow Truck. "Hi," says Krystal from the passenger seat.

"What? Jesus! I take it you rode over with Brandon?"

"You knew we were going to be here! I didn't expect them to put you in charge so early, though. So sad what happened to Mr. Evans' boy!"

"Yeah. Look, don't take this the wrong way, but what are you doing here?"

"Someone's gotta look out for you! You don't know these people!"

"I'm getting an idea."

"Besides, they didn't leave you nearly enough people to clean out that freezer. I'm pretty strong, you know!"

"All right, then. Welcome aboard."

We drive to the back. I'm almost relieved to see the two deaders coming in the other side of the parking lot. I know we're not completely alone out here. It's just a matter of waiting for the party to realize the food trucks (so to speak) have pulled up.

The man walks unsteadily, as if drunk. He sways from side to side, his weight on one leg, then the other. He toddles laboriously behind the thin, intense-looking woman who is hobbled only by the broken stiletto heel on one shoe. She makes a loping, up-down motion as she staggers along, not as awkward as the man following her, but with grim, I-will-have-this purpose. The gore is dried thick and stiff down her power-suit ensemble, with a glistening fresh sheen adding another layer to the man-sized scab accessorizing her white blouse and navy-blue skirt. Her sloppy seconds cake the pastel yellow button-down shirt of her wobbly companion.

I'm wondering whether to back the truck in first or jump out and address this now when the Goth kid comes out with his katana. I stop the truck to let him cross the lot towards the two. He draws his blade from the scabbard along his back, makes a show of whooshing it around over his head.

"I never caught his name," I say.

"That's Trenton," says Krystal. "He wants everyone to call him Oni-bara now. Says it means 'Devil Rose.' More like Devil Dork! I never understood those anime freaks."

The woman makes a course correction to intercept Devil Dork. An angry and wanting moan rises from her gore-crusted lips. Her companion adjusts likewise, rocking sideways, focused on the tall, pale young man wearing the long black coat in the middle of May in humid, sun-baked Kansas.

Devil Dork brings the blade down to one side of the woman's neck. She falls to the asphalt in halves, her organs and entrails flopping wetly to the pavement. The man behind her hesitates. His head is back, sniffing the air. He's backing away when the blade goes through his neck. His head tumbles from his shoulders to the parking lot. His body falls backward and lands across it, putting one shoulder up.

"Great," says Krystal. "As if it didn't stink enough out here already."

I'm backing the truck up next to Randy's at the loading bay. I kill the engine and we get out. Going up the concrete stairs along the side I see Randy's flatbed already has fryers and frozen turkeys stacked in a spill of meltwater. Five cases of burger patties sit off to the side. It's backed in over the lower steps so we have to climb under the rail to get up.

"Didn't you have some shopping to do?" says Krystal. "Now's your chance."

"Yeah, I do," I say, looking around the area. It's a broad lot arcing over either side of the large graded knoll the Supercenter is on, Whatever comes up here will have to lean into the incline. It won't be easy. But it won't stop them, either. Worse, we won't know we're surrounded until too late.

"Well, what are you waiting for?" says Krystal. "We'll be right here."

Krystal goes to help the boys in the freezer. They've found a dolly and are using it to stack the boxes of patties and ground beef from the freezer. Wide puddles of water cover the floor but it doesn't smell like anything is turned—yet. Then again, it's hard to tell with the smell of dead people in the air.

"Where's that chick I saw earlier?" I say, looking in on them.

"Marta's s'posed to be bringin' us some ice from up front," says the guy in the trilby hat. "You might wanna go check on her."

"Yeah, will do. What's your name, by the way?"

"Timcat. Like 'tomcat,' but with Tim."

Jesus. "Great." I nod to the guy in the Chiefs hat. "You?"

"I'm Randy."

"All right. Move fast. Oni-boner or whatever his name is just got two walkers outside. You can bet more are on their way."

Randy and Timcat laugh. "I hear ya, boss! We'll handle it!"

I push out the service doors into the main of the store. The heat, the stench, is gagging. Like Kansas City outside the hotel this stench has layers to it. Just when you think you're getting used to it a fresh wave of putrefaction billows over and it's all you can do to keep your stomach from turning inside out.

A grunting and shuffling to my right draws my attention to the man in the cargo shorts struggling towards me. His difficulty is exacerbated by having only one working leg. Apparently whatever got him worked one side; even his arm has had so much muscle chewed and sucked away it's useless. He's managed to pull himself up along the shelves on the back wall and hop-shuffle towards the sound of our activity.

I draw my panga and walk over to the half-man. Flashing back to Rebecca's smooth motion with her gun, hitting her target along the sweet spot of the curve, I raise the blade and divest the half-man of his one good arm. The fine silvery deluxe claw hammer I found in a tool box in the garage is in my other hand; I bring the blunt end crashing between his eyes before he has a chance to drop. He goes over backward, cracking the back of his skull for good measure as he hits the floor.

These exertions don't make this easy but I have to control my breathing, if only so I can hear what's around me. I turn my head slowly to take in my surroundings, waiting for my panting to quiet.

Eventually it's enough that I can hear the stirrings down the various aisles across the store.

Goddamn it, let's just get that underwear and get out of here!

Panga in hand, I jog down the wide aisle separating the grocery from the dry goods. There are display islands in the middle of this aisle. I'm come to the clothing section and the racks enclose the right side of the aisle like little banyan trees concealing the predators beneath.

A hand claws at me from beneath one of these and I miss a step, my foot coming down on that hand. But that gives the other hand a chance to grab at my boot. It's a small blue hand, with stubby blue fingers and yet I can feel its death-rigored grip through the leather.

I pull my panga and swing but the child is wrapped around my boot now—a little thing with a yellow ribbon in her hair and the fatty child skin chewed away on one side of her face. An eyestalk hangs eyeless from one socket but the muscles about her jaw are intact and working. Her little baby teeth are bearing down hard on my boot. I lift up my foot and kick at the display in the middle of the aisle. A small ribbon of intestine trails beneath her waist; she has no legs, not even bones.

Her teeth bear down harder.

I pull my hammer and smack it into her yellow-ribboned hair. The pain in my foot intensifies and I snap-grip the handle in my wrist as if the hammer was a drumstick and her head the snare. Her little skull cracks open and her body falls limp.

Rigor clamps her little jaw fast to my boot. I shuffle towards the end of the center-aisle display. No one is in this food aisle to the left so I ease towards it, propping my backside against an end-cap shelf so I can figure out how to get little Brittney off of me.

I grab a fistful of her hair and try pulling her head back. I see the gaps in her front incisors; if her adult teeth were in—hell, even if her originals were still there—they would have broken the skin of this boot. I need thicker boots, steel-toed. And thick socks. Save for that strip of intestine (which has since slithered off the rib bone it was caught on) the girl's torso appears to be hollowed out. No insides, no stomach to even hold her meal and yet she crawled along, with this sick, pointless hunger. How many more are scuttling along like this out there?

When I found this deluxe claw hammer in the garage I thought it might double as a convenient tool with which to break into things. I never thought I'd be fitting the broad tines through the top gap of a small child's teeth. The rotten blood in her ruined gum runs down my boot, adding one of those special nuances to the boxed-in stink in the air that makes me gag.

It's when I see the tracks of tears through the dirt on the good side of this child's face that I unload my breakfast into the aisle. I jerk the claw-end up hard and snap this flesh-and-blood reminder from my boot, this notice of how our position on the food chain has adjusted. Just as lions think nothing of culling the young of a zebra herd, something got hold of this once-five-year-old charmer in a pink Disney Princess T-shirt and made a meal out of her. And in turn made her into this....

I let out a furious yell. Goddamn it, come at me, you ugly, fucked-up shits!

I push myself away from the endcap, stepping carefully to the side, not wanting to slip, not wanting to see the remains of the child face up in a puddle of vomit. Unable to rid myself of the sight of her remaining eye, the terror and agony of a little girl's last moments sealed within its dry, dead glaze...

...Claire. Jesus. I think of my daughter Sibyl....

I listen and hear the slow shuffle-slide throughout the store, coming down any of the dozens of dark, hot, stinking aisles. I'll have my chance with whoever-whatever killed this girl soon enough.

I'm jogging down the middle of the aisle, rounding the corner of the Men's section. I find my size in boxers and grab five three-packs. I pick up some socks and colored T-shirts. I need something to carry this so I step out into the broad main aisle between the main goods and the checkout lanes and look for the chrome tree with the cloth shopping bags. There's one by the outside corner near the shuttered entrance.

Now I've got one arm free. Time to find Marta. I see movement in the pharmacy area. I jog down the aisle and find myself face to rotting face with the most distressed-looking dead person I've seen yet.

He's in his late teens. I don't see the terror of his death so much as he looks...green. His chin-to-crotch gore bib glistens with bright yellow gobbets like crumbs of wet rancid popcorn. He staggers towards me. I swing the panga but instead of taking off his upraised arms—which he doesn't seem to have strength to raise—I slash his throat clear back to the spinal column. The rust-brown corpse gravy oozes thickly through the flap, his already discolored face paling visibly as it leaves his skull.

I don't want to step up to him without first taking off his arms and he won't hold them up for me. Dropping my bag I put both hands to the handle of my panga and swing a hard chopping blow between his shoulder and elbow on either side. His limbs tumble to the linoleum, rank blood splats from his stumps. Instead of charging me in a rage, though, he backs off, moaning miserably. I draw my hammer, switch hands with my panga. I do the same snare drum snap with the hammer as I'd done with the girl. He falls to his knees and maybe I'm seeing things but his dead mottled face looks relieved,

"Another one of those, huh?" says a sharp-toned female voice behind me. I turn to see Marta, carrying a cloth shopping bag of her own. "I dropped four of them on my way here. Looked sick as dogs."

I'm looking around the pharmacy area. It occurs to me I might need something while I'm here.

"Don't even think about it," says Marta. "I got all the good shit."

"Good for you," I say. I go to the vitamins and start scooping bottles of Vitamin C supplements into my bag.

"What the hell you want that shit for?"

I go to the aspirin aisle and scoop the shelves there. I consider getting another bag, maybe a cart. On the other hand, there's plenty of places to loot between here and Colorado Springs. We really need to finish this up and hit the road....

"Wait!" Marta says as I turn to go. I stop and she runs up to me. I resume walking as she catches up. "Look, you don't have to be all anti-social and stuff. I'm not gonna give you grief like those other little show-offy shits."

"Nice to know. I take it you're not bothering with the ice?"

"Fuck that! Old Man Kerch got plenty of ice and everything where he is. We'll get the runty and the rotten and the leftovers down at the high school, like since we got corralled in there."

"You're telling *me* this?"

"C'mon. Everyone knows you don't wanna be here. Including

Kerch, I imagine. Better watch your shit, is all I'm sayin'. By the way, was that you hollerin' a few minutes ago?"

"I thought all you were saying was I'd better watch my shit."

"Hey, look, those four I killed? I'm not sayin' I took 'em on at once. I mean, I'm not sayin' you—"

"Shhh! Listen!"

It's a heavy flop-slide, flop-slide. A clattering as the thing gets caught in one of the circular racks of clothing.

"Oh, God," says Marta. "That thing sounds huge."

The morbidly obese woman pushes aside the racks like a squat Tyrannosaurus Rex pushing aside trees to get to its prey. Her curly white hair is a nauseous pale yellow from the dead scalp showing beneath but at least the rest of her looks more or less normal. That is, normal about her head. Discounting the red, gore-clotted teeth and mouth, and the rage to rip, rend, and feast in her face.

The rest of her as seen through the streaming rags of her muumuu is a horrible sea of red-yellow holes in a wide ocean of pale, quivering flesh. Globs of rank, yellow fat fall from some of the wounds, especially the one opened in that broad, naked fleshslide flopping over her privates.

"God, no!" and now it's Marta's turn to give up her breakfast.

I bring the panga up and slice it hard through the middle of the woman's skull. It goes in but not deep enough; it's sticking. Her arms reach out for me and I lean into the blade and push her back. The blade slices further down the middle of her face, squeaking through the groove it carves through her skull. Finally all 300 pounds of this woman spill over. We jump back barely in time as glistening fatty tissue like bright yellow corn kernels in red gelatin bursts forth from all those bite wounds, ripped wider by the heavy woman's impact to the floor.

Marta is coughing and spitting. "Goddamn zombie shit!"

"Yeah, that explains the sick ones," I say through the hand cupped over my face. We're already moving away from the massive spill on Aisle Get Me the Fuck Outta Here.

"Huh?" says Marta.

"The sick ones with the yellow down their fronts. They've been eating the stuff they shit. Off that fat woman."

"*What?*"

We hear the gunfire from outside. "Goddamn it," I mutter under my breath. Mindful of yellow zombie droppings we run down the long aisle to the back of the store where the service doors lead to the prep area and the loading dock.

We burst through the swinging doors to find the freezer door still open and Randy and Timcat on the loading dock fighting off the former citizens of Natalia, Kansas. The stinking mob is pressed against the lip of the five-foot concrete dock, reaching and grasping. The white truck backed against the stairs makes it difficult for them to come up at us from that angle, but not impossible. The Goth kid in the long black coat swings away at their exposed arms. He flips the blade and backswings to take off their heads. Yeah, definitely more than three at once.

But there are so many of them. Their combined moaning is so loud we can hardly hear one another.

"Reckon we shoulda minded the time, huh, boss?" Timcat yells over the racket.

I run to the edge of the dock and begin swinging, hacking through their upraised arms. I have to swing deep enough into the horde so I can hammer at the skulls of the ones up front without getting grabbed by ambitious outliers shoving their way towards me. Hammering at their skulls requires my getting on my knees to reach over and pop them and I don't like that as a defensive position at all. They swing at me with their oozing stumps, snap at me with their foul teeth. I wish I had two hammers; it'd go a lot quicker.

The bodies fall, and now the rows behind them have something to stand on. I'm able to take their outstretched arms off closer to the shoulder. When this new row falls backwards it knocks down the former citizens coming up behind them. It's hard standing on a corpse, with the skin slipping and ripping beneath their feet. Once the bodies get two rows deep towards the back, a pale thing in a tracksuit attempts standing on the fallen ones furthest back. He pitches forward and cracks his forehead open on the concrete lip of the dock before I have a chance to do anything with him.

I take advantage of the buffer of fallen bodies to stand back. "This isn't getting any better," I say. "We're either going to jump in our trucks and go, or plan to be stuck here until our arms wear out."

"Whatchoo think we oughta do?" says Timcat.

"Who had the gun? I heard gunfire."

"Ain't nobody here got a gun," says Timcat. "Someone was horsin' around there at the bottom of the west side of the parking lot. It's drawin' all these things to us!"

"I got a gun!" says Krystal.

"What?"

"Right here," she says, pulling a 9mm Glock from her purse. "It was in the glove compartment of the truck. I'm sorry."

I take the Glock from her. Just like the one I had in Kansas City. Might well be same one, I don't know.

"There was an extra one of these that went with it," says Krystal, handing over a magazine. Thank the dark gods, it's full.

"Good job, Krystal. Here, take these," I say, handing her the truck keys. "I've got an idea."

"If this don't work we're fucked," says Timcat.

"Shit, ya think!" says Randy.

Goth kid cries out. His arm has been caught by an alert young woman who brings the full unrelenting force of rigor mortis into her bite. He drops his katana; it's seized by pale blue grasping hands and pulled into the swarm.

"Goddamn it!" I run down the steep loading dock steps. I have to chop through a forest of fingers and hands clawing from the rail. I backslash off the woman's head and pull Goth boy away, careful to hug the wall on our way back up.

"Marta! Timcat! Somebody mind this gap! Whoever's got the keys to the white truck, have 'em ready!"

I pull Goth boy out just as a little boy crawls up the stairs in his filthy pajamas. Marta takes the boy's head off with her machete and kicks it towards the crowd at the lip of the dock. It hits a white bearded man in the face, knocks him back before tumbling into a dark forest of dead, shit-stained legs. Marta turns towards the stairs where the only thing holding back the mob is their sheer numbers trying to get over and around the flatbed of the pickup and cram onto the narrow stairs.

"Whatever the hell it is you think you're doin' please do it quick!"

"Randy! Timcat! Who's driving the white pickup?"

"I am," say Randy.

"Don't drive your load to Kerch's place. Take it directly to the high school."

"Why?"

"'Because I said so! Unless you don't like eating! I gotta go!"

One thing about our focus towards the stairs is that the mob is massing at this corner. This gives me room to make a run for the far corner of the dock. I'm not a young man, I can't action-hero jump this thing. But I doubt I'll have time to butt-scooch over and let myself down nicely. I've got to move. And pray I don't break a leg doing this....

20

A few blind heads turn as I make my run. I stop abruptly at the edge and hop over, bending my knees as hit the ground. I edge around the back of the mob. The heads that turned to follow my movement have lost sight of me behind their fellows. I look around. No reinforcements. Yet.

My bright idea was to use the Glock to draw their attention. Here with their backs to me, though, I see a way to draw them off that doesn't involve making a racket that brings more dead people to the Supercenter.

I have to put nearly everything I have into these two-fisted swings. I get through one row and half of the second, the heads smacking the pavement, the bodies falling stiffly after, the corpse-gravy red-brown and everywhere. Then the remaining three and a half rows go quiet.

The quiet is so sudden, and such a contrast to the racket before, everyone freezes. The only sound being the scraping of their feet as they shuffle around to face me. I make a quick slash at the ones closest to me, then back away. When they don't come at me right away I run up and take off three, four, five more heads.

At last they scent me. The moaning begins anew as the mob begins moving away from the trucks. I slice away a hand and two more heads, then dart back again.

I look at the (once) people coming towards me. Not all of them have the bib. I see some in the crowd who seem to be there for no other reason than that's where everyone else is. The ones in the more expensive clothing, the suits and the silk pajamas obviously not from Wal-Mart or Target, are the ones who seem to be most aggressive, the most *entitled* to the meat before them. The ones in the more "common" clothing defer to these, though it's clear they've got a hunger, too.

Their faces are deformed in death, discolored. Some are scratched or torn outright where they were attacked. I recognize them all. The smug suburban mom who got my son suspended from school for defending himself (and roundly thumping) her bully child and his sidekick. The smirking cop who knows the four-point ticket he's writing for your being inches over the line at the intersection will financially cripple you, threatening you with worse as the color runs from your face. I see the scrawny teenage slacker who thinks throwing his trash in the street and spray-painting buildings are legitimate acts of self-expression. There's even a trio of well-dressed professionals congregating towards the middle, and looking very much out of place. I almost laugh to see them looking so wide-eyed and lost without their smartphones.

It's like a gift, their coming at me like this. I think of that child in the Wal-Mart, the tears she cried, how she must have screamed as she was manhandled and chewed into by people like these. I think of my children, and this shitpit of stupidity and arrogance and plain taking-up-space of humanity I cursed them to live among.

Did these things get them yet?

Did their own mother get them?

I tease the crowd towards me. They shuffle faster than you'd think but I manage to dart back, watch them reform as they come towards me, gathering closely behind their alphas.

After a while I can't stand it anymore and I charge into them.

They bring their arms and hands up. Some of these things even manage to touch me and it makes me crazier. My arms and shoulders and chest burn with the exertion, the swinging, the chopping, the shocks of impact. They don't falter. The more I look into their faces, their stupid, dust-whitened eyes, the harder I swing.

"Goddamn, save some for somebody else!"

"Fuck you!" I'm chopping into torsos, arms, faces, asses. I swing from both sides, moving up and down the line. By the time I get to the last four they're backing off. I'm kicking their heads

across the lot, watching them disappear over the edge of the knoll. Some are biting and snapping, some are plain dead and bug-eyed astonished for it.

Those last four run into Marta's machete, Timcat's demo bar, and Randy's hunting knife, stabbed through the soft part under one's jaw and into his brain. The fourth one staggers helplessly away. Three quick, long-legged strides and I've got his head rolling over the side of the lot.

"Holy fuck, man!" says Timcat. He looks about the bodies carpeting the lot.

"What?"

"You got over forty of these things! That ain't even countin' the ones at the dock!"

"I got more than that!" growls a voice from the flatbed.

"Yeah, so many you let yourself get wore out and bit!"

I walk over to Randy. "You know a way back to the school from here that doesn't take us down Oak Blossom Lane?"

Randy is wiping his blade on the shirt of the man he dropped. "Yeah, sure. We're not supposed to cut through the Good People's neighborhood anyway."

"All right then, I gotta follow you."

"No you don't," says Marta. "Krystal 'n' me both know the way."

"All right, then." I look at Randy. "You know to take the goods to the school, right?"

"It ain't what we're told to do."

"I know, and I take responsibility for that. I've got a feeling that—"

The very molecules in the air are humming: *THOOOOOOOM!*

"Let's get out of here!"

If the thud of the subwoofer wasn't enough inspiration, the ghastly chorus of dead raising their voices in answer puts a real spring in our steps. I run to meet the Big Yellow Truck as Krystal drives it towards Marta and me. Krystal stops and scooches over just in time for me to leap into the driver's seat. Marta climbs in the passenger side and we're backing up and pulling away in time to see the next wave of walkers leaning into the incline of the parking lot, coming right at us. I turn sharply to dodge them and punch it down the side where we first came in.

"Just turn left and follow it straight out," says Marta.

I note the dead are all coming from the direction behind us. It probably wouldn't be a bad idea to drive as fast as I can down this straightaway lest these things think to follow us. I hand my phone to Krystal. "Text those guys on my phone. Ask them for their status."

"What do you think's goin' on?" says Marta.

"One or more of the squads has gone rogue," I say. "Either all the other ones are working together or one has managed to shut down the other two. No doubt whoever fired that gun outside was looking to take us out. We're damned lucky to be alive."

Krystal is shaking her head. "I've messaged everybody but no one's replying."

"Well," I say, "that's good news and bad news."

"Whaddya mean?"

"The good news is I've done my due diligence as the sacrificial lamb in charge of this mission. The bad news is the bad guys know we're still alive."

The ringtone for a text message fills the cab. "Gitmo says he's fine. He wants to know where we're at," Krystal says.

"Don't respond!"

"Wait, there's another—it's Brick. He wants to know where we're at."

"Great. So now we know."

"Know what?"

"Who the players are. Five gets me ten Brick is with Kerch. And Gitmo is worried he's going to end up like Kerch's personal security."

"You mean Amos and Andy?" says Marta.

"What?"

"That's what they called 'em. They didn't like it, but that's what they called 'em."

"Shit."

"What?"

"Nothing. It just looks like Kerch has gotten a little overt with his ethnic cleansing. Can't say I blame Gitmo for making a move."

"You're up against a beaner named Gitmo," says Marta. "I got a bad feeling about this, chief."

"I'm not up against anybody! If we're doing anything, it's

getting the fuck out of their way. Let's feed our people at the high school. Then we'll work on surviving this."

"I like the way you think," says Marta.

"So don't send any messages out?" says Krystal.

I take the phone from her. "Nope. Radio silence from here on out."

"What do we do?"

"Nothing. Except maybe fight the zombies when they come. If they come. You guys are the labor force. Any side would be stupid to kill you."

"Not that stupid ever stopped anybody," says Marta.

"You are wise beyond your years, grasshopper."

"What are you two talking about?" says Krystal.

"Nothing. Just follow Marta's lead. She'll get you out of this alive."

"You dropping us off?"

"You know of any place you're safer?"

I'm already slowing for the turn as I say this. In under a minute I'm pulling into the high school. I see where Randy and Timcat have already organized the unloading of their truck. Meanwhile, the barbecue is on. I'm no sooner stopped than my flatbed is being unloaded. If I was thinking of getting away with any meat, I was wrong.

"Shit, there he is, man!" says Timcat as I get out of the truck. "The Dead Motherfuckin' Silencer!"

A confetti of hoots and cheers erupt from the people standing around the large grill.

"What?" says Randy. "Oh! Yeah! We didn't think we were getting outta there, we could hardly hear ourselves think over all that moaning and shit! Fuck, man, I thought we were done for! And then this old motherfucker jumps off the dock and starts choppin' 'em up from behind—!"

Timcat finishes for him. "And they all turn like to look at him after a while and it's just dead...silence!" He spreads his arms and hands out and the people go quiet. "Like *that!*" he stage whispers.

"Oh, bullshit!" I see they've got the Goth kid lying in a low folding lounger, which is why I didn't see him at first.

"Yeah, Lonely Boner over here's still gettin' over havin' his ass saved by a man who knows how to dress himself," says Timcat.

The crowd laughs, albeit uneasily. It's obvious to all Goth kid has been bitten and that they're going to have to put him down sooner than later.

"What I don't get is how Kerch is goin' around embarrassin' him sayin' he got three at once."

Marta steps forward. "That's so you'd be all be hatin' on Mr. Grace for being the new guy while you're takin' all the food you risk your stupid fuckin' lives for to old man Kerch! That ever occur to ya?"

"Well, shit, Marta, you don't know that!"

"Why were you gonna take all this food over to Kerch, anyway? What makes you people think he knows better what to do with it? Though to tell ya the truth, I hope you don't eat all this tonight and tomorrow! This is the last meat we're gonna have for a long, long while!"

The people start murmuring among themselves. It's apparent this is the first time most of them have even heard Kerch's name. The highest-up person they've ever known is Evans.

The rest seem merely confused. "You don't have to eat nothin' if you don't want to!" says Timcat.

"Oh, I'll have a plate!" says Marta. "So will our hero of the hour, too! We ain't done yet, today, not by a long shot. We might have to drop everything and board ourselves up in there and hope we don't get broke into!"

"Oh, my man the Silencer is definitely gettin' some of this steak! Got some fries, too, you want some, man?"

I feel Marta nudging sharply into my side. "Get yourself re-fueled. I'm gettin' some Tupperware an' I'll meet you at the truck in a little over half an hour."

Everyone's wanting to shake my hand and cheer me on for saving the squad. I smile and nod, wondering how Marta knew I'd want to get something to eat before hauling ass. She says she's going for Tupperware? Oh, let me guess….

The steak is damn near perfect, seared on the outside and hot pink and bleeding on the inside. The only side I wanted was the fries. I have a feeling I'll need the carbs. Besides, steak fries were one of the few decent things about this civilization fading before our very eyes. Might as well enjoy them while I can.

Krystal plops herself on the opposite end of the cafeteria table they've pulled out of the school. She sighs theatrically to get my attention. I cut another piece of steak, put it in my mouth, and savor it in a way the dead can never know before I give her an acknowledging glance.

"You're going back out, right?"

"As soon as I finish this."

"I mean, you're gonna look for Brandon, right? He was supposed to hit that supermarket. He hasn't texted you, has he?"

"Only Brick and Gitmo were thoughtful enough to get in touch. Either Brandon took up with one side or another or he got shot just to get him out of the way—"

"They wouldn't shoot Brandon! He's too good at what he does!"

"Amos and Andy looked like they were good at their jobs, too."

"Well, what are we gonna do about this! We can't just leave him out there!"

"Krystal, if he's dead, he's dead."

"You don't know that!"

"So we'll look. Marta knows where the supermarket is."

"I'm coming, too!"

"Like hell you are! We're going into a combat zone!"

"So I drive the truck while you and your new girlfriend do your combat thing!"

"It's not gonna work like that."

"How do you know how it's gonna work?"

"That's just it! We don't know, and we don't need your goddamned drama distracting us and getting us killed out there! You want Brandon back, you're gonna have to trust us. That's all there to it."

Krystal gets up. Others take this as a sign they can sit and talk but I get Timcat and Randy to hold them off so I can finish my lunch in peace. After a while I get up, accept a bottle of cold beer and make social for a few minutes, checking my phone for the time. In a few more minutes I see Marta standing by the Big Yellow Truck. I excuse myself, do the thumbs-up soul handshakes, the one-armed hugs, and make my way on over.

I pop the lock with the remote and Marta climbs in her side— loading a stack of Tupperware with steaks and barbecued chicken. "You're sharing some of that with me, right?"

"Oh, I'll treat ya right," Marta says. She situates the stacks of plastic containers in the rear cab and climbs in. "You got any place you need to go before leaving town?"

"I'd like to go back to my house on Oak Blossom and collect my stuff."

"Good. We can do that."

"Nice to know," I say. "What did *you* have in mind?"

"Weapons. I got a cache of 'em."

"Could be useful. Where are they?"

"Let's hit your place first. Make it fast. We need to be settled in before sundown, you know that, right?"

"Yeah," I say as we pull out of the lot. "I think I got an idea."

I speed away down the narrow road between the fields of wheat and soybean. So far, so clear.

"I figgered out why you got that stuff you did in the pharmacy," she says as we speed down the straightaway. "I wanna trade ya."

"One on one, then. That Vitamin C is going to be all that stands between us and scurvy until someone learns how to cultivate some year-round fruit. Even then it's only good for a year. Just like your Vicodin."

"Shit, ya kiddin' me!"

"Nope. Most of the people who live to see all this one year from now are going to have another set of problems entirely. Even the canned food will start going bad."

"Well, shit," says Marta. "One day at a time, I reckon. We gotta live through this day and a whole buncha others before we level up to those problems."

"Yeah," and I mentally kick myself for worrying this far into the future. I'm not getting anywhere until I get through today.

We cross the bridge, make the turn. You can feel the temperature drop ten degrees as we enter the sheltering trees. I race down the empty street to my assigned quarters on this old town aristocrats' street and pull up fast into the driveway. Apparently all hands are on deck with the former citizens of Natalia, Kansas, because I skid to a halt in old, half-dried blood no cleaning crew showed to clean up.

I'm unlocking the front door when Marta says, "Can I ask you something?"

"You just did."

"No, what I mean, is I heard you spent the night with Rebecca last night."

"She drove me home from the party."

"That's all?"

I push the door open. "That's all."

"I guess the fact you're here says it all," she says as she steps in behind me.

"How's that?" I say, heading immediately up the stairs.

"I've watched her kill a man just for smartin' off at her. I bet y'all didn't talk much on your way over."

"No," I say as I reach the second floor ahead of Marta. "We didn't."

"I heard she was here this morning."

"Yeah, they were looking for that girl."

"That's what's left of her out front, ain't it? That girl, I mean."

"Let's talk about something else," I say, unlocking the door to the trophy room.

"Yeah, that was so sad—oh!" Marta is stunned by the array of weapons in the room. "Why aren't you carrying that crossbow?" she says.

"That's why I'm here now."

"Can I have this?" she says, holding up a long, heavy spear.

I don't know what on earth for but, "Knock yourself out."

"All right!"

The crossbow and every arrow in the room is all I can bother myself with. I'm halfway through packing the last quiver when the air horn blats loudly in the street.

Not once, but several times. Ringing the dinner bell on Oak Blossom Lane. I grab what I've got and run to the master bedroom in front.

Through the sheltering boughs I see the bright red fire truck pulling up in front of the house. It pulls close to the curb, thoroughly blocking the driveway. And whaddya know, Krystal: there's your boy Brandon sitting tall in the driver's seat, living every five year old boy's dream.

I turn and run from the room.

"What are you doing?" asks Marta.

I'm tearing through the closets, looking for the luggage I might have had the sense to find and pack last night if I hadn't gotten lucky. I'm damned if I'm hauling ass out of here without a change of clothes.

THREE

BURN

21

I find a small suitcase, the wife's I presume. I shove in all the clothes that fit, zip the toiletries into the appropriate compartment. I shoulder the crossbow and quiver. Marta's carrying her spear and we're on our way out the door.

Brandon sees us coming out of the house. "Yeah, y'all better be gettin' outta here, muthafuckas...hey! *You!*"

I'm putting the suitcase into the rear cab, careful not to disturb the Tupperware stacks. Brandon leans on the horn. "Hey! I'm talkin' to you!" he shouts.

I close the rear cab door. I turn to look at Brandon. "What?" We have to shout to be heard over the idling fire truck, even as I close the distance to stand below Brandon's high perch in the driver's seat.

"You s'posed to be dead, man!"

He's drunk. So is the young man smirking over Brandon's shoulder in the cab. So are the six others who have stumbled laughing from the side and rear panels of the fire truck, pulling cigarette lighters from their pockets and scattering among the yards. One squats to strike fire to the dry debris around the privacy hedge.

"Hey, what are you guys doing?"

"New bossman says clear this shit out! Burn 'em out and feed 'em to the former citizens!" Brandon turns up his beer bottle and throws it to shatter at my feet. "Bossman's orders. Whatchoo gonna do?"

"Who's Bossman?"

"Gitmo!" he shouts. He laughs loudly, as if the very sound of the name tickles him. Brandon leans out the window. "Any man who gives me and my crew beer and tells us to go have fun with the fire truck, I'll follow that motherfucker straight into hell!"

"Haw!" cries the boy in the cab with Brandon, holding up his beer. "*Gitmo!*"

"C'mon, Brandon, why burn this neighborhood! This is nice; your people could be living here!"

"Fuck these snooty-ass houses and shit!" Brandon cackles. "Fuck you, too, you sell-out son-of-a-bitch!" He holds up a black Glock 9mm. "Whatchoo gonna do about it?" he sneers. "Wanna try and make me move this? C'mon! I wanna see you try!"

The crack of a rifle and a high-pitched scream cut through the rattle of the fire truck's diesel engine. Another rifle shot, another scream follows. Then another.

"The fuck!" says Brandon. He and his companion look over. I can't see past this fire truck but it's a safe bet some of Brandon's firebugs are getting stepped on by the residents. The flames are rising by the truck where the privacy hedge is; the two who set the fire have already moved on to another house. I hear another rifle crack. He's opening the door and edging over to jump out. He looks at me, his gun upraised. I hold up my hands, make no threatening moves.

I only need the second he takes to slip to the ground from the truck, which he does with a surprising agility for his condition. Still, he's slow bringing the gun around. When he does my panga is there to relieve him of it. At the wrist.

"My God!" squeals Marta from behind me.

By the prodigious spray it's apparent the arteries aren't convulsing shut. Good. I grab Brandon by the back of his shirt and shove him hard into the blazing privacy hedge. There's a hissing like a fuse as the spurting blood drowns the flames. Stunned, Brandon falls to his knees and shrieks as the heat from the smoldering debris seals his wound with a crackling of seared flesh and steaming blood. The stench is gagging. Goddamn it, I'm so looking forward to living somewhere in post-undead apocalypse America that doesn't stink like a bag of sour assholes.

The other boy from the cab comes running around the front of the truck. He stops long enough to go reeling from pistol fire. He falls over, clutching his side.

"Shit!" I turn to Marta. "Can you hold off any deaders coming this way while I move this truck?"

"It's all right, Mr. Grace," says Mr. Paulson. "I've got the truck." I turn in time to see the muzzle flash of his silver .38 service revolver as he squeezes a round into the face of Brandon's fallen cab mate.

Paulson waits a couple of seconds for the initial ringing from the gunshot to leave our ears before continuing. "In fact, if you and your friend can defend the area around the hydrant we can take care of the fires."

"Yeah, sure. Great."

Paulson climbs into the cab. I hear the tenor of the engine shift as he puts the truck in gear and clears the driveway. So much for my getting out of here right away.

I turn to Marta. She cuts quite the figure, a tiny little woman with a huge spear upright beside her, the pointed stone head of which is half the size of her own blonde noggin and a foot taller besides. "You ready?" I ask her. Marta nods.

The truck pulls away and a mangled, chewed-over woman in gore-blackened hospital scrubs toddles up towards Brandon. Brandon mewls piteously as he watches her approach, too weak from blood loss and burn trauma to flee. I walk towards the former hospital worker. Up come her arms. Off come her arms. Her head tumbles after.

Standing over her remains I see her fellows advancing one by one down the street, following the vibrations of the fire truck—which the old man has brought around in a three-point turn to the hydrant across the street. He's killed the engine but it's too late for these, they're going to keep coming until they scent one of us.

Still, the quiet is welcome. It's just the sound of ringing in my ears now. That, and the clank of the wrenches as the old man and his younger neighbors work to attach a hose to the hydrant. Still, the approaching dead are "in number," as they say, and shaping up to be more than Marta and I can handle. The people putting out the fires are going to need some time to do just that before they join in the battle.

I bring the hammer down on the snapping hospital aide's head. I look back towards Brandon in the steaming, smoking grass and get an idea. I jog across the broad lane to the men at the hydrant. "Where's the other firestarters?"

One of the men gestures up towards one of the yards across the street.

"Thanks."

"You evil son of a bitch, why don't you just kill me?" Brandon says as I cross the street back to him. I grab him by the back of his hair and the top of his pants. I lift him from the smoldering, stinking grass and begin carrying him up the driveway.

I heave him over the tailgate into the back of the truck. He lands with a thump, wisps of smoke and blood-steam still rising from his clothes and skin. I walk around to the cab, start the truck.

Marta looks at me wide-eyed as I back out of the driveway. I roll the window down. "Be right back," I say. "Can you take care of these other characters coming down the street?"

"Where are you going?" We both glance over at a second hospital worker. He looks as if he's trying to decide between homing in on the sound of my truck or on Marta's voice. He settles for a few steps in the general direction of both of us.

Marta runs over and taps him on the forehead with her spear. His head snaps back and she thrusts the spear through the soft underside of his jaw. He falls to the street.

"Swear to God, I'll only be a minute," I say.

Another walker approaches. A patient in a hospital gown. He's got the bloody VanDyke about his face and his pale mottled ass to the wind.

Marta scowls at the thing. "Dammit, you better come back is all I can say!"

"Promise!" and I screech off down the lane. Brandon thuds into the tailgate with the acceleration.

I see a few more hospital characters as I ride down the block. The citizens advancing along the next block are more of a mix of random street people. The discarded homeless veteran, his beard clotted with who knows who; one of the pale chubby peasant women you see at the bus stop, a chunk torn from the tissue flapping about her arm.

They thicken the further down I drive. The furious-looking woman with the wild hair, her entire front a stiff bib of dried gore turns her head my way as I pass. The young man in the baggy shorts lifts a grasping hand. The trick will be to get as close as I can to the middle of them, bring them all together. After a while I feel I have no choice but to stop. If I keep going the mob behind me will be too thick and I'll never get back.

Of course, I could just keep on going. Fuck Marta and all those people.

I wish I had just a little more time to think about it but…no. No.

I stop the Big Yellow Truck. I leap from the cab. The ones closest already sense me through the vibrations of the truck's engine and are beginning to close in. I vault over the lip of the flatbed.

"Hey, man, whutchoo doin'!" Brandon squeals.

"You brought over guests, son. It's your responsibility to feed them."

"What?"

As before, I pick him up by the hair and the back of his pants. A group of teenage boys who look a lot like him, maybe a little younger, are homing in on the back of the truck. All wear fresh bibs. The eatin's been good today, I take it.

"Krystal's not gonna like this!" Brandon says. "She's not gonna like you anymore if you do this!"

That gives me the adrenaline spike I need to duck with my knees and clean-jerk his body over my head. The mouths of the approaching dead fall open as if they know what I'm about to do. Bending my knees again I raise and hurl Brandon at them.

They fall back a few steps. Save for one dangling foot, though, Brandon doesn't even touch the pavement. His screams barely cut through the *"ooooooh!"* and *"mmmmm!"* of the mob as they take his arms, his legs, and as many clawed scoops into his ghost-white belly until the packaging breaks and they can get to the good stuff.

I jump out of the flatbed and for a panicked second I can't get the door open to the truck (apparently it locked after I closed it). I end up bumping a 30-something mom type in the face with the door, dropping her in time for me to climb in.

I start the engine and pull away fast, making a wide arc right to circle around the gathering crowd. I wish there was a sidewalk for me to drive down but the broadness of the avenue serves just as well. I cut around the edge of the mob, clustering like ants about the gobbet of living flesh dropped in their midst. The ones closest to the hydrant have already turned around to see what their fellows are making yummy noises about. Bless her heart and that ridiculous spear of hers, Marta has widened the margin enough for this to happen. The men at the hydrant are free and clear and already working the blazes in the lawns along Oak Blossom Lane.

Marta has this look on her face when I pull up, though. "You all right?" I say.

She looks down the street at the massed dead. "Did you really do what I think you just did?"

"Take out the son of a bitch who came here to kill us? Use him to draw off the undead killers he brought on us in the first place? Yeah, I did."

"What are going to tell Krystal?"

"If I ever see her again—which I won't—I'll tell her I did her a favor. You got a problem with that you can stay here. I've got one more thing to do before I go, and I doubt you'll like that either."

My foot is halfway off the brake when she says, "Wait! Let me in."

I jerk back to a halt. She runs around the front of the truck and climbs into the cab. "All right, then," I say. "Let's save this little piece of paradise and we're out of here."

"I can't believe you care about these people."

"I don't. Not for what you'd think."

"Why are you doing this?"

"These are the only people who know how to appreciate and take care of these houses. I want them to keep on doing that."

"Why? I mean, it's nice here and all, but—"

"Marta, if you want to continue riding with me you'll shut up. Now."

I pull into the driveway of the house where Brandon's crew is kept. One is laid out on the grass, dead or the next best thing. Two more sit next to him, holding their torn shirts to the wounds in their arm and chest respectively, their faces contorted in agony. The remaining three sit on the driveway, their legs out, their hands bound behind their backs. A man with a shotgun stands over them.

I stop just in front of them. "You have any plans for these?" I say.

"What are you looking to do?" says the man with the shotgun.

"You've got a herd moving into the neighborhood. If we can hang them off the fire truck as bait we can lead them back out of here."

The boys' eyes widen. I nod towards them. "We don't have to feed these to them outright, just tie them to the side rails—"

The man with the shotgun delivers a swift kick to the boy nearest him. "The hell with that! I was voting for shooting this white trash filth anyway!"

"We gotta move fast, though."

"You're not feeding me to those motherfuckers!" says the boy next to the one who got kicked.

The man with the shotgun aims at his legs. "You can get in yourself or get carried in. Me, I'd just as soon shoot every last one you for what you've done! This way you *just* might get out of it, depending how fast Mr. Paulson drives!"

The three young men on the driveway get to their feet. They march obediently to the tailgate. When the man is done helping them up into the truck he goes to the boys on the grass. They struggle to their feet and with much more time and effort than we can afford he too takes his place in the flatbed.

"What are gonna do with that one?" I say, glancing over at the boy laid out on the grass.

The man gives a look to his young charges. He steps over the grass at the boy's feet. He drops to one knee, tucks the stock into his shoulder. He squeezes off his round. The spray at this range obliterates the boy's skull. Red, living blood pumps from his neck, pooling blackly in the dark green Kentucky bluegrass.

"Who's next?" he says to the boys in the flatbed as he walks back to the truck. He steps up from the tailgate. I back out down the driveway. We need to move faster. There wasn't that much of Brandon to go around. Not for that many "guests."

As I back out into the street I can see the assembled mob four blocks down the lane. They're breaking up, stumbling about. Their heads are back as if sniffing the air.

I pull up to the hydrant and kill the engine. We should be as quiet as possible to buy ourselves maximum time but the man with the shotgun is jumping out of the flatbed and yelling at his fellows working the wrench on the hydrant. "Don't cut that water off yet, we're gonna need it for cleanup!"

"What the hell is going on here, Frank?" his companion says, eyeing me and my truck.

"Mr. Grace and I are trying to save the Oak Blossom Lane Homeowners Association. Now who had the duct tape?"

"Duct tape? For what?"

"To fix our zombie problem, you idiot!"

Mr. Paulson walks up. "What's going on?"

I get out of the truck. "This is my idea. I figure the fire truck brought them in, it can lead 'em back out. We tie these boys to the handrails on the back of the truck and between the noise and the promise of fresh meat they'll follow."

"Why can't we just let them walk on through to the other end like they did last night?" says a younger man by the hydrant.

Mr. Paulson turns abruptly to him. "You do *not* want these things getting used to walking through here! And if their scat gets on the ground anywhere out here, that's it! Dr. Hearn figured out that's how they mark their territory! You'll never get rid of the smell—and you'll never get rid of *them!*"

"Huh," I say aloud to myself. "So where's there's crap, there's food?"

Mr. Paulson turns to the men at the hydrant. "Get those boys taped up to the back of the fire truck! Now!"

Frank already has two duct-taped to a rail, including the injured boy. It's slow going because there's only one roll of tape to go around.

Mr. Paulson looks down the street to our approaching guests. A few loud grunts and moans can be heard as they catch traces of our scent. "Now what I'd like to know is how we've going to get this truck through the thick part of that mob. This isn't an all-terrain vehicle; we can't afford to ruin the tires and undercarriage on a bunch of rotten flesh and bone."

"How far can these men pull this fire hose? How far does the spray go?"

Mr. Paulson's face lights up. "Mr. Grace, I must say I underestimated you. You are indeed Evans' superior. I will be sorry to see you go." He turns to the men at the hydrant and shouts orders. He indicates Frank with a nod of his head as he binds the last teenage vandal to the fire truck.

The men get to work pulling the hose while Frank stands by on pressure. "How'd you know I was going?" I ask as Mr. Paulson turns back to me.

"We all know your story, Mr. Grace. We'd all do the same thing."

"Thanks for understanding."

"Let's get you on your way," he says, and turns to go to the fire truck.

"Uh, wait!" I say. Mr. Paulson stops. I can tell by the look on his face he'd really rather I was on my way.

"You don't have to actually feed those boys to the walkers," I say. "It's best you use them to draw them along as far as you can until you circle back."

Mr. Paulson's eyes narrow. I shrug. "After all, they did bring the fire truck."

"Which we may yet need," Paulson says, nodding slowly. "If Brick did his job Kerch is out of the picture. With him gone I wouldn't be surprised if all the other crews weren't getting a little overly jubilant."

I hardly know what to say in the face of this confession. Fortunately the roar of water rushing from the hose changes the subject. A loud *hrrrrrrrn!* erupts from the herd as the force of the water clears a path down the middle of the lane. Any deader who doesn't get out of the way is pushed bodily across the pavement, the smear of his road rash washing up behind him.

"Let's go!"

Mr. Paulson turns away to climb into the fire truck. I spare a glance for the boys trussed to its rear before I get into the Big Yellow Truck. Only one meets my eyes, and with blazing hatred and defiance. The rest lean against the tall chrome rails, looking at nothing in particular, their faces empty and waiting. Just boys, waiting for the final terror that must come. I try and remind myself of the ugly smirks and laughter from those same faces as they sought to turn Natalia's sole shady oasis into an inferno. Besides, Paulson doesn't have to kill them. Just ride them through the mob and put the fear of righteous upper-middle-class retribution into them.

I settle in and turn the key. The fire truck's big diesel matches the roaring water decibel for decibel and I have to look at my gauges and test the pedal to make sure the engine in the Big Yellow Truck turned over. I put the truck in gear and drive towards the cleared area, a wall of wet, angry dead on either side.

The hose is directed to my left, pushing back the dead on that side. I power down the window and hang my panga out to take swings at random citizens who somehow miss the wrath of the Oak Blossom Lane Volunteer Fire Department. The hose lifts over us and the water rains down on us in fat, splatting drops before being directed into the flailing, furious dead on our right.

"A shotgun like that Frank guy had would be really nice right now," says Marta.

"Yeah, it would. Where do you want me to drop you off?"

"I got a shotgun at my place."

"So that's where I'll drop you off."

"No! I want to—I want to get out of town. Like you. Drop me off next town over. In Salina."

"Christ! Fine! If we ever get out of here!"

I see shreds of Brandon's clothes cupping eddying pools of water in the street. A leg bone rolls and bounces along the weakening flow, the flesh red and furry on the knobs. Mr. Paulson sounds the air horn and run the sirens. Marta and I both jump when we hear the horn. It's more than enough to wake the dead. Based on what I'm seeing in the mirror former citizens pushed over by the hose are getting up to stagger after the big knocking diesel, the skull-rattling honks of the air horn.

I drive as fast as I dare, weaving among the once-people swaying down the lane towards us. I use the forward momentum of the Big Yellow Truck to add force to my panga swings. My arm is killing me. The mob is thickening and I see why: we're passing the turn to Kerch's place. All I see is dirty hair on pale rotten scalps, a roiling sea of the things. Someone flooded Kerch's estate with the former citizens of Natalia. All the racket Brandon made is bringing them our way.

We have to draw this new flow of undead off. I slow down. Mr. Paulson does likewise; he's already a few car-lengths back. From what I see in the side-view mirror the masses are turning towards us. But we have to keep them with us. There are way too many former citizens for the wide avenue to contain. A few will find themselves pushed uphill into the yards and driveways by simple physics, where they will find the windows with the smell of living flesh behind them. They will find that the glass breaks easily beneath their numb fists….

"A little help, Marta?" My left arm is killing me.

She powers down her window and braces her spear. "This ain't as easy as it looks—oh!" The spear recoils with the force employed to crush a fat woman's face.

We're coming out of the trees. The dead are very few and far between in the bright sunlight. Mr. Paulson was right; you can't have these things getting used to being in your neighborhood. These former citizens are definitely the wrong kind of white people. As are the boys they so eagerly tied to the back of the truck.

The boys are doing their job, though. The dead are following them into the blistering early summer Kansas sun. We might very well be winning.

"Turn left when you get down to the intersection," says Marta.

"Yes, ma'am."

We're free and clear in the punishing sunshine. We pull our weapons back inside the cab and wave at Mr. Paulson in the fire truck behind us. He leans on the air horn. The *ahhhhhhhnnnnnn!* of the walkers in response makes Marta and me laugh.

I make the left and pull away towards the heart of Natalia. I slow, then stop. In my side view mirror I see the fire truck stopped, as if waiting for traffic at the turn. But the only traffic to speak of are the platoons of dead piling up behind him. And given the way they're clustering it's apparent the front line has finally caught up to the morsels duct-taped to the rear of the fire truck.

"No!" cries Marta.

Meanwhile, Mr. Paulson composes a text on his phone. Like an ordinary jerk in ordinary traffic. And that's an ordinary crowd gathered behind the big red lunch wagon, jostling for a taste of what's on the counter….

"Huh."

"Let's just get out of here!" says Marta.

The air horn blatts as we pull away into town.

The most obvious thing we see on the way in isn't the lurkers detaching themselves from the shadows to follow our vibrations as we go by. "You sure we want to be driving into this?" I say as we approach the nearest fat column of smoke over Natalia. "We could be on the Interstate now and hauling ass. In fact, I'll be that's where Paulson leads his herd off to. I can only hope he doesn't point them west."

"Turn right," she says.

The cloud of smoke is blocking the sun. We drive on through a sickly brown light, making the squat little clapboard houses in this neighborhood look even uglier than they are where they squat on flat, packed brown dirt. The fire is very close.

The little houses, each and every one of them, have sine-wave patterns of holes across them. All the way across them. High caliber rounds that clearly pierced the walls, maybe all the way through the backs of the houses.

"Stop here."

We pull up in front of a house, one with a small cyclone fence with a gate at the front walk. "Wait," she says, and jumps out of the truck.

She's no sooner inside the door than I'm surrounded by some hard-faced *cholos* pointing their assorted pistols at me in that sideways "gangsta" pose. I raise my hands. The door is opened for me and I'm yanked out by the sleeve.

"Take it easy with him!" I hear as I stumble to the asphalt. "He's a cold-blooded killer, this one!"

Amid ugly laughter I push myself up from the street and look up into the hard brown eyes of Gitmo.

22

Hands reach under my arms and yank me to my feet. I feel them groping for my panga, hammer and pistol. My fists go out, catching one of Gitmo's people alongside his head. I lash out and the second one drops.

A third comes rushing out and my panga is out. I'm about to relieve someone of his gun fast and sloppy for the second time this morning when Gitmo shouts, "*Alto!*"

I can sense people backing down from 20 feet away. If they didn't swarm me they could have dropped me. As I'd rather be shot than suffer any number of horrors sure to happen should anyone lay hands on me, I raise my panga. Bring on that final hail of bullets, you bastards. I'm past sick of this.

"That's enough! Mr. Dead Silencer, you can keep your weapons! So long as you keep your hands to yourself."

"What about my food?" I nod towards the crew unloading the Tupperware stacks from the Big Yellow Truck.

"If Marta told you any of that was for you she lied. This was lunch for the crew. We've had a busy morning."

"Great," I say. I put my panga back on my belt and begin brushing myself off under the watchful eyes of the gunmen.

"Ah, but you've been busy, too! Marta told me all about it!" Gitmo calls out to everyone around him. "*Hermanos!* I heard you laughing when I told you this man is a killer. Remember those silly white boys who couldn't hold their *cerveza*?" He reaches up to clap me on the shoulder and pull me close: "This man you see here personally took out the stupid filth that was Brandon and threw him to the *muertos*. Drove down into the thick of them and threw him into their midst!" Gitmo tugs at me with his arm. "Tell me, my friend, what happened to the others?"

"Dead."

"Shot?"

"A couple got lucky."

"Lucky. Huh. Did they start the fires?"

"They did."

"Of course! I sent them to you in a fire truck! All you had to do was get the fire truck away from them. And *el jefe* Paulson will organize everyone to put it out. You see what I did there? I, too, appreciate the finer things. Especially fine homes! Marta is just a silly *puta*, she can't understand. A man who would be king should live like one!"

"I wouldn't go that far. I just like a nice house in the shade. As it is, I wasn't planning on staying."

Gitmo laughs. "Yes, yes! Just a man trying to get back to his family! Brought down by spike strips! Set up to take the fall for that *pendejo* Evans while that coward and his master hunkered down in their castle! You see, he knew. Kerch *knew*! He knew there would be blowback from killing DeShaun and Tavon—you know, Amos and Andy?—but what he didn't count on was how much bite *el jefe* Paulson still has. My people have known that mean old police dog for many, many years. You don't even think of threatening someone like that unless you've already killed him. That stunt Kerch pulled with the parade, he opened up the war on a whole new front, know what I'm sayin'?"

"I've got an idea."

"You're lucky he didn't kill you for being associated with Kerch! Of course, it's obvious you were set up. You don't want anything to do with this. You're just trying to get home. *El Silenciador de los Muertos*, I respect that!"

Gitmo turns to speak to the others. "For that matter—everyone, listen!—I also respect how you got Marta and those others out of Wal-Mart. We cut into that mob for you. Did you know that? We cut that mob to one hundred from one thousand! Even then we weren't sure you would make it but you pulled through for everybody. That was brave. You're braver than any other white man in this sad little village!

"But for some, that is not an excuse. These are all I know of my people from my old barrio. There are others."

"Did the Flu hit you guys that badly here?" I say.

"The flu?" Gitmo's face changes for the uglier. "The *flu?*"

"All right, apparently I missed some stuff when I was out…."

"Yes!" Gitmo nods vigorously. "Yes! You were out! But did you not see or hear anything while you were in Kansas City? I got word from my people there were black ops going on all over!"

"Gitmo, I got a feeling I'm going to regret the answer, but what the hell happened while I was out?"

"Not even a week ago. Sunday. You crashed Saturday. Okay, okay…you never seen anything like it. Not in this country. I imagine anyone or anything on the road either got out of the way or they got run over. A mile-thick wall of men and materiel rolling west across all lanes of the Interstate. Hummers and tanks. Blackhawks in the air. Behind them were the fuel trucks. Lots of fuel trucks, one tanker after another. Then more Hummers and tanks. You know there's a lot of 'em there at Fort Riley outside of Topeka. I'm still trying to figure out how they found all the personnel to move all that hardware. I noticed not everyone driving was in uniform. In fact, most of them weren't, come to think of it.

"No, they had all their dogfaces out on the perimeter. And they decided to stop here. And you know, it's the strangest thing. You know how blacks and Latinos are generally overrepresented the enlisted ranks, right? These grunts were white to a man. To a man! No women. People thought, We are saved! Here comes the U.S. Army! But me and everyone else who ever served, we knew right away these aren't the same kind of people we served with."

"Shit."

"Yeah, you know what happens next! At first people thought, What are they doing? You see them running from building to building. So maybe they're going to try and take out the *muertos*, right? They're shooting every one they see, we figure, yes, good!

"No. They are also surrounding all exits. They are shooting tear gas canisters through the windows. The kind the cops like. The kind that sets the room on fire. Women and children are the first to run out the door. And you know what's really messed up about that, Mr. Grace?"

"Aside from shooting the women and children?"

"Everyone who saw this, they say they let the first ones out the door run for a bit. They led them so they could draw more out before they started mowing them down. One line of fire across the adults' faces, another across the children's! They had people assigned! And they did the same in every apartment building, every house. They trained for this, Mr. Grace. *They trained for this!*"

"I was kind of in a bubble in Kansas City. I heard gunfire when the Flu victims started coming back, but I figured that was…well, natural." Of course, being a white guy with the slightest idea what's going on is liable to make me complicit in the eyes of seriously pissed off people looking for someone to hurt. Honestly, though, I wasn't sure what that gunfire was about at the time. Tanner said it was because some black families were resistant to giving up their dead. I could kick myself now for not appreciating the obvious absurdity of this notion when he told me this. Of course, things were getting so weird so fast it was just one more weirdness among legions.

I'm also having trouble with the idea of the U.S. military working to ethnically scrub the cities and towns while a more universal apocalypse was already in progress. That's some boss-level multitasking. Not something I'd credit any government agency with, let alone the Army. And as Gitmo asks, where the hell did they get the personnel when one person out of every three was out with the Final Flu?

Fortunately, Gitmo seems satisfied with my reaction. "Yes. Yes, we are all guilty of living in the bubble. We live our lives, just trying to pay our bills, you know? Other men you never see are pulling strings, and they pit us against each other, brown versus white, man against woman, gay and straight, while they sit back and laugh. I'll be honest with you, Mr. Grace. I look at the *muertos* and I realize even they are victims. They were once people, *our* people! But whoever came up with the Final Flu denies us even the peace of the grave! And, as always, turns us against each other!"

This from the man who got a bunch of white kids drunk and sent them off to get killed by their social betters. "All right, then," I say carefully. "What do we do now? You realize we can't hang around here."

"No," says Gitmo, "we can't. I tell you, I understand one more thing Kerch did not. You can't take on thirty to fifty thousand of the dead with a few dozen people. Not at a hundred per day, and sure as hell not at a thousand a day! We can run and cull herds here and there, sure, but you are always losing people doing this. Always! There are simply too many! We will run out of people before you put all the *muertos* down. This all belongs to them at last. All of it!"

"So what do you need from me? You know I don't mean harm or disrespect. I just want to be on my way."

"So do we, Mr. Grace! So do we! We need your help to—wait." Gitmo holds up a hand for everyone to be quiet.

Holy shit, I hear it, too.

Gitmo says, "Did you see which way *el jefe* Paulson was turning we he came out of Oak Blossom Lane?"

"No. But it is funny how he waited to make his move after we'd made our first turn out of sight."

"We gotta get outta here!"

"It's what I've been trying to do all along!"

"We need a fighter to help us get our families out!"

"Oh, goddamn it. Explain it to me on the way!"

We run to the Big Yellow Truck. Gitmo and his right hand man slide in the passenger side. These are smaller men, thank God, so it's not so crowded.

The flatbed thumps and rocks as half a dozen young Latinos jump in. "Don't you guys have your own cars and stuff?" I ask.

"We keep a lower profile if we don't drive so much. Everybody sneaks around like ninja commandos. And again, I tell you, it's the problem—we need to move houses out of here!"

"Houses?" I start the truck. "Where am I going, by the way?"

"Go straight, take a left at the second light," says Gitmo. "We got entire families of people—well, not entire, everybody's lost somebody—but we got little kids, mothers, fathers, uncles, aunts, grandmothers. They can't stay here. Nobody can stay in the cities and towns. If the *muertos* don't get them, those people in Army BDUs—I can't call them real Army!—will come back and clear it out all over again."

"Again? These people haven't been back, have they?"

"I was talking to my cousin in San Ysidro, in Cali. He says they came through the barrio three times already. That was before I stopped hearing from him."

I make the left. "Keep going," says Gitmo.

"By 'clear it out,' I guess you mean they got the *muertos*, too? I can't get over how empty these streets are." As far as Dr. Hearn was concerned, that's what they were here for, but I don't dare mention that.

"Turn right here. Yes, they took out all the *muertos*, too. I dunno 'bout you, man, but it makes me wonder if they couldn't have done this in the first place. How hard could it have been? Shoot them as they rise and be done! But you notice at the mass burials how they had these young kids—the real Army, black and Latino and poor white—running the show. They were told there 'might be trouble' and nothing more, and when our people started coming back they just freaked out. Meanwhile you had these squads putting down the ghettos, the barrios. Even trailer parks. Section 8 houses. These *chingados* took class warfare to the next level!"

Up ahead I see two tractor trailers standing nose to nose as they straddle the lane street. Cars of various makes and models stand parked in front of the trailers and various heavy items put in front of the cars—an old clothes dryer, a refrigerator, etc.—against the hungrier dead who would crawl under those. I see a few desiccated corpses on the sidewalk. Funny how the scavengers, even the bugs, avoid human bodies now. "So who set this up?" I ask.

"Building on the work of the Big Red 1, or whoever that was who came through here. We packed in most of the stuff at the bottom. They got it like this on the other side, too. It's just a channel they've worked out. I'm thinking they might close it off soon and burn them out, like with that fire they got going now, but there's still a lot out there in town walking around. Forty-nine thousand people might not make a big city, but it's still a lot of people. They're lucky if they got half of that in the street on the other side."

And half of them would still be too much, I think. I take a right and drive on, giant abandoned warehouses to my left, Section 8 projects to my right. Three blocks later: "Stop here," says Gitmo.

We stop in front of a five-story building with wide black streaks tapering out of the first-story windows. It looks burned out and uninhabitable. Gitmo has his phone out. "One of the boys should have called ahead. They all understand we have to move today."

"That fire to the east will get you if the dead don't." I look over the building. "You got your people living here?"

"They burned it once," Gitmo says, phone to his ear. "Figure they won't come back. Besides, it's only bad on the first floor and we don't have—*hola!*"

Gitmo speaks rapid-fire Spanish into his phone. He begins to ease his way out of the truck as he talks. When he and his henchman are out, I lean into the back cab to see what's left. All the food is gone, along with my crossbow. At least they left my suitcase and clothes, but not before someone opened it and went through it. I put the suitcase up on the back seat, settle everything in as best I can. I had stuff packed in pretty tightly to begin with, though, and I'd have to repack altogether if I'm going to get it.

It's one thing to take my weapons, my ammo, even my bag of vitamin supplements and over-the-counter meds—but to put your grubby hands all over my clothes? I back out of the truck. I slam the door and lock it with the remote.

"Why you locking that?" Gitmo laughs. "We're—"

I reach down and grab him by the hair and pull him to me. I've got the barrel of my 9mm jammed beneath his chin. "I want my crossbow. I want my ammo. And I want Marta. Now!"

I hear the clicking and sliding of many a firearm around me. "Nice to know you're all armed to the teeth," I say loudly. "You know what else I hear? Listen!"

The knocking of the diesel echoes loudly through the streets. The low moaning of the dead is just becoming audible behind it. Paulson has to drive slowly. But he'll get here soon enough.

I look at the men holding guns on me. One is not holding a gun. "Tell me, is there a reason you haven't tried going north out of here towards I-70?"

The man nods at Gitmo. "He knows."

"I need to talk to somebody who isn't going to waste my time with bullshit. Look, I'm sorry you guys got fucked over here. But I had nothing to do with it. All I want to do is get home to my kids, and the next thing I know some lying whore is drawing me into a trap. Then you go through my truck and steal my stuff. You guys wanna cap me for disrespect—shit! The ultimate goddamned disrespect is I'm trapped here with you, between the fire and a mob of hungry dead!

"Thing is, I can get us out of here! But you're going to have to get your heads out your asses and work with me. And work fast, because I'm guessing we have ten more minutes before Paulson and his crew show up to picnic!"

There's a brief pause where we hear the diesel snort a little as Paulson gives it the gas to take a corner.

"I sent scouts north to the highway," says Gitmo. "They haven't called back. It's just a big open pasture before the Interstate. I guarantee you they got snipers waiting for us to cross into their sights."

"That's what's happening, then. Paulson is coming this way. He's driving us into the final ambush."

"Not even trusting the fire Brick started to finish us off," says the man without a gun.

"We're fucked, then, eh?" says Gitmo. "Think you can let me go?"

"No we're not. And we have some things we need to understand before I let you go."

"Come on! You know we don't have time for this!"

"First, I resent—really, really resent—that I was brought here under false pretenses only to be delayed—again!—and robbed."

"Look, man—"

"I want my vitamins, I want my crossbow, I want every little thing your thieves took, and I want them at that barricade. Now. Or you and I are riding out to meet Paulson and his crew. By the way, did you know the dead routed into Kerch's place are now following him? That's a lot of dead people."

"Looping them back on us," says the man without a gun.

I shove Gitmo away from me. "You're smart," I say. "Why the hell aren't you in charge?" The man doesn't answer. "Paulson has to drive slow to lead them here but he'll be here in ten minutes, maybe less. We can let Chuckles down there make speeches. Or we can get organized and get out of here. But we're on the clock. Whatever we do has to be done now!"

"So what do *you* think we ought to do?" says Gitmo, getting to his feet.

"We can't go north for snipers. We can't go east because that part of the neighborhood is on fire. We can't go south because we'll run into Paulson and all the dead they routed through Kerch's place. That leaves west."

"That's a big, roiling river of dead on the other side of that barricade!" Gitmo says. There's no way we're getting through it!"

"My concern is the barricade," says the man without a gun. "Even with the grenade launcher we've got, we're not getting through those semis."

"There's got to be some construction equipment around here somewhere. Earth movers. Snowplows."

One of the gunmen runs down the front windshield of the car he's standing on. He jumps to the street and disappears around the burned apartment building.

"Berto works on a crew," says the man without a gun.

"Good. We need to get everybody at that barricade. We got to be ready to go in five minutes, maybe less. Nobody's got time to move households. It's just like when some of you got here—you're going to have to move with nothing more than the clothes on your backs!"

Another *vato* runs away, this one into the building.

"Are we going to help each other?" I ask the man. "Can I get your name?"

"Tracy." That's what it sounds like, and it seems absurd given his hard features.

"Like the number 13 in English," I say.

Tracy can't help but raise an eyebrow. "*¿Habla Español?*"

"No. I just know how to count."

"You have a plan?"

"Nothing more sophisticated than busting through that barrier with the heavy equipment, firing whatever you picked up from the National Guard when they got overrun, and crossing that river of dead people until we get away. Where's that auto dealership Gitmo was saying you needed to get to?"

"Half a mile on the other side of that street you want to bust through."

"Then we have a destination. Me, I'll find the Interstate from there, and you guys enjoy shopping."

"All we got from the Guardsmen are their guns. They didn't bring much in the way of heavy weaponry with them."

"We got that one M203 on the M4!" says Gitmo.

"With all of two grenades!" says Tracy.

"M433s! You'll flatten everyone in the intersection! At least long enough to bust through the other side!"

I have no idea what on earth Gitmo is talking about. I can only hope they really have stuff like this. "Got any of those tear gas grenades that burn things up?"

"Let's get down there and find out," says Tracy. He nods to one of the gunmen. He drops his aim at me and they go to a little white pickup parked by the curb.

There's nowhere else to go and not much time. I run to the Big Yellow Truck. I noticed Gitmo coming up behind me. "Oh, no," I say. "I'm done with you."

"My family's using my truck. They're carrying two more families with them."

"Ride with Tracy."

"I'd rather not, if it's okay."

"Goddamn it, politics is going to be the death of us all!" I say. My eye is caught by two *vatos* carrying my crossbow and bag of vitamin supplements. Coming my way. They hand them off to me. I nod. They turn and run away.

"Now that's what I call timing!" I say. "Go ahead, get in!" I have to shift my burden to one arm to get my keys to unlock the truck. The locks click and we climb in.

23

Women and children emerge from the burned apartment building in groups of three and four, assisted by at least one young man whom I presume is somewhat related. This started shortly after we'd pulled up; I was counting on their presence inspiring restraint in the gunmen. So far, so good.

One of these women looks like she's a hundred years old. She's moving slow as Christmas. Nor will she let the young men pick her up and carry her as they've already done with so many far less needful.

Gitmo rolls down the window and yells at the young men. It's in Spanish, which I understand only slightly better than his Army terminology. He yells at the old woman, who waves Gitmo off contemptuously.

After a moment bent to snapping the young men say something that sounds like, "Sorry, grandma" and begin walking quickly away. The old woman shouts after them.

"I had a feeling we were going to have a problem with her," says Gitmo as I put the truck in drive. "Been nothing but a pain in the ass since this got started."

We quickly cover the three blocks to the intersection. I see the fire truck down the street to the left, maybe seven blocks away. He honks/blasts his air horn when my Big Yellow Truck comes into view.

"Man, I hope you know what you're doing," says Gitmo.

"I'm open to better ideas."

"No, cuz," Gitmo says, "this one's on you."

I pull over to the far side of the street. There are half a dozen little cars and pickup trucks loaded down with bedding and children and toys and God knows what else in the Intersection. I park the truck and jump out. "Get these cars and everything to the side! The plows and earth movers have to be able to get up the middle here!"

The oven ranges and dishwashers and refrigerators have been removed. It's just the big semis now. You can see the legs of the shuffling dead through the underside of the trailers. The women urge the children to lie down on the flatbeds of their pickups before covering them in quilts. The don't let the children look lest one sees that impenetrable forest of legs and screams.

Between the fire and the dead walking behind the barricade it already smelled bad here. But we can smell the others coming up from behind. Paulson hits his horn, runs his sirens. "Keep cool!" I say, standing on the running board of my truck. "He's trying to panic us!"

I'm yelling this for myself as much as anyone else. That forest of legs is slowing down for all Paulson's noise; it's only inertia that keeps them moving on. All one has to do is peek under, get a whiff of our living meat, and the rest will follow. And Paulson is already another block closer behind us.

I go up to Tracy, who is supervising the distribution of weapons. "I imagine we don't have a lot of ammo."

"Actually, we're fine on that," says Tracy. "At least for M4s and 9mm sidearms, but we can go through guns blazing."

"Your people know to aim for the heads, right?"

"We know what we're doing, Mr. Dead Silencer."

"Is anyone using that?" I say, pointing to a flare gun in the flat bed of what I presume is our munitions truck.

"What, are you calling for help?" Tracy says. The young *vato* next to him snickers.

"Testing a hypothesis," I say. I reach out and take the gun. Bright orange plastic. Hard to miss. With a plastic strip of flare shells, too.

"Test a what?"

"They burn down your shit. Let's burn down theirs. Did you find any tear gas?"

Tracy's face turns serious. "Yeah. Yeah, actually we did."

"You want to get through this, you need to start thinking outside the ammo box. Keep in mind we might run into trouble on the other side of that second barrier. They're thinking you're nothing more than a bunch of dumb Glock-carrying gangbangers. You want to hit 'em with something they don't expect."

"Shit, man," says the guy standing next to Tracy, "you some kinda general or somethin'?"

I look down the street. Paulson has closed another block. "Nope. Just trying to get out of here. Just like you."

"I hear ya, cuz."

What I'm hearing is Paulson's diesel engine, loud and getting louder as it closes the distance. The moans from behind the barricade, from behind Paulson's fire truck—they're not so loud, but I can feel them. Feel them in my bones. My bones, and every ounce of juicy, living meat around them....

I wonder why Paulson doesn't speed up the street towards us. The walkers would keep walking towards us while he cut north along the warehouse road and—well, whose snipers are those at the Interstate? Maybe we're lucky here. There's so little I know about the politics here. And if it weren't for me getting pulled into this stupid, Mean Old Rich Fart drama, I'd care even less.

Paulson is three blocks away. The seething mob massed behind the fire truck and boiling around its sides are visible as individuals now. The remains of those teenage firebugs still drip down the fronts of the ones closest to the truck. I look through the big window of the truck towards Paulson. He's a little harder to make out through the glass but he shows no expression. Naturally. Nothing personal. Just business.

I glance towards the three big white trucks with the women and children packed in the cabs and lying down in the flatbeds. The women who sit up in the flatbeds watch Paulson's approach with characteristic hard peasant faces used to grief of one form or another. No one has yet died, so there's no cause to weep. Not much cause for hope, either, but unlike softer souls who would already be losing themselves to hysteria these women will not crack until their doom is actually upon them. Three blocks away is still three blocks away.

Though now it's two and a half blocks away, and getting closer every second....

Tracy is on his phone. Judging by his expression he's not getting an answer.

I'm eyeballing the parallel street one block away. I might make a break for it that way. Being shot up by snipers is infinitely preferable to getting pulled apart by grubby, grasping hands and eaten alive.

Paulson is crossing to the second block now.

Then Berto rounds the corner in a large snow removal truck with a de-icer unit. A regular snowplow comes around the corner. Someone else found a tow truck, the kind in which the vehicle goes on the long bed in back. He's followed by one lumbering bulldozer grinding up the street on wide treads, then another.

I wave the units into position, one eye on the advancing mob. The snowplows and bulldozers line up side by side in the broad intersection before the tractor trailers. Gitmo takes his position many paces back from the middle, reckoning the trajectory of his shell. I look back to Tracy. Berto and the heavy equipment operators are waiting for his signal. And Tracy is waiting on us.

"Think you can get it right between the barricades?" I ask Gitmo.

"I'm working on it," he says.

Gitmo takes another step back. There's a terrible *hrrrrrnnnnn!* behind us. Paulson's entourage has scented our party.

Gitmo fires. You can't even hear the soft click of the launcher over the moans of the dead, the unholy clatter of large diesel engines.

The shell goes up, tall and steep. It comes down.

If that isn't the middle of the intersection it's going to have to do.

The multi-ton semis rock with the impact. A dozen or so charred limbs whirl out beneath the trailers in smoking pinwheels, banking off the blades of the 'dozers when not gonging square into them. "All right!" shouts Gitmo, raising an arm. "Let's move!" He brings that arm down and we hear the terrible grinding and crunching as the 'dozers and the plows slam into the semis and begin pushing them aside.

I'm turning to go to my own truck. Halfway there I turn and see Gitmo loading the second shell, looking square at the fire truck and the graying cadavers shuffling up behind it. Paulson has stopped his fire truck. He can't back up; there are too many dead behind him, pouring around the big red machine to get at us. The dead move quicker than you'd think once they've got a purpose.

I run for the shelter of the Big Yellow Truck. Gitmo has the M4 pointed up just so. I pray he's doing what I think he's about to do.

I jump in the cab and look back towards the fire truck and the hundreds, maybe a good one thousand dead walking tall behind him. I'll give Paulson credit. He knows what's coming. And like the rock-ribbed Old Family man he is, he accepts it with dignity. The grenade goes up, and Gitmo throws himself down in the street, his arms about his head. Thank the dark gods Gitmo was smart enough to aim the grenade behind the fire truck, and into that thick scrum of walkers behind it to absorb the blast. The blast is still enough to lift the back of the fire truck slightly and push it forward a foot. It lands a little low on the back end. I'm guessing the rear tires got blown.

Then the diesel tank on the fire truck explodes.

I duck behind my seat. The pressure of the blast wave on the rear window of the cab makes the glazing creak loudly in its frame, but the glass holds. (It helped that I parked along the side of the street instead of in the middle, directly in front of the fire truck.) As the smoke clears I see there are still a lot of dead on their feet behind the burning remains of the fire truck. They're over one hundred yards back, though. To get at us they would have to wade through wall-to-wall burning and pulverized flesh.

They sway from side to side, shifting weight from one foot to the other, as if trying to build courage to cross, or turn and walk the other way. They can't smell us, can't reckon our movement through the heat shimmers off the smashed, burning bodies. An eerie blue-green flame flickers over the denser clumps of blast-smashed bodies. An occasional puff of sickly yellow flame blooms over this hellscape of broken bone and scorched flesh, expanding rapidly as it hits less putrid, more oxygenated air.

These dead won't be coming back at us. But even if there weren't hundreds more dead turning away on the other side, we'd never be able to cross that toxic, superheated mess. Beyond that, the blaze Brick's people started on the far end of the barrio is creeping up from the other end. We're still trapped.

The roar of outraged metal fills the air as snowplows and 'dozers and the big tow truck push against the semis. The blast on the other side was intensified by its containment between the heavy barriers and the heat blew the tires out on the semis all across the way. Only the blades of the huge 'dozers prevented the rest of us from getting flash burned. A taller pile of bodies and bubbling necrotic flesh presses against the cabs and their trailers, smoking pieces of them blown under the trailers and around the heavy equipment.

Eventually it's all Berto's crew can do to push the semis over, cabs, trailers and all. They fall awkwardly across the vast, lumpy carpet of blast-pulped bodies. The young man driving the biggest bulldozer backs up as the other trucks back away. He positions himself in the middle where the cabs lay with their scorched undercarriages facing us. A gap has opened between them in the fall. Not big enough to drive through. Yet. The young man revs the engine once, twice. He charges the gap.

The blade smashes into the cabs. They slide with a sickly ease on their sides across the smoldering, liquefying corpses. For a moment I panic, remembering these semis have huge diesel tanks of their own. Apparently the black ops people drained the tanks— and I can see where they thoughtfully (or carelessly) left the caps off. In any event we were damned lucky. That I didn't think about this until now…Christ, it's a goddamned miracle we've come this far.

As the first bulldozer backs off from his push the second one charges in. He sends the cabs sliding far enough apart that he can plow a little ways in. The mothers in the backs of the white pickups cover their eyes as the gases from the smoldering corpses billow out of the gap. They sit at the edges of the flatbed and draw their knees up close, burying their faces in their skirts. Even in the cab I catch a whiff of the caustic stink. A huge yellow bloom of bubbling putrefaction rises on a stalk and flares out wide and high over us as the 'dozer's blade collides with the three-deep carpet of bodies.

And here's something else I didn't think about: my concern getting through the barrier was the remaining walking dead coming towards us. As it is the blast probably funneled along the lane and flattened—and ignited—bodies for far beyond the documented casualty radius. I'd thought I might use the flare gun I'd taken from

Tracy's munitions truck to light the bulging pants seat of a walker, see if it blew up as Hearn said it might. Now it's weirdly colored flames and noxious gases from the superheated cadavers and their necrotic fat. Berto's men have to keep those blades low and scrape the asphalt good if the trucks are going to pass through. And they still have to break through the other side. And deal with whoever is waiting for us there.

Gitmo is on his feet. He makes reassuring gestures as he talks to the women in the trucks. He goes over to Tracy and they bring out the tear gas shells. They're checking to see if they're compatible with the grenade launcher on the M4.

Berto now has the two dozers side by side, scraping back bodies, pushing across the broad four lane street towards the barricade on the other side. The bodies, red-black and ruined, crack and bend into grotesque shapes, arms bent this way, legs bent backward behind their shock-faced skulls as they ebb and flow up the sides of the tractor trailers with each push and retreat of the bulldozers. The 'dozers make three quick pushes and then rotate drivers. They're not taking chances with overexposure to the toxic air of the zombie cattle chute.

Gitmo and Tracy take turns sending incendiary tear gas canisters into the buildings across the barricaded street. They drop another into the street between the buildings just as Berto's crew begins banging into the semis parked on the other side, the charred and broken cadavers piled high against the 'dozer blades. As the gap opens between the cabs the gas catches the hot white flame coming from the tear gas canister. We see a hot blue-green flash consume the block beyond. It's at this point I notice that the warehouses on our side of the street have smoke pouring through their windows. As do the buildings on the other side.

Paulson shouldn't have wasted that fire truck bringing it here. Hell, I shouldn't have bothered trying to save Oak Blossom Lane. Aside from Paulson and the families there being far from grateful, the fire on the east side has grown so that it's bringing in hot Kansas prairie air. This wind will happily feed the other blazes of houses and human flesh about Natalia. All because the very few can't share with the other very few. And someone always has to be in charge. And that asshole always has to be so full of himself he gets everyone around him killed.

As the bang and shriek of metal-on-metal continues, the cabs of the semis on the other side parting much too slowly, I resist the urge to drive the Big Yellow Truck out the north road and take my chances with the snipers in the fields before the Interstate. I realize I could have, should have, hauled ass the other way out of Oak Blossom Lane, told Marta to find her own ride. This is another hour that would have been better spent on the road back to Colorado Springs. As it is I'm going to have to find someplace to camp for tonight. I'll never make it by nightfall.

Assuming I get out of this, that is. The sunlight is darkening beneath the smoke on both sides. The ghastly color of the air Marta and I first drove into has found its way here. The women in the backs of the pickup trucks flap the quilts over their children before tucking themselves beneath the heavy material. At least the sun doesn't beat down as hard. But it's still hot, and getting hotter. The only saving grace is the wind coming in from the west, keeping the worst of Paulson's black-smoke belching truck and burning lake of bodies off of us.

The hellish clatter of two multi-ton semi-cabs falling over and pulling their trailers down behind them is the sweetest music I've heard since this all started. The man in the tractor, a wet rag over his nose and mouth, backs up behind the breach in the first barrier and charges through full speed, taking himself well down the avenue on the other side. The second 'dozer follows through, this time grazing the cab on the left on the way out. The snowplow behind him bashes the cab on the right a foot or so over.

Seven *vatos* climb to the tall flatbed of the tow truck. They're crouching along the edges with their M4s at the ready as it rolls through.

Tracy is talking on his phone. He puts it away and waves towards the trucks with the women and children. He goes alongside the drivers' sides and shouts instructions in Spanish, with expressive motions indicating directions to be taken. He's saying something to the women whom he's called from beneath their quilts when another woman's voice calls out and everyone looks to see the grandmother from the burned out apartment building hobbling around the corner.

She cuts a curious figure, moving so slowly and stooped before the flames and smoke. Tracy nods at the driver of the truck nearest her and he backs his truck up to meet the old woman. The women in the flatbed help the grandmother in. Once that tailgate is slammed by another M4-toting young man, the driver does not wait for the women to tuck themselves beneath the quilts with their children. He takes off at speed behind his fellows, wasting no time getting across the toxic intersection. Like the heavy equipment before them they disappear down the avenue. The cars sit too low and heavy to be driven as fast. They follow as best they can, though.

I don't live here so I have no idea where they're going. All I know is the Interstate is north, this avenue leads west, so I'll keep driving and hang right somewhere. I'll wait until everyone clears out and then....

There's a knock on my window. It's Gitmo. "Hey, can you keep an eye on that last car? Follow behind it until we get to the dealership?" he says when I roll down the window. "Once we get there we can upgrade and you're on your way."

How big of you, I want to say. "Where are you gonna be?"

"Me and some of my men are gonna be tagging on that last snowplow, bringing up the rear. It's gonna be all right, man. Nobody's seen nothin' out there and it's a straight shot to the dealership. We've driving as fast as our slowest people can."

"All right," I sigh. The last car has disappeared through the gap. I roll up my window and follow.

I take my time going through the formerly barricaded area. I try, anyway. Even with the windows up the stink makes my eyes water. A greenish-yellow haze of flame still flickers like a will-o-the-wisp over the nearer piles of bodies. The flesh is burned black on the bones. The mouths of the skulls hang wide as if screaming, tendrils of the whitest smoke pouring through the eye and nose holes. For blocks on either side it's a hilly, rolling vista of ruined humanity. If any are on their feet they stand well behind the haze, and I don't see how they can get to anyone in this bulldozed path between bodies before all these gassy, superhot fires go out.

The burning in my nose and throat is going beyond merely irritating to painful. I tap the accelerator and push through quickly. It's not just the bodies, though they're obviously the most poisonous. The pall of smoke from the east side is merging with the blazes on the west, and the warehouses on either side of this street are catching fire.

Beyond the second barricade I notice a rifle barrel sticking from a third-floor window, the muzzle pointed to the sky. Smoke billows through the open window. This was one of the buildings Gitmo hit with the tear gas from his launcher. But the smoke from the fires across town is also thick up there. No telling what got him first.

I speed to catch up to the car in front of me. The truck carrying the loot from the liquor store as per his original assignment—it's the one pickup with a hardtop, while the women and children ride open—closes the distance behind me, as does the snowplow behind it. Can't blame these guys for not wanting to linger, either. No doubt pissed at me for rubbernecking.

We come to another broad intersection, the black-eyed stoplights sagging hangdog from their rigging, marking the boundary of the poor neighborhood of warehouses and Section 8 housing. Beyond I can see where the western sky is purpling from one end of the horizon to the other. There's a mean line of thunderstorms in the far distance. Far, but still coming our way. Wherever I'm camping tonight I'll have to find it fast. Resign myself to a long drive in the morning....

I follow the car as it turns right behind the rest of the convoy. The air clears as we go over another low ridge. The sun almost looks natural. Then we climb to another short, artificial plateau, this one vast enough to accommodate a large auto mall complex. No super high-end stuff like BMWs or Mercs or Ferraris, but pretty much everything else. If they don't have it, you don't need it.

Me, I've got what I need right here: the Big Yellow Truck and a clear line of sight to the next Interstate exit, this one a good mile up from the one the snipers are watching. Of course, they might be here, too; it only takes one asshole with a scoped rifle to ruin your day. I should take the road we were driving west before the turn and drive until the road runs out, and then zig-zag my way up to the frontage road....

The truck behind me is right on my tail. I follow the last car into one of the dealerships and find myself in a narrow lane between rows of used cars. The car in front of me stops. I stop, and marvel how the truck behind me doesn't plow into me. But I'm pinned in. If I push against either vehicle in front or back I'm pushing against a truck and a snowplow in back, and every other goddamn thing up front.

I shut off the truck and jump out. "What's going on, Tracy? I say, slamming the door behind me.

Tracy is at the front of the convoy talking to his lieutenants. He ignores me. After his lieutenants leave to carry out their order Tracy spends a leisurely minute with his phone.

Finally he puts it away and looks at me. "What?"

"I understood I could go free after this. You've got me blocked in. I figure it's a misunderstanding, but I really need to be on the road by—"

"Gitmo's in charge of that. You'll need to talk to him." He walks away.

The *vatos* standing here and there, guns at the ready, smirk at me. Son of a bitch.

I walk back to my truck, and then back to the snowplow where Gitmo is holding court. I wait for the requisite time they make white men wait until I'm acknowledged.

"Gitmo," I say. "I gotta go."

Gitmo makes a point of pulling out a cigarette and lighting it. I wait for him to go through his ritual of doing this before he says, "My friend, you have a decision to make."

"Like hell," I say. The sound of M4s, Glocks, and who knows what else clicks in the air as my hands position themselves above the handles of my panga and hammer. "I didn't want to be here. I was the one who figured out how to save you and your people. Now you're fucking me over? Again?"

"That's just it. How were you fucked over? Don't you have everything back that was taken from you?"

"Yeah, I'm good. Now I'd like to move on."

"Thing is, I'm still owed."

"For what?"

"You put that gun on me. Treated me with disrespect."

"Were you giving me my stuff back otherwise?"

"You got your stuff back, right?"

"Yes."

"So you're good. But that still leaves me."

"What the fuck do you want, Gitmo?"

"Take it easy on the language. No need to talk to me like that."

Oh, for fuck's sake: *"What do you want?"*

"Just 'cause we're not in the barrio anymore doesn't mean we're safe. Rumor has it they've chased some people down in the mountains with drones. Taken 'em out, every last one. You know they can computer target faces with those things, put a bullet in every one."

"Sure," I say, assessing my tactical situation. They're all standing well back. They'll have me leaking out of a dozen holes before I get my panga off my belt.

"I know it sounds crazy but I've been in touch with a lot of people. Too many people disappearing off the grid without telling me what's what. People talk to me, you know? Somebody always gets back to me!"

"Did it ever occur to you they lost the bars on their phones? Or maybe their phones just died? Service was spotty as hell before the dead overran Kansas City." Or maybe you're not the Well-Connected Man you'd like everyone to believe. Goddamn it, this is the fool who's going to end it for me?

"You know," Gitmo says, "you did all right back there."

"If saving everyone's lives is 'all right,' I'll take it."

"You didn't bust through those barricades, now."

"No, but until I brought up the idea of using the heavy equipment to do it, and how to pacify the area, you guys were standing around eating grilled chicken and waiting to die."

"Well, see, that's the deal. All you have to do is think of things. I mean, yeah, use that fancy cane-cutter of yours from time to time on the *muertos*, that's good. Still. A hell of a deal! You just use your mind and suggest ways to go and me and the boys will do all the heavy lifting."

"I got a home and family to go to."

"No you don't," and my hand goes to my Glock when I see the sneer on his face. His *vatos* all point their pieces at me, and I'd love to shoot them too for their stupid pseudo-gangster poses with the guns held sideways.

"What I'm saying is they're gone. You know it, I know it. This is your chance for a new family. You help us, we got your back. Win-win, man. You live. We all live."

"And what if I just want to live somewhere else?"

"Then you owe me for your disrespect."

"Which means what?"

"Gotta take you down. Just the way it is, man."

On one hand I'm flattered they think little old me is worth keeping around for the brains they expect a white guy like me a couple of steps up the social ladder to have. On the other, this passive-aggressive doubletalk pisses me off even more than the guns when it comes to getting me to join the team.

I take in my final scene. My last opponents. There are four goons to the left and three to the right of Gitmo. It's a sure bet I've got shooters behind me but there's not much they can do when I'm making my final charge at these guys. As Marta said, though, stupid never stopped anyone.

However it plays I'll be sure to inconvenience at least two, maybe three of these shits before I go down. Enjoy the rest of the apocalypse with no arms, asshole. I'll be the lucky one, free of this sticky-stupid flypaper of power games and bullshit.

Gitmo is looking at me looking his boys over. "The alternative to death is family. That's what we're offering here! How can you turn down family?"

I look over the tops of their heads, breathing steadily. I'll go after the kid on the far left first, maybe use him as a shield while I hack away at the others. (Breathe.) It's got to be panga and Glock, not panga and the hammer because Gitmo will run and I do so want that ugly motherfucker dead. (Breathe.) (And breathe some more, because you need to be cool....)

"What's it gonna be, Mr. Dead Silencer? You can't be silent forever!"

I'm bringing one last, deep draw of air through my nose, mentally rehearsing the motion of my hands to my belt. I'm going to have microseconds to make this move. I listen for what sounds like distant thunder. A sign? Wait....

That's not thunder.

"You hear that?" I say.

"What?" Gitmo laughs. "You hear another fire truck I need to blow up?"

But the screams from the other end of the lot, where the rest of Tracy's *vatos* are organizing the new trucks, indicates they see the helicopter coming in ahead of the storm front, a shiny black speck against the deep bruise of the sky. Gitmo turns slowly—he's so terrified he doesn't want to look. When he turns back around to face me he's whiter than a Goth. "You need to make a decision," he says.

"No, cuz, this one's on you. You need to figure out whether you're going to try and take out that chopper with your launcher, or if you're going to try and hide everyone. If they're really looking for you in the barrio and you're not there, what's to stop them from a little search-and-destroy?"

"I'm not gonna ask you again!"

"Do what you have to do. I'm going home."

My hands rise to my panga and Glock. All they have to do is squeeze their triggers. As the sound of the helicopter grows louder I wonder if I'll feel the bullets rip through me or if I'll get lucky and die immediately....

24

The men at either end of the line flanking Gitmo fall. Before the ones standing next to them can turn their heads to look, they fall, too. This time I notice the slugs obliterating their faces in such rapid succession it gives the illusion of happening all at once. I drop to the ground in time for the next two to meet me on the hot asphalt.

The seventh *vato* has enough time to get his pistol aimed at what he hopes is the source of the gunfire when his head snaps back. Gitmo is fumbling with the M4 hanging at his back by the strap. He takes a slug to one shoulder, then the other. Not square on the shoulders, but grazing. Enough to make the son of a bitch hurt, which is all I ever wanted to do before I died.

I hear footsteps crunching behind me. Gitmo raises his hands, tears now fat and hot in his bulging eyes. "Aw, come on," he says. "We don't have to do this!"

I glance over my shoulder, then roll back to my feet in time to get out of her way. At first I don't recognize her in her khaki Great White Hunter shorts and blouse, complete with matching bush helmet. The surgical mask she's wearing against the soot isn't helping either, but that's definitely a woman in that outfit. And who else can handle such a ridiculously long-barreled pistol with a suppressor? It looks like a Klingon Wild West sidearm if the Klingons had a Wild West phase. The bright chrome gleams even in this corrupted sunlight. Especially as she steps towards Gitmo and raises the suppressor to press it to his cheekbone. The sizzle is horrific; I can hear it even over Gitmo's shrill screaming. Christ, aren't we all sick of the smell of burning flesh already?

Rebecca turns to me, pulls down her mask. "Mr. Grace. Mr. Gutiérrez here is my final assignment. Given your relationship with this dirtbag, would you like the honor of completing my mission?"

I look at Gitmo when I say, "No. I'm good." I turn to Rebecca. "Besides, a macho dumb-ass like him would resent it more for being killed by a woman. Even if she is the best sharpshooter in Saline County, Kansas."

"Try, 'First in Class' at Quantico," she says flatly, her silvery eyes flashing in the shade of her brim. Her eyes still on mine, she lifts her pistol again and shoots Gitmo in the face. The muzzle is so close he falls with a circle of powder burn arcing about his brow and just beneath where his nose used to be.

Rebecca glances towards the approaching helicopter. Black, two rotors. A Chinook? My son Jack could tell me if he were here. "I need to get something from your truck," Rebecca says, her eyes on the helicopter.

"Sure." She's already on her way before the syllable leaves my mouth. The sight of her taut, perfectly rounded backside as she climbs up and leans into the cab is a divine gift in a day full of hella-fugly sights.

Rebecca emerges with the flare gun. She's hanging off the doorframe with one hand when she fires the gun into the air. A hot pink ball of light ascends into the yellowy air. She tosses the gun back into the cab and swings over into the flatbed of the Big Yellow Truck.

The dual-rotor chopper angles towards us, coming in low. Low enough for me to see the man standing in the open door, in all-black battle-rattle, black aviator glasses, black flak helmet, the works. The chopper slows to hover and the wash is ferocious but Rebecca is signing something to him. She indicates the general direction of the women and children and the young men shepherding them. The man nods, signals to the pilot, and the chopper roars off across the city, towards the brown-black columns of smoke towering from the east.

"They're coming back to get Tracy and his people?"

Rebecca looks at me as if that's the dumbest thing she's ever heard. "I scratched off those punks long before I got to you. There's no one left but a couple of dozen scared women and children and maybe a handful of teenage boys trembling under the SUVs in the northeast lot over there."

She swings back around from the flatbed to the cab, reaching through the door for the pistol she'd tossed to the seat while reaching for the flare gun. "It's going to be a while before this thing cools down," Rebecca says as she emerges with the chrome beast. "A good thing we're here because I'm tired of carrying this thing on the bike." Rebecca looks at me. "You know the snipers in the fields left once the mansion got overrun. Kerch called them back as soon as his back lawn started filling up with the dead Brick sent over. You guys could have left out that north road. You'd be halfway home now."

"Goddamn it!"

"Oh, calm down. You're not the one who had to race a mountain bike through toxic fumes to catch up! It's okay, though. I'll take the liquor truck back, and be a big hero for the Death's Head bully boys."

"Back where?"

Rebecca's eyes flash. "Where I come from. Anyway, I saved these clowns for last. I knew Brick was going to give me trouble. It was worth it for this sweet custom Desert Eagle of his, though." She runs a finger down the long barrel. "These 14-inch jobs usually only come in black. I'd have loved to found out where he got it but he wouldn't stop screaming after I fed his dick and balls to a walker. The look on his face, though…so precious…."

"Sorry I missed it."

"Oh, it was just *tedious!* Like most wannabe super-badasses he was surrounded by wall after wall of goons. I had to come up with different ways to kill them just to keep myself focused."

"Oh."

"My favorite was their silly little command center. I shot the hands and legs of eight of those fools, then killed the last one with a shot to the heart. Then I locked the door behind me. I got one of their webcams and set up a video stream to go straight to my phone. I'm curious to see how long it took for the one I killed to turn. Of course, the looks on those poor crippled little boys' faces—mmm! So *hot!*"

"So the area's pacified? We can drive around and not get shot at?" I say, looking towards the stormy horizon.

Rebecca's eyes follow mine and she nods. "That was the mission. Neutralize Brick, Gitmo. Liquidate their soldiers so they don't fall in with other wannabe warlords, wherever they are." She smiles as if laughing at a private joke. "Just honest refugees out here now."

"How about Kerch?"

"First order of business. You thought he fed some dinner guests last night; well, he had some people over for breakfast. In bed, no less. Of course, I'd tied him to it. Getting the guests up through the garage elevator and into the main part of the house, that was the challenging part."

"Great. Another mattress ruined."

"They'll fly in another. We'll make a training exercise of it for the junior Death's Head crew. Find a deluxe mattress place and shoot their way in and out for a king-size luxury pillow-top. I might insist on going with them just to piss them off. Funny you should bring that up, though. I thought you liked your 'patron.'"

"It's not a matter of like or don't-like. I'm just trying to get home."

"Yeah, like you were driving real hard to get there last night."

I look her straight in the eyes. "More than you'd know."

Her Desert Eagle comes up in my face. I try not to blink at the heat still coming off the suppressor. "What do you think I know?" she says.

And all of a sudden it's very easy not to blink. I can feel the blood slowing down inside of me. Heating up to match that suppressor just an inch from my right eye:

"That's it, Rebecca. I don't know. I don't want to know. And I don't fucking care. All I know is that I was jumping through hoops long before this all got started. Now I'm hundreds of miles from my home, my wife's sick and dead, my children are God knows where—and you want me to jump some more? You'd think a man could catch a break after everything collapses under the weight of its own bullshit! Instead I'm being sucked into crap by total strangers who think their drama is the only drama that matters in a whole planet full of people suffering and dying!

"If this is life after the apocalypse, fine. Be the Queen Bitch of this fucking hell! But don't expect me to beg for my life. I've sat across the desk from many a sadistic little HR cunt who wanted to make the big bad old man who reminds them of Daddy squirm. I don't have anything to do with her personal misery, I have a family and pets and a home on the line but none of that matters because Princess has a grudge and I'm handy for a smackdown I can't do shit about.

"So do it! Pull your trigger, bitch! You're dealing with another kind of trained professional here. One who sees you as nothing more than a stupid-bitter piece of ass who's really handy with her substitute penis. Fuck me, then. Fuck me good and hard, you sick whore! *Do it!*"

Her eyes narrow at me beyond the barrel. She's got the thing right in my eye but I refuse to look at it. Thunder rolls in the distance, a long rumble culminating in little booms like some drunken giant stomping across the uneasy prairie.

As the rumbling fades, Rebecca pulls back her weapon. That ridiculous 14-inch barrel against her shoulder, she says, "It would seem you and I are a lot alike, Mr. Grace."

"Fuck you! When you kill, you're killing the same man over and over again. I'm killing *all kinds* of people!"

The corners of her mouth turn up in a joyless smile. "Yet you wouldn't kill Kara."

"Kara who?"

"Kara McConnell. The girl from this morning. The kind of rich bitch out of McMansionland who's looked down her nose at struggling stiffs like you for as long as you remember. Who wouldn't have looked twice at you if she didn't need someone, anyone, to save her worthless life. You actually felt bad for her!"

"For God's sake, she was just a child!"

Rebecca laughs bitterly. "Not quite. Certainly not how the Powers That Be saw her and her girlfriends, which is what got Emory Kerch taken out of the picture."

"So my hatred isn't pure. Is that it? You're shaming me for that?"

"Worse." Rebecca brings the Desert Eagle away from her shoulder. "Mr. Derek Samuel Grace, for the crime of Gross Sentimentality, I, Queen of Hell, hereby condemn you—to live!" She taps me on either shoulder with the barrel, careful not to touch me with the still-hot suppressor.

"So I'm finally free to go?"

"Silence! For the ancillary crime of Giving a Shit, I, Queen of Hell, curse you with *success*. That you may suffer for it. Which, for the most part, you already are. Therefore I wish you more success. Lots and lots of success!" After tapping me again on the shoulders Rebecca pulls the muzzle back until the suppressor is level with my cheekbone, as if she might do my face like she did Gitmo's. I hold her stare. Rebecca once again rests the Eagle on her shoulder.

"Success for me, right now," I say, "would be to hit the road and never interact with another living human for the rest of my natural life."

"And that, Mr. Dead Silencer, is the one thing you will fail at. You can't escape the world."

"Oh for God's sake, Rebecca, the world ended about a week ago!"

"Not at all. It was just *born*." She smiles coldly. "It'll take a while to find its feet but believe me, in one more year or so you might wish I had killed you."

"If it ever comes to that I'll be happy to handle it myself."

"You think you're free because civilization has collapsed and it's every man for himself. What if I told you this was all deliberate? That everything is going more or less to plan?"

"I'd say it's a hell of a plan. Sweeping off the game pieces and setting the board on fire."

"If I tell you anything more I'll be under orders to kill you. Just know that the reset has been pressed. If the Powers That Be are taking their time reasserting their authority, it's because they like the idea of the strong and clever culling the weak before they step back in."

"Huh. Okay. Can I go now?"

"Just one more thing. You'll want to go by your crash site one last time. Say goodbye."

"Okay, sure."

"I mean it. Get back on the road, take a right. It'll take you straight there. You'll be close to the exit, too. It'll just take you a couple of minutes out of your way."

I look towards the approaching storm front. "All right. I'll chance it."

213

"You'll be glad you did," she says, squatting to lay her Desert Eagle flat on the asphalt. "Closure is a powerful thing. Which brings us to this."

She rises, threads her arms around my neck. I take her in my arms in time for her open mouth to meet mine. Another roll of thunder rumbles and booms in the far distance, adding a dramatic urgency to our coupling.

But the rumbling fades…slowly…as does the kiss. "Want something out of the back before I take off?" Rebecca asks, nodding at the pickup truck with the liquor in it.

"Sure."

"You're not going to have time to browse," she says, picking up her gun. "Just grab a bottle of something. I've got to meet those people from the chopper."

I follow her to the back of the truck, where she unlocks the topper hatch and I reach in to grab a bottle of Tennessee whiskey. I've no sooner got the bottle out of the back and closing the hatch when Rebecca has the truck started and in reverse. I step aside and she takes her foot off the brake and rolls back.

"Take care, Derek," she says from the open window. "Long live the legend of the Dead Silencer!"

"Right. Long live the Queen!"

She has the surgical mask on already so I can't see her reaction. Just flashing gray eyes and a hand raised farewell as she drives off. I walk quickly back to the Big Yellow Truck. I've got all the room in the world to back out now.

Pulling onto the main road through the auto mall I look for signs of the "honest refugees" but wherever they are they're keeping their heads down. I think of the signals Rebecca flashed to the man in the chopper. The chopper moved on to wherever it was already going so I can't imagine what that was about.

I drive as fast as I dare down the road. It comes up alongside the Interstate in due time. Still, I wonder why I'm doing this. I'm finally free, right? Just get the fuck out of here! But there was something in Rebecca's voice that would be bothering me all night if I don't get that "closure" she's talking about.

The fields rise with the corn, fall with the soybeans. Between the smoke and the approaching storm the sun takes an eerie cast. It's as if it's evening at—holy shit! The clock on the dash says 1:30. I check my phone. The dash clock is running fast by all of three minutes.

Lord, what a day.

Even at 80 miles an hour it feels like more than a couple of minutes but eventually I come upon the crash site. It's hard to miss a wrecked airplane. It looks so much smaller than I remember it. I let my foot off the gas and let inertia bring me alongside.

The hatch is open. No sign of our luggage inside. I guess someone got to eat all that lovely bacon I'd stashed away after all. As for the thing catching fire, it looks like someone threw something burning into the cabin on a goof, maybe to try and make it blow up. It scorched a few chairs, blackened the area above the hatch with smoke. Still, whatever the cause of the fire, it didn't start with the plane.

To see all this, though, I have to avoid the most obvious feature of the wreck, the one that first catches your eye. Other than the open, smoke-stained hatch, the smashed wing with the chunky dried brown splatter of corpse gravy fanning over the tip.

It's in the cockpit.

Tanner.

He's hard to recognize; a week's constant exposure to the sun has baked his skin to a leathery red-brown. Even the polo shirt I remember him wearing is discolored and disfigured by the wheel column in his chest and the blackened heart's blood that soaked it. He rocks violently back and forth against the column pinning him to his seat as he senses my presence.

I have to climb the berm leading to the Interstate's eastbound roadbed to get to him. I can see how it was easier to pull me out of the passenger seat than it was to get to Tanner. Still, I'm surprised no one else took him out, especially after he reanimated. I suppose he was part of the tourist attraction bringing potential new workers to Emory Kerch's plantation.

I'm about to step down into the tilted cockpit when I'm distracted by the sound of a helicopter. It roars over fast, in the general direction of Kerch's mansion. Coming in from due north. What the hell?

I look down and realize this may have saved my life. Tanner has somehow worked a big enough hole in his chest cavity where he can slip the wheel behind his open rib cage and swing around to the passenger side. If I'd stepped down there he would have had me. Judging by the blood scabbed on his chin I'm guessing this has worked at least once.

Tanner's arms are flopping and waving blindly across the empty cockpit seat at me. Ordinarily I'd take my panga, eliminate the threat of those grasping hands and close the deal with the hammer. I can't bring myself to mutilate this poor son of a bitch, though. I pull my Glock and edge as close as I dare. Rebecca makes it look so easy. Me, I have to take a full minute to get myself situated just so I can get that bullet right where it needs to go. I've only got so many of these things.

Christ. All this for someone like Tanner. A McMansionland douchebag who let me get chased around by a dead old cougar just to see how I'd react. Still, who's to say we'd have gotten this far if we'd made it to the Interstate with an intact Luxury Tank? It took something a lot of people don't have to fly an actual plane based only on simulator experience. If he hadn't acted as he did when that imperious bitch and her special needs spawn held us up we'd have been overrun.

I squeeze the trigger. The slug catches him over one eye. His movements are jerkier, but he isn't stilled. I have to fire a second shot in the vicinity of his mouth to stop him.

Me and my gross sentimentality. I really need to think things over. It's a world just getting born, all right, and God knows it's even more unforgiving than the one whose morbidly obese chest it burst out of to get here.

Okay, Tanner's down. Closure, and all that. Let's go home.

25

I don't bother with the exit. I turn the Big Yellow Truck around and angle it up the berm to the roadbed. I scan the white asphalt ahead, glowing brightly in contrast to the indigo darkness of the storm on the horizon. Nothing to suggest spike strips.

I'm in the eastbound lanes pointed west. Let's floor this bitch.

One mile down the road something catches my eye. I slow to look at a trio of walkers shuffling along the dirt frontage before a wind farm. Like me they're moving westbound into the storm.

There's something about this group, and then I realize—it's not three walkers traveling. It's two following a questing alpha. This one's head is up; he's walking near normally while the others shuffle and drag after him, hopeful for whatever he might find and eventually toss aside. Or maybe they'll push him aside and take what he works so hard to catch. Looking at this group, I doubt that latter scenario will happen. But he does seem cursed for his success, doesn't he?

Another thing that occurs to me is that if they're out and walking towards their next meal it's because the alpha missed getting corralled like the others. By avoiding the herd they avoided manipulation and deployment as weapons. Therefore they missed getting shot and burned and blown to pieces for their troubles. No curse to that success, it seems, unless facing into the storm to get whatever's next is a curse. Like living itself can be a curse. It's a concept I'm all too familiar with.

Still. They're on their feet. They're moving. There's a chance.

The third lesson isn't particularly Zen, but it makes me sit up straighter, forces me to mind my surroundings and my speed. That is to say, if I wrecked, and God help me survived...and there I am, pinned in the wreckage...and these guys walk up....

Slowing to more or less normal highway speed serves me well when the double-rotored helicopter roars overhead. It all but rakes the roof with its landing gear before rushing ahead to lands astraddle the lanes in front of me.

For a rage-blind moment I imagine putting my foot through the floor and plowing right through them. For God's sake I'm not even past the auto mall! The men in black battle-rattle are pouring out. Two stand facing the Big Yellow Truck, ready to cut me to ribbons. Others fan towards either end of the Interstate. They're taking aim and dropping random walkers attracted to the racket of the rotors. Meanwhile a second chopper lands at the auto mall to my left.

When I see Dr. Hearn step into view in the open door of the helicopter, smiling and waving me over, I push the shifter into park and kill the engine.

I emerge carefully from the truck, my hands upraised to show the two on standby at the door I've got no quarrel. Dr. Hearn seems to find this amusing. I step up to the helicopter and immediately a black-uniformed man takes my forearm and pulls me up. I'm plopped down into a chair opposite where Dr. Hearn has seated himself. Someone shoves a pair of headphones at me. This is good, I think. As I can't imagine how else we're talking over the racket of two churning rotors and men with M4s screaming at each other, I put the headphones on, pull the microphone stem to my mouth.

"Mr. Derek Samuel Grace, the Dead Silencer!"

I can't help but smile for the old man's enthusiasm. "Dr. Hearn."

"Did you know you're driving in the wrong lane?"

"I didn't think it mattered anymore. Are you giving me a ticket?"

Dr. Hearn laughs. "Oh! We haven't quite come back to that! Yet. But it still matters. The old ways haven't entirely left us. We just buried them. Under so much...well, we've done away with all that now. Just a friendly tip."

"I'll cross right on over, then."

"Good, good! Just so you know, that's a strong cold front coming up on us. Severe thunderstorms, possible tornadoes. We're just doing a quick mop-up before the rains come in and help us put out the fires. By the way, thank you so much for your efforts on behalf of Oak Blossom Lane! I'm sorry about Paulson. Just so you know, he was off the reservation. Got what was coming, though, don't you agree?"

"It was a shame to lose the fire truck," I say.

Dr. Hearn nods. "Yes! Yes! You understand! With every destroyed vehicle, every burned building, every wrecked house, that's one less until we learn to make them again! Will we ever make them again? That's probably the biggest problem ahead of us. We gave up a lot for this—but it will be better!" He looks out the door where a squad of three take positions to shoot something or someone outside our own line of sight. "But that's neither here nor there," the doctor says. Now he snaps forward, his hand out and a huge grin on his face. "Anyway, I'm glad you're here. I had to shake the hand of the man who slept with the Mantis and lived!"

I lean forward and shake his hand. "Uh—what?"

"Ms. Rebecca! Special Agent Rebecca Anne Donaldson, to be precise. She's got issues, in case you haven't noticed."

"Uh, no. She seemed fine to me. Very dedicated to her work. I'd be honored to take firearms training under her. Could come in handy."

Dr. Hearn looks at me incredulously. "They call her the Mantis because she eventually takes the head off of every man she sleeps with! I don't know what's going on between you two but apparently you work well together! According to her we would never have rid ourselves of the mestizo infestation if not for your help bringing them here. God forbid they had escaped into the countryside!"

Infestation? "Glad to help."

"We're glad to have it! You've saved the oldest neighborhood in town from fire and ruin! You've neutralized almost exactly half of the walkers brought together from all over town to funnel into the Dougherty estate! Of course, it helped we had them in a tight corral, but still! Inspired! Then you bring them to a more or less dead-free area for cleanup!"

"Heh. Shucks."

"And, dear God, I'm forgetting! You rescued that group from the Wal-Mart with that beautiful sword of yours! And you stood for that poor girl this morning when those jackanapes killed her! Your one and only failure in a long and busy day, and you still showed courage of character!"

Well played, Rebecca. "I really regretted losing Kara. That was such a waste."

"Indeed! But you and Rebecca *destroyed* the malefactors! Such a team! My people won't forget this, Mr. Grace!"

"I'm just a guy trying to get home."

"In Colorado Springs! Yes! We wish you the best! There's a farmhouse just up the road we've secured! You'll want to stop there before the storm hits. It has a shelter if it comes to that...."

So he gives me full directions to this place on Exit Something-or-Other, drive north and it's completely clean, etc. I thank him and we shake hands. "We'll be in touch sooner than later!" Dr. Hearn says "We can use a man of your talent! To mate you with a Rebecca Anne Donaldson, imagine the warrior!"

"Imagine trying to get the little son of a bitch to do his homework."

Dr. Hearn grabs his chest as he laughs and the black-suited bastards on either side glower at me like they're really going to resent the paperwork on this one. After a scary couple of moments he coughs, cackles, and regains his composure: "Yes, I understand what she sees in you! Very good! We will be in touch, Mr. Grace!"

I'm not quite escorted from the aircraft, but I know their eyes and gunsights are upon me as I smile and nod my way back to the Big Yellow Truck. I hear a woman's scream from the auto mall, the cry of a child, followed by the gunfire, as I climb to the running board. I turn to look and see a familiar face commanding a squad of black-uniformed goons coming away from one of the dealerships off the highway. Yes, it's Evans. Pointedly ignoring me. Which is fine. I imagine it's galling to see me getting ready to drive away in the truck he'd picked up just days ago.

For that matter, I can only imagine what his story was after this morning. At least he was on the correct side politically. And now he has a new job. Looks nice and secure. So what if they run out of brown-skinned women and children to kill? There's always going to be someone at the bottom of the social totem pole who needs "ordering."

I drive at an angle across the median into the westbound lanes. Now I'm on the proper road, driving like a good citizen. Good for me. The quicker those helicopters and columns of smoke disappear from my rear-view mirrors, the better.

It was kind of Dr. Hearn to give me an exit number and an address to stay at. With that woman's scream and child's last cry in mind I'll take any other exit but that one and go as far as I can in the opposite direction.

Fields surround me. The wind turbines spin furiously in the face of the coming storm. There's not much between here and Colorado once you're out of Saline County. After several miles of clean sunlight the clouds overtake the sun. Soon I'm surrounded by that eerie, greenish glow in the air you see just before a tornado. Powerful downdrafts rock the truck on its frame; fat drops of rain smack the windshield.

I look to either side of the Interstate. An old farmer here, a good old boy in a T-shirt there, stumbling along, their sightless heads turning uneasily about them. I wonder if they're sensitive to barometric pressure. Me, I'm about to get blown away on the open Interstate so I slow down and pull off at the next exit.

I have no idea where I am. All I know is that Hearn's secured area was north, so I drive south. The sign promises a town in three more miles. The clouds thicken, as do the hungry dead along the sides of the road. Their heads follow the movement of my truck. Soon the rest of them are staggering after. I see them following in my rear-view, leaning awkwardly into the gusting winds.

I keep driving, with an eye on the rear view. I'll need to hole up somewhere and soon. So far it looks like I'm the only living soul out here.

Good. I feel so much safer. God bless the Middle of Nowhere.

THE END

ICE STATION ZOMBIE
JE GURLEY

For most of the long, cold winter, Antarctica is a frozen wasteland. Now, the ice is melting and the zombies are thawing. Arctic explorers Val Marino and Elliot Anson race against time and death to reach Australia, but the Demise has preceded them and zombies stalk the streets of Adelaide and Coober Pedy.

www.severedpress.com

The Coalition

When the dead rose to destroy the living, Ron Cutter learned to survive. While so many others died, he thrived. His life is a constant battle against the living dead. As he casts his own bullets and packs his shotgun shells, his humanity slowly melts away.

Then he encounters a lost boy and a woman searching for a place of refuge. Can they help him recover the emotions he set aside to live? And if he does recover them, will those feelings be an asset in his struggles, or a danger to him?

THE STATE OF EXTINCTION: the first installment in the **COALITON OF THE LIVING** trilogy of Mankind's battle against the plague of the Living Dead. As recounted by author **Robert Mathis Kurtz.**

www.severedpress.com

RANCID

Nothing ever happens in the middle of nowhere or in Virginia for that matter. This is why Noel and her friends found themselves on cloud nine when one of their favorite hardcore bands happened to be playing a show in their small hometown. Between the meteor shower and the short trip to the cemetery outside of town after the show, this crazy group of friends instantly plummet from those clouds into a frenzied nightmare of putrefied horror.

Is this sudden nightmare related to the showering meteors or does this small town hold even darker secrets than the rotting corpses that are surfacing?

"Zombies in small town America, a corporate conspiracy, fast paced action and a satisfying body count- what's not to like? Just don't get too attached to any character; they may die or turn zombie soon enough!" - Mainak Dhar, bestselling author of Alice in Deadland and Zombiestan

www.severedpress.com

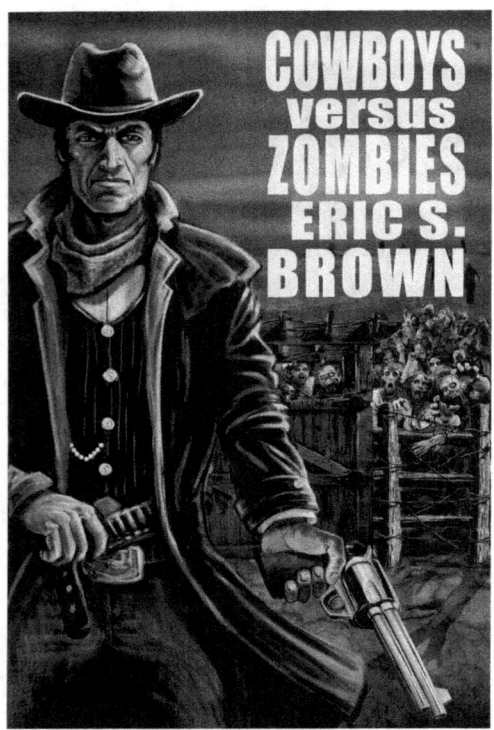

COWBOYS VS ZOMBIES

Dilouie is a killer. He's always made his way in life by the speed of his gun hand and the coldness of his remorseless heart. Life never meant much to him until the world fell apart and they awoke. Overnight, the dead stopped being dead. Hungry corpses rose from blood splattered streets and graves. Their numbers were unimaginable and their need for the flesh of the living insatiable.

The United States is no more. Washed away in a tide of gnashing teeth and rotting, clawing hands. Dilouie no longer kills for money and pleasure but to simply keep breathing and to see the sunrise of the next dawn. . . And he is beginning to wonder if even men like him can survive in a world that now belongs to the dead?

www.severedpress.com

TIMOTHY
MARK TUFO

Timothy was not a good man in life and being undead did little to improve his disposition. Find out what a man trapped in his own mind will do to survive when he wakes up to find himself a zombie controlled by a self-aware virus.